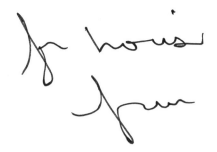

Skygrass Reunion

Tales of the Skygrass Kingdom
Volume III

෬

Lynda J. Farquhar

Cover Art by Maeve Pascoe

www.skygrasskingdom.com

I dedicate

Skygrass Reunion

to

*All the women in my family:
my mother, my sisters,
my daughters & my granddaughters*

**With all that I have and
All that I am
I honor you,
For you are the circle of life.**

Settings

Talin	One of Twelve Valleys in the Blue Mtns.
Namché	City at base of Mountains
Maidenstone	Ancient school for Healers and Priestesses
Natil	King's Valley, government for all twelve valleys
Skygrass	Legendary valley, location of blue diamond mine
Halfhigh	Way-station on journey from Talin to Skygrass

Names of Major Characters

Sab-ra	Healer, Empath and Priestess
Ruby	Sab-ra's twin sister from Island of Viridian
Ellani	Sab-ra's Grandmother, Midwife
Silo'am	Sab-ra's Grandfather, Head of the Silversmith Guild
Dani	Sab-ra's Father, died before her birth
Ashlin	Mother to Sab-ra and Ruby
Linc	Ashlin's brother, died in Angelion cave

Names of Characters at Maidenstone House

Falcon	Mistress of Maidenstone, Priestess and Empath
Conquin	Best friend of Sab-ra, aide to the Queen Verde
Honus	Cook at Maidenstone House
Jun	Empath Teacher, Maidenstone House
Marzun	Head Empath, Maidenstone House
An Mali	Physician, Healer at Maidenstone
Te Ran	Head Priestess, Far-Seer

Soldiers at Garrison

Capt. Grieg	Captain of Garrison, obsessed with Sab-ra
Justyn	Translator in love with Sab-ra

Carmac	He and Jaime are soldiers from Viridian

Ruisenor	King of Twelve Valleys
Verde	Disgraced Queen of Twelve Valleys, Hakan Queen
Ion'li	First Consort. Becomes Queen of Twelve Valleys

Say'f	Warrior King of Kosi tribe
Hozro	Wants to unseat Say'f, killed his father
Ghang	Mercenary Kosi, guard at Maidenstone
Argo	Kosi Assassin
Rohr	1st Blood Arrow, Guardian after Avalanche
Ten Singh	Bearer guard, Member of the Resistance
Norgay	Horse Captain for King Ruisenor

Cloudheart	Puppy Sab-ra earns for passing the Empath test
Shine	Colt Conquin earns as part of Empath test
Yellowmane	Sab-ra's pony
Kys	Say'f's warhorse
Tye	Rohr's warhorse
Angelion	Mystical animal, spirit of Sab-ra's mother
Sumulus	Baby Angelion found by Sab-ra's parents
Daybreak	Gazehound, belongs to the Kosi King
Dusk	Gazehound found starving in the Citadel

Names of Months in Skygrass Kingdom

Moon of Snows	January
Hunger Moon	February
Vernal Moon	March
Waking Moon	April
Planting Moon	May
Flowering Moon	June
Ripening Moon	July
Thunder Moon	August
Harvest Moon	September
Red Leaf Moon	October
Black Twig Moon	November
Long Night Moon	December

The Story of Volume I, "Journey to Maidenstone"

I am Sab-ra of Talin. I was raised in the Twelve Valleys country high in the Blue Mountains. As a child I was taught to hate the Kosi, copper skinned barbaric warriors who stole the future of my People. They abducted our young women because their tribe was dying; their women were sterile. The Elders trained me as a spy. Following a horrible raid in which many died, my spy partner Hodi and I were sent on our first mission. The Elders commanded us to bring Lethal Sleep berries to our women held captive by the Shunned at the Green River Camp. They were to poison their kidnappers. Even now my mind shrinks from the horror of our failure, of Hodi's scalping and burial in a garbage pit by our enemies. The Elders of Talin blamed me for Hodi's death and banished me to Maidenstone, an ancient school in the city in Namché. They said my home village of Talin was closed to me forever until I brought our women home. So far away from the Twelve Valleys country, I could only nurse my grievances and swear revenge on the White Eyed Kosi Wolf who took Hodi's life.

Despite many attempts, I was unable to escape Maidenstone. Over time, I learned to love my life as a Novice there and became devoted to Mistress Falcon, head of the school. My roommate Conquin and I became best friends. We studied mind reading skills with Brother Jun. When I passed the final Empath Test, Jun gave me a puppy named Cloudheart. My loneliness vanished. I began working with An Mali, Maidenstone's Healer and in time qualified for the Healer's cord. Later, I worked with a Priestess called Te Ran who taught me to see the future in a scry bowl. On our first trek up the mountain, we witnessed an invading force of Harn soldiers coming to seize the city.

During the Occupation, Captain Grieg, head of the Harn Battalion ordered his soldiers to take two Novices from Maidenstone. While negotiating one girl's release, I learned the true objective of the Harn Army. It was the plunder of the blue diamond mine of my People hidden deep in the secret Skygrass valley. Its location was a closely guarded secret. Captain Grieg threatened to take me prisoner and when I said I would stab him with a poisoned knife, he vowed he would strip me naked and hang me by my long red hair. Grieg's handsome young translator, Justyn, offered his help. Both of us knew my life was forfeit to Grieg's power.

Desperate to alert my People to the impending Army attack on the blue diamond mine, I disobeyed the powerful Mistress of Maidenstone who had told me not to leave the Lamasery. Ignoring her counsel, I returned to the Garrison to help rescue the last Novice. Mistress said she could trust me no longer and directed me to leave Maidenstone, the place that had become my only home.

On my final day at Maidenstone, Mistress told me my mother had not died at my birth, as grandmother said. The truth was that my mother left Namché and abandoned me. Heart sore and dreadfully fearful I would be captured by the Army, I left Maidenstone late at night with Mistress Falcon commanding me to complete my original mission by going to the Kosi. It was dark in the garden when I turned to lead my pony Yellowmane down the back path with Ghang clattering behind me. We trekked through descending terraces of budding flowers, beyond the gate and around the city to the Wool Road. The mist rose. Crying so hard I could hardly see, I bade farewell to Maidenstone.

The Story of Volume II "The Songs of Skygrass"

Thus I began a frantic trek into the mountains to warn my People of the coming Army attack. Justyn, Captain Grieg's Translator, deserted the Army to warn me that soldiers had been set on my trail. Desperate to elude our pursuers, we were forced to take refuge with the Kosi, ancient enemies of my People. To my dismay, I fell in love with Say'f, the Warrior King. Fearing my pacifist culture would never take up arms in defense of the Skygrass stone mine, I sought to hire the Kosi warriors to repel the Army invaders. I hoped having the Kosi defend the Skygrass valley, sacred to all the People of the Twelve Valleys, might lead to peace between the two warring cultures. The Elders ruled that King Ruisenor, monarch of the Twelve Valleys, should decide whether to hire the Kosi. Grandfather, the Warrior King and I departed for the Twelfth Valley to meet with King Ruisenor. In a conversation with my grandmother before we left, I learned that I was born a twin. My mother left the city of Namché shortly after my birth, taking my infant sister and leaving me behind because I was not expected to live.

When we arrived in the Valley of the King, Lance Ruisenor approved my idea to forge an Accord between the People and the Kosi. The treaty protected the Skygrass valley, the blue diamond mine and stopped the kidnapping of the People's women. When the Army attacked Skygrass, the Kosi were victorious, but Captain Grieg discovered a way into the valley and took me prisoner. Leaving Grieg near death, I escaped and married the Kosi King the night before an avalanche destroyed the mythic Skygrass valley. I fled the Valley, but his warrior's creed compelled Say'f to stay and kill Captain Grieg. Travelling with Rohr, First of the Kosi Blood Arrows, I journeyed across the vast mountain range in winter, finally reaching the King's valley where I was certain I would find my ally, my lover and husband. I was wrong; the Kosi King was not there. I would face pregnancy and motherhood alone.

Chapter 1 – In Natil, the Valley of the King
Moon of Snows, January

The Moon of Snows had buried the high country in tall snowdrifts before Lord Rohr, the First of the Kosi Blood Arrows and I, Sab-ra of Talin, reached the great circular caldera within which lay the castle of Lance Ruisenor, King of the Twelve Valleys people. Rohr left me at its rim and plunged straight down through snowdrifts that reached his stallion's shoulders. I was so weak I could not stand. I closed my eyes, sank to the earth beside brave Yellowmane's feet and slept on the windswept ridge with nothing to cover me but blowing snow.

Many of my People, the Kosi, our horses and livestock lost their lives the day the Avalanche roared down upon the Skygrass valley, but my husband's last words were that he would meet me in the Valley of the King. I knew Rohr would return bringing Say'f, the dark Warrior King of the Kosi—my ally and my lover.

When I learned my husband was not in the Valley of the King, I cried until my eyes were dry as the upland salt flats. When my best friend, Conquin, told me I carried his child, grief took me into a different world. I watched myself through what seemed an impenetrable glass window as I stumbled through the days—looking alive but feeling dead.

My pragmatic dark-haired friend consoled me. She reminded me the baby would absorb my feelings and be sad his whole life unless I raised my spirits. She asked me if I had seen the King's revenant, his spirit, riding his stallion among the clouds. I told her I had not.

"Then he may yet live, Sab-ra," she said. "A Warrior always keeps his word. He said he would meet you here. I believe he will come."

I forced the dark cloud in my mind to lift a little and went to work, serving others in the Kingdom as a Healer. The back kitchen of the castle became the clinic where patients came for me to look at their skin, their throats and listen to their bellies. Some of the children even came without their parents. They stood silently waiting until I came to look at them. Most of them had nothing at all wrong with them, except a yearning to be the center of attention. They giggled when I felt their tummies and backs. As huge snowflakes fell on the flanks of the Blue Mountains, I fought against despair while my son grew strong inside me.

I was walking down the hall of windows one bright blue day when I glimpsed two dark-skinned Kosi Warriors plunge down the vertical cliff into the Twelfth Valley. They were shouting war whoops of victory, high-pitched keening cries of triumph as the stomping feet of their warhorses churned the sparkling snow. I leaned against the window breathing deeply and closed my eyes in joy. Just as he had promised, my King had come. But, when I opened my eyes again agony raked my soul. It wasn't Say'f. Two Blood Arrows, nobles who guarded the King of the Kosi, and a young child riding a pony had come to the Kingdom. The pony resembled Sorrell, my former spy partner's mount. I had last seen Sorrell at the Kosi Citadel. I felt the wave of grief grind me, cold as the remnants of melting snow.

The Blood Arrows dismounted and King Ruisenor strode out to greet them. They stood together on the stone forecourt and locked arms reinforcing their status as allies. Then the King turned to the child. He lifted her from her pony and she knelt on the stone forecourt. He raised her face and I could see her golden skin. Her features were small and fine. I knew this little girl. She was the child I had seen at the Citadel— the one who fell in love with my spy partner's pony, Sorrell. A second warrior came up, carrying a baby. I hadn't seen the little one riding behind the other Warrior.

"Welcome to my Kingdom," King Ruisenor's voice resonated, "Please come in."

The men walked through the great doors of the castle with the slender older child running beside them. King Ruisenor, who longed for an heir to his Kingdom, carried the baby. I turned my face away from the scene, tears wetting my eyes.

All winter I scrutinized the towering cumulus clouds, gray and heavy with snow, drift over the Valley of the King. I watched to see if Say'f, the King of the Kosi, rode the thunderheads. Although I didn't see his face in the skies, each day that went by my hope that he lived grew weaker. I felt blood pound in my temples; I dreaded the news brought by the Blood Arrows. I feared they brought word of his death.

The next morning a servant came to my apartment. "Lord Sta'g wishes to speak with you. He is in the Throne room with the two children."

"He will have to wait." I spent an hour trying to compose myself. Outside the palace windows the winter winds stirred the tops of drifted snow banks. I trembled like the dead leaves of the Rholam tree, wondering what news Lord Sta'g had of my husband. When I went down to Throne room, Conquin came with me. Lord Sta'g rose when we entered the room, holding two young girls by their hands.

"Wife of the King," he said, "I bring you the King's daughters. Their mother, Martyn, rides the skies. They are yours now."

The silence rang as he finished speaking. The oldest of the little girls walked forward and knelt at my feet. The little one toddled after her sister. I was shattered. I lifted their little faces up with a finger. The eldest had her father's beautiful golden eyes. The baby was pudgy and bewildered looking; she started to cry.

Poor little mites, I thought, they are motherless, just like me. "What are their names?" I managed to whisper.

"They are Kim-li and Kensing."

"Thank you for your gift, Lord Sta'g, but such young children need a family. I am a Healer and Far-Seer. I am no family for the daughters of the King."

"It was the King's command. If he didn't return from the War, his daughters were to be given to you." Sta'g met my eyes unyieldingly.

I hesitated, feeling tears sting my cheeks. If I took the children, it would be like accepting my Say'f was dead.

"Lord Sta'g," Conquin said, after giving me a scorching glare, "It would be my privilege to care for the Kosi King's daughters until Sab-ra is ready."

She turned toward me and whispered fiercely, "Do not say another word." Her dark eyes snapped in anger.

The Blood Arrow went down on one knee to the children and the oldest girl made a circle blessing above him in the air. He patted the little one on the head.

"Have you any news of the King?" I begged.

"Nothing since the day of the Avalanche," Lord Sta'g replied. "Soon the choosing of a new King will commence."

His eyes said this was something of great import. I felt dizzy and the room swayed around me. No other man should serve as King of the Kosi. That honor belonged to my ally, my lover and my husband. Lord Sta'g drew a black fur cape around his shoulders and strode from the room, taking all my hopes with him.

Conquin took Kim-li by the hand and picked up baby Kensing holding her tight against her pregnant belly. Once inside her home, Conquin set a kettle boiling, called the girls to the table and gave them Ghat milk and sapritet fruit. They were not used to sitting at a table to eat, at the Citadel everyone ate together on the soft white sand around the fire. They took their food and sat on the floor by the window. Kim-li sang quietly to her baby sister.

"I can't believe you would tell Lord Sta'g you didn't want the children," Conquin hissed. "I wonder what Brother Jun would have said." Her voice was disgusted.

Only a little over a year ago, my Elders sent me to attend school at Maidenstone. Brother Jun, my compassionate Empath teacher, had taught me to read the minds of others and ease their sorrows. How I wished I could ease my own sorrows—how I wished I could heal myself.

"Truly, I am appalled, Sab-ra." Conquin shook her head.

"I didn't say I didn't want the children, but I am a Healer, Conquin, not a mother. I don't know how to take care of such young children, especially without a father."

"Well it looks to me like you better figure it out soon," she said, glancing at my belly. The corners of her mouth tightened in aggravation. "Sab-ra, these children are Kosi royalty. If you don't have a son, Kim-li will become Queen of the Kosi. She will marry the new King when she comes of age, and I remind you," she scowled, "they are the sisters of the babe you carry. I don't understand you sometimes, but I will keep them until you come to your senses, Idiot Lakt."

Chapter 2 – On the Isle of Verdantia
January

The day Lord Sta'g brought the King's daughters to Natil, half a world away Sab-ra's twin sister Ruby was about to hear a long-buried family secret.

Ruby cuddled in a mass of hand-pieced quilts with her young setter puppy, Maeve. Her red hair cascaded over the embroidered linen pillowcase, the same color as the dog's curling fur. Her eyelashes were dark against her fair cheeks. Freezing rain fell outside her window taking her deeper into slumber. A brisk knock on the door and her mother's voice brought her from her dreams.

"Get out of bed now, Miss, it's time you had breakfast with your family."

"Ma," Ruby groaned. "What time is it that you are waking me on my school break?"

"Don't be bold, and it's Mummy, not Ma. The breakfast is ready. Get yourself down here. Your Da and I have some things to talk to you about."

Ruby looked at her clock gloomily. Nine o'clock on a bloody Tuesday morning. During vacation no less. What in the world had induced Ma to make a full breakfast in the middle of the week? She put her feet on the wood floor, winced at the cold and reached for the skirt and sweater she had pulled off the night before. She stepped into her clothes, yanked a comb through her long curly red hair and stomped down to breakfast.

She looked at the table in dismay. There were rashers of bacon, sausages, fried eggs, black pudding and toast—burnt to a crisp. Baked beans, fried tomatoes and brown soda bread were already on her plate.

"Do I have to eat all this? What's the occasion, Ma?" she asked, looking at all the food.

"Don't be giving me grief my girl, and it is Mummy, as I told ye before. Sit down while I get your Da his tea."

Ruby's father, a tall skinny man with freckles and an easy smile came in and joined them at the table. It was an eat-in kitchen with a pine table and four old gray chairs. The table had been scrubbed so often, it was nearly white. The rain outside the antique leaded glass windows had turned to snow, making the world look soft and out of focus.

"Mornin' Ruby."

"How ya, Da."

"Say grace, you," her mother said.

Ruby recited the usual prayer, made the sign of her God and dug in.

"So what's the big deal to get me up out of bed at bleeding

dawn?"

Ruby's mother didn't answer. She was unusually quiet, looking out toward the back garden. She was in her late thirties with red curly hair that had only a few silver threads. Her eyes were far away. Then she straightened her shoulders and exhaled as if she had been holding her breath a long time.

"Okay, here goes, my girl. I have a tale to tell you and I don't think it's going to be easy," she hesitated. "When I was about your age, my older brother Linc talked my Da into sending him on a trip to see the Far East. He had dreamed of seeing the Blue Mountains since he was a tot. My Da was sick with the cancer and wanted Linc to have his dream. Half the place was on the dole, but my Da had some money stashed away so he buys Linc a ticket. Linc was beside himself with joy. He was headed to this place called Nam-shay."

"Can ye not come to the bleeding point here?" Ruby said, rolling her eyes and thinking about meeting her boyfriend Shane later at the shops.

"Language," Ma snapped. "I was planning all the time on following him, but I didn't tell Da. I figured I had to wait until he was welcomed into heaven before I left. Linc and I were goin' to live together when I got there, the pair of us. Linc was all for studying the animals of the place, Goddess love him. Nobody thought those animals were real, but the day I found my dear brother, I held a baby white cave lion in my hands. You can't image how beautiful he was."

Her voice was soft and dreamy. For just a moment, she looked seventeen again, holding a cup of tea, the warmth making red tendrils around her face. Tears came to her eyes and she blinked them back.

"Ma, I swear, I'm going back to bed if yous can't come to the point," Ruby half rose to leave.

"Did I say you could leave the table?" her mother asked angrily.

"Sit girl," Da said calmly. "Your Mum is trying to tell you something important here. Go ahead, Ashlin."

"So, we hadn't heard from my brother for almost half a year. Sure, we'd no phone when he left, so how would he ring us? And he always did things in his own time. At first, we thought he was just not for writing, but when Da died and Mum turned fifty and we still didn't hear a word, I left our beautiful Isle of Viridian to find him. Makin' a long story short, for Miss Impatience here, I found him up in the Blue Mountains. He had died of starvation, giving all his food to the cave lions."

"Jaysus. Oh Ma, I'm so sorry. I knew he died, but this is awful, truly awful."

"I'll go on then, shall I? Unless this little wagon needs her bed more 'un the story."

"Okay, okay, I'm staying," Ruby said, settling in for the duration.

"There was this big Monastery, part school and part hospital in that town. They called the place Maidenstone. When I got to the city of Nam-shay, a monk sent me to the Wool Market. I found this man, named Silo'am, who had brought his wool down from the high range to sell in the city. He had a son named Dani, young and dark-haired. Oh he was lovely, he was."

"Ma, you didn't, did ye? Did ye fall for this dark mountain lad?"

"Maybe I best tell the next part," Da said gently, patting Ma's hand and she nodded.

"Dani guided your mother up into the Blue Mountains. It took weeks, even in summer, but eventually they found her brother. It was like she said. He was dead of starvation in a mountain cave. They had no choice but to bury him with rocks, trying to save his body from the mountain lions eating 'im. They call them Angel lions in that country."

Ruby looked at her mother who gazed down at the table, blew her nose and wiped the tears from her face.

"Your Ma and Dani found this baby Angel lion near Linc's body. The lion's Mum ran into the deeper tunnels and disappeared. They stayed and took care of the wee one. When he was big enough they left him to fend for himself."

"We named him Sumulus," Ruby's mother said softly. "He had the most beautiful eyes and the tips of his ears had white fur tassels on 'em. When he played in the mountain meadows, I would sit down on the grass and after a while, he would come and put his head in my lap. His eyes were near to silver. My Dani loved him too." Ashlin's voice was low and sweet. Ruby could feel the room grow tight with her mother's profound love for the little lion.

"Ah, you were a bold little rebel then, were ye Ma?" Ruby said.

"Now, Ruby, none of that. Your Ma and Dani fell for each other hard," Da looked away for a minute, saying it seemed to hurt him even after all those years.

"You'll be having another cup of tea, Frank," Ma said. Da nodded. Ashlin stood up and re-filled his cup, handing him a ferocious dark brew.

"Go on then," Ruby said.

"So, they got married, your mother and Dani and your Mum got herself pregnant."

"Hold on a minute here, Mum. You were married to somebody before Da?" Ruby asked. She felt the palms of her hands start to sweat.

"Ah now, Ruby girl, you have to try to understand, it was an eon ago and a long ways away from our beautiful island. I was terrible lonely, I was."

"So how did this fall out? What happened to this Dani, to the dark-haired boy?" Ruby asked. It troubled her deeply that Ma had married someone else besides her beloved Da.

"Dani died in a mountain climbing accident," Ma said, her voice low and sorrowful. "He screamed my name as he fell," her tears came down hard. After a bit, she cleared her throat, striving for control. "I tried to climb down to him, but the rocks were slick with ice. I could not reach him. I called until my voice went."

"And you are the kid, Ruby," Da said, his voice so gentle, so very kind.

"Am I not your child then, Da?" Ruby could hear the anguish in her voice as she turned to her father, tears filling her eyes.

"No, Darlin' you're my child all right. I adopted you right off the bat. Your Ma used to say I fell in love with you before I even knew for sure I loved her."

"What happened after that," Ruby said, with a worried frown on her face. She dreaded what other deeply buried secrets she would hear.

"I came back to Viridian afterwards, to tell my own Ma what happened to Linc and to show her my baby. Ah, but you were a sweet little dote, a giggly small one. I met your Da and we got married right away."

"I can't take this all in, Ma." Ruby stood up. Her stomach clenched and her palms left sweat marks on the back of the chair. She was desperate to leave the kitchen. "I want to go talk with Nana about this."

"You're going nowhere, you. There's more to say. You were born a twin, and I am going to Nam-shay in a few weeks to get your sister. There," she said, "now I told ye."

"What?" Ruby looked at her parents in stunned silence, sitting down suddenly.

"You have a twin, a sister. It's been seventeen years, but I learned last week that she lived."

Ruby sat at the table, shaking her head, unable to say a word. Nothing in all the years she had been the child of these two had told her she wasn't an only child. She shook her head, trying to register a sister, a twin. Everyone was silent and Ruby nibbled on her toast as if in a worrisome dream.

"If I have a twin, why isn't she here?" Ruby demanded, lifting her face to her mother angrily.

"When she was born, she was very poorly, a weak little thing. Couldn't even raise her head. I left her with the Healer in Nam-shay, because they didn't think she would live. It was a horrible time and there was a war in that country. The Army ordered all the white people to leave the city. I brought you back here to our Island and married your Da. I left your sister behind at the Infirmary at Maidenstone." Her voice trailed off into silence, tears in her eyes.

"I don't understand. It's been seventeen years and suddenly you remember this child that you left. Could you not just give this up? After all, you gave her up," Ruby's mouth tightened in disapproval. She glared at her mother.

"You have no idea how hard this has been for me, Ruby. A few months ago, I wrote to the Mistress of the Maidenstone School and she sent me back a letter. That's when I learned your twin lived. Her name is Sab-ra, and she's been raised by her father Dani's parents. They have been training her to be a Healer. I got the letter and ever since then, I've been dreaming about her. In the dreams, she is calling me, needing her Mum. I'm going to the Blue Mountain country and bring her back to Viridian."

"So, Ruby girl," Da said, "You are going to take language lessons so you can speak to your twin when she gets here."

"Oh Da, no," Ruby wailed. "If Ma can even find this girl, can't she leave her there?"

"I'll get the letter," Ma said, "You'll see why I have to go. There is war in Nam-shay again and your sister left the city almost a year ago. She was travelling up the mountains to warn her People about the Army that plans to invade the high country."

Chapter 3 –In Natil, the Valley of the King
Hunger Moon, February

While Ruby struggled to accept her mother's revelations, Sab-ra slept alone in the palace of the King of the Twelve Valleys waiting for her Warrior King's return.

At the beginning of the second month, I woke to hear Conquin calling my name. "Sab-ra, help me."

I sat bolt upright in bed and looked around. It was the middle of the night. There was no one else in my palace apartment, but I heard Conquin's voice as clearly as if she stood beside me. She sounded like she was in pain. I knew instantly that she was in labor. I dressed quickly, pulled on my coat, grabbed my Healer bag and ran through snow drifts to Conquin's home.

Pushing through the door, I called out, "Conquin, it is Sab-ra. I am with you. You will bring this baby into the world alive, warm and whole."

"Sab-ra?" Conquin's voice was weak. I whirled toward her women in a cold fury.

"How long has she been in labor?"

"Nearly ten hours, Healer."

I was enraged, "How could you let her get into this state without calling me?" They said nothing. "Where is Thron, her husband?" They wouldn't look at me, but one finally admitted he had been there, but they had sent him away. My mouth tightened in displeasure.

"One of you go and find him," I ordered. Turning back to Conquin, I lowered my voice. "Together we will bring this baby to the light. The Goddess called and woke me, Conquin. She spoke to me with your voice." Conquin managed a tired smile.

I sent the other attendants for broth for Conquin to drink, warm water, towels and the beautiful clothes Conquin had made for her child. My dearest friend labored until morning, but my certainty she would have a healthy baby bore her up from the depths of watery pain, to the surface of the warm sunlit world and the child was born. She came to us with her eyes wide open. She looked directly at me and I gazed back at her. Thron had returned and was standing shyly at the back of the room. His eyes pleaded with me for reassurance.

"Your wife will live to bring you more children," I told him, smiling as I handed him his daughter. I looked at the little mite cuddled in her father's arms, knowing I would give birth myself soon. Goddess of the Winds, I prayed, let Say'f be here to hold his son.

"We will call her Sab-ri," Thron said, his voice heavy with emotion.

It meant "little Sab-ra." She smiled at only three days. The Goddess had used me for her purposes, but for that one moment in time, I was content. I had received a gift beyond price. I felt born to do her bidding.

The following day, a servant came to my rooms to tell me that King Ruisenor wished me to attend him in the Throne room. I pulled on my fur coat and hide boots. It was icy cold outside as I walked from my apartment to the wing of the palace where the King received petitioners.

When I entered the room, I saw the King and young Queen Ion'li sitting on their thrones. No one else was there. Ion'li sat at his right hand. Before I went to the war, there were two Queens of the Twelve Valleys. Queen Verde, as first Queen, sat at the right hand of the King in those days. I banished her from the Kingdom when I discovered they planned to murder Ion'li. I came forward seeing Queen Ion'li smile radiantly.

"I have told the King that I am again with child," her face was pink with pleasure.

"I am so pleased," I told her. "Queen Ion'li, I wish to know this baby you carry. May I place my hands upon you?"

She nodded and I put my hand on her stomach and called out, "She will bear you a healthy son by the end of the year, my Lord."

"So you know already," the King said. His voice was deep with pleasure. 'Truly you can see the time-coming-to-be. Tell me, Sab-ra, will my son be born alive and well?"

Ion'li had lost two babes before I told her to stop riding her horse and bathing in the hot springs—advice from the jealous Queen Verde who could not conceive the King's child.

"My Lord, unless the life of his mother is taken, you and I will help Queen Ion'li bring him into the world. It will be my pleasure to lay him in your arms."

The King smiled and Ion'li's fears evaporated like the dawn-mist rising over the mountains at sunrise. I started to leave the Throne Room, but the King stopped me with a gesture.

"There is another reason I called you here, Sab-ra, I wish to award you the cords that are mine alone to grant," the King smiled.

When women get married or become mothers they are given beautiful braided cords to wear around their waists over long gowns. One of the Ion'li's serving women entered and laid a small inlaid gem-encrusted chest in the King's hands. He opened the container and pulled out the golden Cord of Marriage. I felt my heart race. Had he heard something? Was there any news? Could my Warrior have lived through this brutal winter?

I knelt before them.

"There is no need to kneel, Sab-ra," he told me. "Rise. I will thread the Marriage Cord around your waist. When you have your child, return and I will grant you the silver Cord of Motherhood."

"I have no husband," I murmured softly. "It wrong for me to wear the Marriage Cord."

"He will come," the King, pronounced. "If he is not here before your child is born, I believe he will be here before mine enters the world."

He and Ion'li looked at each other, holding hands. Their happiness and love wrenched my heart. I walked from the Throne room gazing down at all the threaded Cords around my waist—red for the Healer and ivory for the Far Reader—cords I had earned at Maidenstone when I was a novice there. Superstitiously, I unthreaded the golden Cord of Marriage from the other two. When I returned to my apartment, I placed it on the windowsill where the moonlight would glaze its satin surface. I would not wear it again until I knew my warrior's fate.

Two weeks after baby Sab-ri was born, one of the Bearers brought me a message. It was a drawing etched into the bark of a lily tree, showing a body wrapped in the shroud of the dead. A second sketch showed a woman holding the hands of many children. In the background, I saw a small building, a river and a waterfall. I felt a frightened tingling across my shoulders and my belly tightened. I sensed the message came from the ancient Kosi Healer woman, Wirri-won. I took it to Rohr, my Guardian—the Blood-Arrow who brought me safely to the King's Valley after the Avalanche.

"I think this message is from Wirri-won," I told him. He nodded. "Do you know where I can find her, Rohr?"

"In the Blue Mountains above the ninth valley. She lives in the river."

"What do you mean, in a river?" I touched the base of my throat, feeling anxiety rise.

"On the Island of the Eaten," he said, ominously. Despite all my questions, he would say nothing more. He looked troubled and left me abruptly.

Perplexed, I took Wirri-won's message to Conquin.

"This is a message from the powerful medicine woman for the Kosi. She came to me during the War at Halfhigh, the way station between Talin and the high range. Wirri-won tended the wounded there so I could go to the front. I asked if I could study with her when the war was over. She said I should come to her when I was pregnant, if I survived the final battle."

Conquin was nursing baby Sab-ri. They made such a lovely picture, with the sun lighting Conquin's hair as she held out a finger for baby Sab-ri to grasp.

"I am not sure the King will permit you to go, since Ion'li is pregnant. Perhaps you should wait until the baby prince is born. Or at least until you deliver."

"Conquin there are times you infuriate me, but you are probably right. Don't you get tired of *always* being right?" I asked. She shook her head at me, smiling. I feared losing the opportunity to study with Wirri-won, but knew I could not leave the Kingdom without the King's permission.

Chapter 4 – On the Isle of Verdantia

As Sab-ra prepared to ask the King's permission to leave the Twelfth Valley, Ruby stormed from her parents' house, slamming the door behind her in a blind rage.

Ruby walked the cobbled streets with their brick houses and narrow-minded windows watching her splash by in the freezing rain. She stomped in all the puddles. Water soaked into the sides of her boots making her toes ice cold. She reached her Nana's side yard just in time to see her leaving by the front door. Ruby called out to get Nana's attention and her grandmother turned around.

"Ruby, me darlin' I'm about to go to the market. Did ye need something?"

"I need to talk to you," Ruby said and at her despairing tone, Nana knew her granddaughter had at last learned the family secret.

"Come in, I'll get your tea," she said putting her arm around Ruby's shoulders and leading her into her kitchen by the side door. "Take off those boots and your coat before you catch your death."

The teapot whistled as Ruby removed her wet things and sat on the red painted stool at the old yellow lino countertop.

Pouring the tea, Granny sat down across from her granddaughter. "So your Mum told you the whole story, did she?"

"You knew all this time?" Ruby said, frustration apparent in her rising tone. She felt her heart beat faster.

"Yes, dearie, I knew. I have told your Mum a hundred times you needed to know."

"She says I'm not Da's kid."

"That's not true. He's your Da. He adopted you right away. I am glad you know. I've been waiting years for your Ma to tell you."

"Nana, Ma got married to some dark-haired boy from the mountains when she was my age," Ruby's voice was outraged. She rubbed her hands on Gran's soft old dishtowel.

"Yes, she did and had the two of ye—you and your sister. Her husband's name was Dani and he died in a mountain fall," Nana's voice was calm. "It happened a long time ago, Ruby, and your Mum was all alone in that God forsaken country. My son, Linc, was dead by the time she got there." Her voice still held old traces of pain, remembering her beautiful son lying dead in the Blue Mountain caves.

"So was she married in the Church at least?"

"No darlin' they don't have the Church in that country."

"She probably wasn't married at all. They were just sleeping together. I know it. Oh, Nana, it means I'm illegitimate!"

Nana rose and walked over to Ruby's side of the counter saying, "Nonsense, Ruby girl. You're grand, yes you are. You know your Ma believes in other things—something she calls the Sacred Feminine. She doesn't even go to church with you and your Da. And you've been baptized, you will go to heaven, I have no doubt."

"How do we know this Dani lad is even dead? She could be married to the both of them." Ruby felt her body grow hot and queasy at the horrible thought of bigamy.

"He's gone from this earthly life. Your Mum saw him fall into a dark crack in the mountain. She told me she tried to climb down to him, but she fell and could hardly escape. She waited at the top of the crack for weeks and nearly starved herself before she gave up."

"Sora Margaret says if a girl lets a boy have her before their marriage, she cannot be cleansed of that sin. Sora says a girl's greatest treasure is her virginity and that boys are just nasty little burglars! Oh Gran, my Mum is going to hell," Ruby cried.

"Ruby, my darlin' your Mother is much like me own dear grandmother who was of the old Celtic people. My grandmother believed she saw the face of the Goddess in the spirits of animals. She lit a candle every night to a white statue of a lioness she called the Goddess of Fertility. It worked, you know. The woman had twelve little children. And, my grandmother had the Sight."

"The Sight, it's all pagan nonsense, that's what the Sora tell us."

"God's Church was built on the foundation of those old beliefs, Dearie. You know the Church honors the spirits of animals. Last year they had a Mass and your brought your Irish setter for the Priest's blessing, didn't ye?"

Ruby nodded reluctantly. Bitterness made the corners of her mouth turn down.

"What matters now is that your Mum has told you about your sister. You have no idea how much your Ma has suffered worrying that the little dote died. She had the light of the risen Lord on her face when she showed me the letter from Maidenstone."

"I'm still mad. She kept this dark secret from me my whole life, and then she expects me to forgive her!"

"Give yourself time, Dearie. She's your Mum and a fine one. It will be good to have another young one around here. The only thing I can't understand is why she isn't sending you."

"You think I should go?" Ruby's eyes widened. "I wouldn't set foot in that God-forsaken country."

"I think it would be the greatest adventure you could ever have," Nana's eyes crinkled and she smiled.

I would chain myself to the altar first, Ruby thought, as she sipped her tea.

Chapter 5 – In Natil, the Valley of the King
Vernal Moon, March

While Ruby's grandmother tried to convince her to consider going to Namché, Sab-ra petitioned King Ruisenor for permission to leave Natil.

Waiting for my turn to kneel before King Ruisenor, I vividly recalled standing here when I suffered from the drumbeat. It had been a year since I begged the King to let me go to war. I was thin and white lipped then, addicted to opium, with dull eyes and lifeless hair. Now I was in perfect health, glowing with the gloss pregnancy gives a woman. When I reached the front of the line of petitioners and knelt to ask for permission to leave the Kingdom, his immediate reaction was to deny my request.

"Sab-ra, I must have you here in the Kingdom for Queen Ion'li," he said. "Your request is denied."

"I know my duty lies with Queen Ion'li," I told him, "I would never fail her. However, she will not give birth until winter and I will return in a month. I would remind you, King Ruisenor, that it is Wirri-won who asked for me."

After talking together longer, the King reluctantly granted my request. Wirri-won's fame as a Healer was known even in Natil. For the first time since I arrived in the King's Valley, except for the night Conquin delivered, I felt needed. Wirri-won, the ancient Healer with white hair that flowed down below her waist had called for me, Sab-ra of Talin. I felt a tiny breeze of relief wave across me, insulating me from the dark sadness of my husband's loss. The Wind Goddess, my own totem spirit had brought me a message.

I went to the Clinic and gathered all the medical supplies I could fit in two saddlebags. I took pearls of the poppy, feverfew and boneset. I took Deepsleep leaves and Lethal Sleep. I grabbed long white bandage rolls and soap grasses. Then I went to the kitchen and asked the cooks for extra food. When I told them I was travelling to work with Wirri-won, they raised their arms and crossed them over their faces, backing away. They practically threw the food at me, running from the room.

Rohr was grooming his stallion, Tye, in the stables. When I told him the King had ordered him to take me to Wirri-won, his dark features blanched.

"You will not go," he said fiercely.

This Warrior had led me safely across the top of the Blue Mountains in winter. Why would a short trip to the ninth valley in spring scare him so badly? It was baffling, but I was unmoved. Wirri-won had called me. Like the time I felt called to war, I knew I would erase whatever barriers stood in my way to heed her summons.

We left for the Island of the Eaten on a cool spring morning several days later. I could hardly mount Yellowmane. I had to try several times, vastly amusing Rohr. I was almost six months pregnant and already very large. Conquin kept teasing me, saying I carried more than one baby. I told her she wasn't funny. When I turned back to wave farewell, I saw Conquin's husband holding her. She collapsed against him, sobbing. Clearly, she thought this journey a profitless adventure, or worse. My dearest friend didn't have the ability to see the future, but she was highly empathic. I quivered inside, wondering what she had envisioned.

We rode through lands dripping with spring rain. Yellowmane was excited to be on the trail and pulled hard on her reins. Rohr kept a relatively slow pace beside me, but it was obvious he was deeply unhappy. He kept pointing at my belly and shaking his head.

Two days later, we reached the valley of Tinsen, where Justyn's grandparents lived. Justyn my dearest friend had begged me repeatedly to marry him, but I had chosen the Kosi King, against all the mores of my culture. I hoped for a welcome, perhaps even an invitation to stay overnight. When I knocked on the door, Justyn's Grandmother came out on the stoop.

"I greet you, Grandmother of Justyn," I said, smiling. The muscles in her face tightened when she saw my pregnant belly. The lines around her mouth deepened.

"Is it Justyn's child?" she asked, pointing at my belly.

"No Honorary Grandmother, I carry the son of the King of the Kosi. We were married before the Avalanche destroyed the Skygrass valley."

She took a deep breath and then turned around, gently closing the door between us. At first, I was dismayed, then angry. I could understand her disappointment, but it hurt that she didn't invite me to come in the house. The last time I saw Justyn was just before we left Talin to return to the Skygrass valley after the War. We planned to mine blue diamonds to pay the Kosi for their services in protecting the valley. After the Kosi King and I were married, I sent Justyn a letter telling him my decision. I wondered if he ever received the message. Now he would hear the news from his bitter grandmother.

Rohr and I spent a cold, wet night sleeping on the ground as the wind rose. The warrior asked me to stop the rain, but I shook my head. Since becoming pregnant, I had not been able to command the Wind Goddess. Pregnancy had removed my gift.

The Blood Arrow and I arrived at the White River the following day. It was evening and the rain had finally ceased. The trees were dripping, but the afternoon sun lit the leaves and nature shone around us. We looked north at a great waterfall cascading down the Blue Mountains. In the wild roaring waters at the very pinnacle of the falls, tall trees walked across the rapid churning river. I could see no land up there at all.

"Island of the Eaten," Rohr said, pointing up to the trees.

"How do I get up there?" I asked him, starting to realize why Rohr was frightened, why the cooks warded off evil spirits and Conquin shook in her husband's arms.

"We wait," he said and so we did.

The following morning, I saw three riderless donkeys pick their way slowly down the steep walls of the Dhali Ra. The Dhali Ra is the most sacred peak within the Blue Mountain range. My People believe it is the home of the Great Mountain Goddess. When the donkeys reached us, out of breath and wet with sweat, they stopped. Their small bulbous knees, ears like furry brown arum lilies and huge dark eyes captivated me. I scratched them between the eyes. Only one wore a saddle. The other two had empty pannier packs on their backs.

"Am I supposed to ride this donkey?" I asked Rohr. "Up that vertical cliff?"

He eyed me in dismay. "Don't go," he said. He reached out his hand to touch my belly. "I beg you, Wife of the King, please don't do this."

I felt his fears and my own rise up inside me. My heart quickened but I slowly put my supplies in the donkeys' packs and clumsily mounted the lead donkey.

"Rohr, my Guardian, Wirri-won asked for me. I cannot deny her summons."

"I will wait here for your body," Rohr said and turned his back on me. It was a chilling farewell. When he and I left Skygrass after the Avalanche, Say'f commanded Rohr to protect me. He told Rohr his life was forfeit if he failed to bring me living to the Valley of the King. Rohr clearly believed this foolhardy venture would mean my death. If that happened and Say'f returned, Rohr would have failed and would pay with his life. I felt a ghost shiver-walk across my shoulders.

The ascent was almost vertical. The path was narrow as a snake, filled with slippery shale. The lead donkey picked her way carefully, but I could feel her fears. I tried desperately to calm myself, knowing donkeys could feel human panic. I dared not look down. I kept my eyes raised to the trees where many birds waited. They were green with long beaks and curving tails; a species I didn't recognize. I saw one returning to her nest. She carried a small furred body in her mouth. It was an ominous sign. They were carnivorous and lived by the trail, waiting to eat the bodies of those who died. Lovely air orchids bedecked the stunted pine trees. Tiny blue dipper birds dashed in and out of the falling waters, catching caddis flies under splashing water.

About twenty thent below the top, we reached a landing carved out of the mountain. The donkeys were breathing hard. I let them rest and gave them water from my waterskin. When my donkey's breathing slowed, we began the final ascent. She got a running start and plowed straight up. I leaned as far forward as I could with my belly in the way. My heart rose in my throat as the donkey slipped, clambered to her feet and dashed up again. Behind us, the other two donkeys waited patiently until we reached the enormous flat stone at the top. I struggled to calm my breathing and my terrible fears.

Two small men emerged from the shadows of a stable made out of green branches and moss. Both wore dark scarves across their lower faces. Between the scarves and their long hair, I could see nothing but their eyes. In this land of water and mist, I wondered why they needed such protection. Neither man spoke. They took my donkey, leaving me standing on an enormous rock beside a vast sheet of moving water. The men unloaded the leather packs from the two donkeys with my supplies.

I looked across the wide river for a better view of this island that so threatened a Kosi Warrior. Now that I had reached the summit, I felt calmer, more in control of my fears. It was only an island, nothing that frightening. A small building made of white stone stood in a grove of Rholam trees toward the rear of the island, but I saw no bridge leading from the landing where I stood to the island. Above the island, the river disappeared into a tall black crack in the high range.

Then I noticed a floating platform, a barge made of tree trunks lashed together with leather lacings, tied to a nearby tree. I motioned to one of the men in the stable. He walked over and I reached for his hand to read his thoughts. He yanked his whole body away from me, looking terrified. He pointed at my belly. I was confused, wondering if he was worried about my baby. He gestured for me to step on to the barge. I touched it with my toe, but the roaring river rocked it precariously. Terrified, I leapt back on to the bank. The donkey minder and I looked at each other in silence.

"I can't ride on this barge," I told him, my heart pounded so hard I shook.

He pointed up into the trees where I saw a small woven seat attached to a liana cable hanging above the icy river. The cable was tied to the stable on our side and to one of the trees on the island. The donkey man pulled the seat down and indicated I should sit on it. The little seat looked old and had started to fray. I looked down a thousand thent to see Rohr standing on the riverbank below me. We were so high above him; he looked like a black beetle—a black beetle who waited for my dead body.

"Wirri-won?" I asked the donkey man. He nodded. "Help me," I said and the donkey man helped load medicines, bandages, food and soap grasses onto the barge, but would not lift me into the seat. Holding my terror at bay, I climbed very carefully into the small rocking seat. It was not wide enough for a pregnant woman. The wind grew stronger. The man pulled on the cable, hoisting me jerkily high above the river. I screamed in fear and clung desperately to the ropes as he propelled me furiously across the foaming water. It seemed forever, but in truth took only moments until he lowered me down on the island.

Dozens of people ran toward me, screaming, greeting me with high-pitched cries. A roaring horror took my mind. They had no faces. Their hoods covered nothing but skulls made of skin. I held my arms up, screaming for them not to touch me.

"Wirri-Won," I shrieked. "Help!"

Chapter 6 – On the Isle of Verdantia

While Sab-ra screamed for Wirri-Won to save her, her twin sister Ruby took out a pen to record her thoughts in her Diary.

Dear Diary,

It has been a month since I heard the devastating news that Da is not me father and Ma married a mountain lad (or maybe didn't even. I am still disgusted with her) and got herself pregnant. I talked with my Nana, my best friend Jackie and me boyfriend, Shane. I told them all about it. Shane just kept kissing me. He was trying to distract me and make me stop crying. He tried to unbutton my shirt and I said, 'Would you ever just hump off.' He left me, all mad.

Jackie said I should have known my mother had loved another man before me Da. She reminded me my Ma taught all that old Celtic stuff at the University and those old people thought a woman got a child from a god, a tree, or some such heathen nonsense.

My mother got her tickets to go to Nam-shay a month after confessing her sins to me. At least her conscience was clear. I was still furious. Da defended her to the hilt, like all'us.

I went to see Dar. Patrick and told him all about it. He said I was probably right. Ma was a truly sinful woman, not even believing in one God, but said I was keeping the sin of anger. He told me to pray for the wisdom to forgive my mother. He said he would talk with her again about her pagan beliefs. He thought she might give them up and join the church if she could find my sister. I have me doubts.

Signed, "Hard Done By" Ruby

Dear Diary,

Despite myself, I have decided to go to the Blue Mountains. After Ma got her ticket, she got the bursitis in her shoulder and the doc said she couldn't go. Ma begged me to go with tears in her eyes. Nana turned in Ma's tickets and bought me a boat ticket and the train tickets too. Da said I was too young to go on such a long trip; something bad would happen to me. Nana said he was living in the past. Girls took protection with them these days, like knives and that. In the end, Da said it was my choice, but he didn't want me to go. It wasn't really a free choice for me though, Ma forced me. She said she could never forgive herself if she didn't try to find my sister. A mother's tears, how could a daughter refuse?

I had to meet with all my teachers. They gave me stuff to read and I'm going to have to take a passel of tests when I get back, but they didn't think I would lose the whole year. My Science teacher said I should have known. When we did the Genetics last *year, she told me I couldn't have these dark eyes with two blue-eyed parents.*

I am going to tell this moochin' sister of mine that she can just stay in her country. I'll be giving out when I see her, you can just bet.

Signed "still outraged" Ruby

Dear Diary,

I leave in the morning. Mum is still in hospital from the bursitis. It's turned into some form of pneumonia. I wanted to stay and see her home from hospital, but she said she didn't want me to wait any longer. She was afraid for me sister. She gave me her small green book; the one she reads at night. I couldn't read the language it was written in, but Ma had drawn pictures in the flyleaf. They showed grass as high as her shoulders and grasshoppers flying in formation. In the margins, she drew a picture of the Lion Baba, with his mane and tufts of hair on his ears. She wrote his name, Sumulus. She wrote other shocking stuff too, I closed the book it was so bad. Something about how she felt when Dani made love to her outside in the grass, no less. Good thing Dar. Patrick doesn't know that stuff.

Signed, "Shocked and Dismayed" Ruby

Chapter 7 – On the Island of the Eaten

While Ruby recorded her consternation about her mother's long held secret, Sab-ra trembled at the top of the waterfall screaming for Wirri-won.

An Mali, the Healer from Maidenstone, had taught me about leprosy when I studied with her in Namché. She said it began by consuming the nose and mouth. Then it ate the fingers and toes. The ears go after that. These people had no features at all, only holes in their heads. They were nightmares wrapped in white rags. They circled me screaming in a demented dance and I remembered Rohr waiting patiently a thousand thent below. Dread coursed through my heart. He had been right. I had put my life in jeopardy. I had risked the King's son. I reached up desperately for the swing, but donkey man had already raised it high above the waters, pulling it back to his side of the river. I was trapped. The non-humans would eat me alive.

"Wirri-won," I screamed frantically. "Help me."

The door to the white building opened and the ancient Healer came walking out. She was wearing a bright yellow dress decorated with beads forming shining suns and red flowers. The sun hit the bald top of her head making it look as if she wore a halo. Pride and pleasure suffused her features. Walking toward me, she stopped several times speaking to the eaten, even touching their wasted faces. When she reached me, she raised both arms in the air saying, "Welcome, Wife of the Kosi King."

Remembering my manners, I knelt and murmured, "I greet you, Great Healer. I came because you sent for me."

When she reached her hands toward me, some innate memory from my ancestors hundreds of years before, made me flinch. I wrapped my arms around my belly, my skin crawling. "Don't touch me," I cried.

Wirri-won looked at me with deep compassion in her eyes. Her empathy reached all the way to the bottom of her soul. When she turned back toward the white building, she called over her shoulder to me.

"Maidenstone Healer," she said. "Your babies will never have Terosi." It was the People's word for leprosy.

I stood there breathing deeply. I wiped the sweat from my brow and prayed to the Wind Goddess, asking her if I should enter the building. A trace of laelia perfume washed the island, the sign and blessing of the Goddess. Straightening my shoulders, I followed Wirri-won slowly into the Clinic, fearing I would never see my Grandparents, Say'f or Conquin again.

Toward the right of the entryway, I saw a massive table. Like Maidenstone's medicine table in the Infirmary, it was crowded with cures wrapped in leather packets, deer hide and Ghat skin. Exquisite drawings of plants had been carved into the leather pouches and animal skin packages. The poisons were marked with the symbol of the hangman's noose.

When Wirri-won opened the door to the next room, a barrage of happy voices called out. To my immense surprise, I saw many children. Some were babies, standing up in tiny hanging beds. Others were older and a few were adolescents on the verge of adulthood. I dreaded seeing their tiny noses and ears eaten, but when I looked closely, all of them were perfect. They astounded me. Not a single blemish marked their brimming vitality.

I realized then what Wirri-won had done. This amazing woman was not a Healer. This woman was a Goddess. Alone, on this island at the top of the waterfall, she had somehow placed a healing membrane around each child. The evil tentacles of leprosy hadn't touched a single one. She had not cured the flesh-eating disease; she had prevented it.

Wirri-won led the way toward the back of the building. All the children followed. They were speaking patois, a mix of Kosi words and those of the People. Some were laughing; others sang. We reached a kitchen with several tables, enough for all the children. A young woman came out of a doorway bringing trays of food. I thought she was whole, but then noticed that she had only two fingers on one hand. I wondered if she was the first person Wirri-won had tried to cure. The Healer took the food trays over to the tables for the children. All of them took their places cheerfully. Wirri-won lifted the smallest ones up into high chairs.

I looked out through the windows. The terrible people with no faces hovered around looking inside. I knew they were the parents of these children. Even with no features, I could feel their longing and love. I wondered if Wirri-won permitted them to touch their infants even once, before she took them away to vaccinate them. Later the Healer took me to a small room at the back of the white clinic.

"This is where you will sleep," Wirri-won informed me. I put my things in the room, noticing the sleeping hammock sway and hearing the tumbling waters rushing by. The sound was an ominous sign of the river's power. I looked out the window at the grass verge where the land met the river. The constant thrust of the water tore another hunk of the sod away.

At night the Isle shakes," she said, "The White River is strong. Blanda must leave soon." Blanda was the Kosi word for children.

My fears roared across my spirit again, fearing the cold muscularity of the river. I felt the beginnings of a headache, something I hadn't had for many months.

"Walk with me," she said.

We left the building and walked around to the end of the island. She pointed down at the rear bank. The fierce current battered against the earth, sharply undercutting the land. Wirri-won pointed to the trees in the river above us. Some still stood, although the water rose to their leaves. The river had tipped over others; their roots rose in the current. If the island was once large enough to hold all those trees, the White River had eaten half of it already.

I thought I would never again experience the paralyzing fear I felt when Captain Grieg captured me and took me inside the

Great Dhali Ra Mountain, but I was wrong. I had risked everything to be here and now I would die and so would my son. Wirri-won and the beautiful Blanda she had saved—all of us would fall victim to the White river. I should have insisted on leaving right then, but it was already dark. Once it was daylight, I would inform Wirri-won I had to go. I could not risk my child a moment longer.

We walked back to the front of the clinic, unloaded the barge, took food into the building and gave it to the kitchen helper. I spent a horrible night, lying in a hammock that seemed to rest only inches above the wild waters. The White River growled beneath me all night. In the morning, I helped Wirri-won give the children their breakfast.

"It is good you came," she said. "You can help the Blanda escape. It is time."

I shivered, wondering when she planned to get me off the island. After they ate, she led the children singing to the barge. She lined them up, two by two. Each older child held a younger child by the hand. She gestured for them to sit down on the wooden platform. We strapped them together with long leather harnesses. The cracks between the boards were wide enough for a person's hand to reach down into the frothing waters. She told the children to huddle close together in the center.

"What if they fall off?" I asked her, terrified for them.

"The Island dies tomorrow," she said, ominously. "There is no other way."

Chapter 8 – The City of Namché
March

While Sab-ra helped Wirri-won arrange an escape for the leper children, Da took Ruby to the Docks. She would leave for Namché on the rising tide the following morning.

Ruby was to depart for the Nam-shay on a gray rainy day in March. Da was so sad looking she almost decided not to go. He told her it would take two weeks to get to the Blue Mountain country. He brought her young red setter dog, Maeve, with them and Ruby could hardly stand to say good-bye to the two of them. She felt the tears well up whenever she looked into her dog's dark loving eyes.

"When the Ferry reaches the mainland tomorrow, you're going to have to get to the Train Depot. You should hail a horse-drawn cab. Here, I drew this picture of a train. Just show the driver this. I still think you're a right eejit for going." He shook his head.

"Da, you are lookin' absolutely shook. I'll be fine. Now, you have to promise me not to get langered every night while I'm gone. Only have a pint or two with the lads of an evening, will you? Please keep track of me dog until Ma comes back from

Hospital. And I need you to write me and let me know she's getting better."

Da held her hands and begged her to promise she would return as soon as she found her twin. Long after the boat pulled away from the dock, Ruby stood at the railing and waved at him. He was a dark speck, still waving, when the storm clouds hid him from sight.

The winds were horrendous, the boat wallowed and Ruby threw up over the deck railings repeatedly. Her red hair was soaked from the rain; pressed flat against her cheeks. By the time the boat landed, she was exhausted, already regretting having left Da, her Mum and her dog Maeve.

She hailed a horse-drawn cab and showed the cabbie the picture. The little puck took her from the waterfront to the train station. He held out his hand after, wanting money. She pulled some silver groats from her bag and he took two, smiling and bowing. The station was so big and dark it looked like the mouth of the Fiend himself, belching red smoke. There were like a hundred trains. She found the ticket office by reading the signs and handed the small gnome-like man her ticket.

"You already have your ticket, girlie, just get on the train," he said looking at her like she was mental.

"Which one?" she asked.

"It's that one there," he said pointing.

Once on the train, she talked with a man in a uniform who took her to a little curtained alcove. It had a tiny settee with bright cushions resting on a green metal bench. There was a window to the outside. Above the seat, there was a door. She opened it; inside there was a fold-down bed. The tiny nook had a sink and a pitcher full of water, but no latrine, not even a hole in the floor of the train. Barbarous form of transport, Ruby thought. Nana had sent apples, hard bread and cheese. She figured she would run out of food in about an hour. She wished she had chained herself to Viridian's High Church.

In the night the train stopped. Ruby dashed from the rails into the brush and did her business. She was climbing back on board when the uniform stopped her.

"Ticket," he demanded.

"It's in me room," she said outraged, whispering 'eejit' under her breath.

"All right then," he said. "I'll come by later to punch it."

Ruby had no idea what he meant. She was walking along the swaying aisle when a woman with a backside the size of a sheep, opened the door into the hall. Ruby looked in and saw a whole row of toilets. It was the jacks for everyone. Heaven forbid the boys used it too!

When the uniform came, he took her ticket and cut a little circle out of it.

"You don't have to stay in here the whole time," he said. "You can go out and sit in the regular seats if you want."

Later, when she was bored of looking out the window in her alcove, Ruby discovered the part of the train where rows of benches faced each other. She was surprised to see two of the Garda sitting in the seats. They were police officers; law-keepers on Viridian. They smiled and tipped their hats to her. They wore black uniforms with golden triangles on their caps. The color of the uniforms surprised her, usually the Garda wore blue uniforms.

"Where are you off to then, girlie?" one asked after her.

"What's it to you then," she said. "Bold 'un."

"We wuz just wondering if you were going as far as the east. We're going all the way to the folded land."

"Fair play to you," she said walking down the aisle and taking a seat. Shane had warned her off the fellas. He said the Garda were a bunch of bollix who were getting above themselves because of the uniforms. She had to admit the uniforms were sweet.

The Garda moved seats until they were sitting across from her. They opened their lunches and offered her poms and nuts. Ruby accepted one gingerly. She was starving. Her food was already gone.

"Give us a kiss then for the pom," a red haired freckled one said. "Or at least tell us your name."

"Ah, he just never shuts his gob," the dark haired one said. "I'm Jaime, this numbskull is Carmac." Jaime hit his friend in the head with the flat of his hand saying, "He just thinks he's God's gift. I'm the one who knows how to properly kiss a girl."

"I'm Ruby," she said and laughed at them. What harm could it do to speak to the lads? This stupid trip was already starting to feel like it would never end.

"We're going to supply a Garrison where all the soldiers went on some bloody quest up into the Blue Mountains. They all died, so the call came out for soldiers wanting a bit of action to come and help 'man up' the Garrison. That's why we are wearing the black uniforms."

"It's in this god-forsaken culchie town called Nam something or other," Carmac said.

"It is Nam-shay?" she asked.

"Tis," Jaime agreed.

"I'll be goin' along then with ye then," she said. "I'm headed there meself."

The young men looked at each other and at her, grinning.

"Yous can sleep in our bunks if you're tired like," Carmac said.

"I have me own bunk and I expect you to watch out for me like I was your little sister," she said, "and not be a bunch of jackeens. I'm under the age of consent and Dar. Patrick will be waiting to be sure I've done no sin when I get back."

"Yah, sure, we will. We were just slaggin' you," Jaime said. "You'll be safe with us."

Later, when Ruby returned to her small cubicle, she pulled down the bed, climbed up into it and pulled out a pen to write in her Diary.

Dear Diary,

I've met some gom Island lads on the train. They are Garda and going to Nam-shay too. They like to act like bold maggots, but I think they will watch out for me. It's making the trip go easier. Yesterday we passed the first set of mountains; the train went up and down like a little toy crossing miniature hills. The Garda told me I could eat one meal a day in the dining room. The cost was included with the ticket, they said. Gran might have mentioned. I was darn near to having a weakness before those boys gave me some of their food.

Da had this language teacher come to the house before I left. She taught me how to say, "My name is Ruby," and "I'm wanting to find Maidenstone," and a bunch of other phrases like, "Where is the toilet?" I actually got quite good, at least I could understand it, but my accent was funny, apparently. The Garda lads were most impressed.

As soon as I get to Nam-shay and see this twin sister, I'm going to make her promise to stay where she is. I'll turn right around and go back to Viridian.

Signed, Ruby the bold girl

Chapter 9 – On the Island of the Eaten

While Ruby travelled in the pleasant company of the Garda soldiers, Wirri-won and Sab-ra got the children ready to depart.

Wirri-won and I continued to ready the children for evacuation from the Island of the Eaten. At our signal, the donkey minders on the other side would pull the barge to their side of the river. About a third of the children were able to sit on the barge in the first crossing. When the raft started to move, they screamed, clutching each other desperately. Three fell into the river, gone before a hand could reach for them. I could hardly watch. My stomach heaved. I retched into the reeds.

When they reached the landing, the men put the babies in the donkey packs to begin the vertical descent. With only three animals to carry the children down, it would take many hours to evacuate everyone.

We assembled the next group of children, putting fewer on this time. All of them made the other side and took their places waiting for the donkeys. When all the children stood on the other side of the river, Wirri-won and I gathered her medicines and supplies. The whole island was shaking by then, several trees creaked as they came crashing down. The wind lashed the trees. I tried desperately to hurry the Medicine woman, but she calmly made trip after trip until at last she sat down on the barge, surrounded by her medicines and those I had brought with me.

I stepped onto the barge with her, but she pushed me back on to the island. She held her hand out to the kitchen woman who stood beside me, indicating she could board the barge.

"Maidenstone Healer," she said pointing to the woven seat floundering in the air high above us. "You ride the air."

I looked back at the ghostly parents standing behind me. They were all huddled together, sobbing. Tears streamed from empty eye sockets. The donkey men levered the seat across the water to me. I jumped into the air repeatedly, trying to grab it. It was my one chance to reach safety. The Island throbbed. Once I got a hand on the seat, but it slipped from my wet hand and I fell in the mud, near the edge. Several of the Eaten came forward. I waved them back shrieking; afraid to have them touch me. Clumsily, I got to my feet. One of the Eaten managed to pull the seat down for me. He held it, careful not to touch me in the roaring wind, as I climbed awkwardly in. I heard a horrific snap and the donkey man yanked the seat high in the air.

The sound increased and I saw the whole island begin to move. I sat in the air, buffeted by the screaming wind, high above the tragedy. More trees fell. One crashed beside me; its limbs nearly ripped me from the seat. The white building crumbled. Time slowed and I saw the Eaten parents tip over, one by one into the water. Those who still had hands not yet eaten by leprosy held them together in prayer. The whole island disappeared over the verge and the waters closed over the heads of the last swimmers.

Not one of the Eaten had tried to board the barge. Not one tried to get into the flying seat. They chose to save their children; they chose to save me. For themselves, they chose death by water. Although my People believed those who died in water could never walk the sky world, I said the prayer for the valiant dead. I asked the Mountain Goddess to take their souls to the heights.

All the children who reached the riverbank alive, made it to the bottom of the mountain over the next two days—before the last donkey died. I grieved for him; he had saved so many children, only to lose his own life. I swallowed hard, honoring the flame of his steadfast courage.

Wirri-Won, the girl from the kitchen and I were still waiting at the top when Rohr sent Yellowmane running, falling, slipping and breathing as if her heart would break, up the vertical slope. When she reached the enormous flat stone, I held her quivering until her heartbeat slowed. I took her into the stable for food and water.

Wirri-won handed me a small packet containing a powdery substance. "For you and the babies," she told me, pointing at my stomach, "When they are one year old." She held up one finger.

"Thank you Great Healer," I said. "I honor your achievement with the Blanda." We stood in the pounding rain looking at each other, drenched. I shook from the cold and the emotion of our escape. We were hardly able to believe that we had lost so few and saved so many.

"I must go now, Wirri-won. Will you descend with me?"

She shook her head. "Maidenstone Healer takes the Blanda. You find them families."

"I have to find homes for all these children?" I asked, wanting to be sure I understood. I was daunted.

"It was for this task that I called you," Wirri-won replied. She made the Kosi sign of farewell and entered the dark stable. She and the kitchen helper weren't going with me. I felt a lurch of despair in my chest. How in the world was I to find families for all these children of the despised lepers?

It was a desperate descent, Yellowmane fell several times, once pinning me beneath her. I was terrified for my baby. When we reached the bottom at last, I was exhausted and filthy. I looked at the children standing quietly in the rain. They were hungry and terribly afraid. I didn't know if it would work, but I called on the Wind Goddess. Raising my arms into the air, I begged her to stop the rain. Blessedly, she did so.

We started out walking to the Valley of Tinsen in the morning. It had been an awful night. Rohr had constructed a brush arbor for the children, but they all had to sleep on the ground. In the morning, I put one young girl on Yellowmane's back and gave her a baby to hold. I put another baby in Yellowmane's saddlebag. I put one larger boy on Rohr's horse and bade him hold the littlest infant in front of him. To his disgust, I made Rohr walk. I gave my shoes to an older child who had none. His toes were white with cold.

We trekked up and down the folded earth. Many of the younger children couldn't keep up and stragglers made the line longer and longer. I ordered Rohr to return for them and carry them up to the front. He did so repeatedly, but grunted saying it was no work for a warrior.

We reached the house of Justyn's Grandmother at evening the next day. I decided I would not tell her where the children came from. The prejudice was very strong against anyone with leprosy. Wirri-Won had inoculated the children against the disease, but I wasn't sure a non-Healer would understand.

"I greet you Grandmother of Justyn," I said when she opened the door. "I have ten children who need families and five more that are old enough to help the Fur Trappers. Will you please, in the name of the Goddess, will you please help me?"

She looked at me; wet, bedraggled, pregnant and barefoot. She hesitated and I fell to my knees. I begged her with my eyes.

"Come in," she said.

I hugged her so hard she could hardly breathe. In three days, we had homes for all ten of the smallest children. The remaining five who ranged from nine to sixteen, followed us out of Tinsen on foot. I was grateful to have my shoes back. The valley of Royenal needed laborers in the salt flats and took three children. The last two came with Rohr and me—a boy around ten, whose name was Bumpy, and a girl of nine. Her name was Belaro. We were fortunate that Justyn's Grandfather had a dweli, the warm folding shelters we use in the mountains. We purchased it to take with us.

Chapter 10 – In the City of Namché

While Sab-ra and Rohr took the remaining leper children toward the King's Valley, Ruby and the Garda arrived in the city of Namché.

Ruby opened her eyes to a cloudy day with gusting wind as the train came to a stop in Nam-shay. The train station was very small compared to those she had encountered on the trip. She looked around, excited to see the place where she was born. The town had been built in layers, like a wedding cake. A wavy wall made a circle of protection around the city. Terraces that looked like massive green lily pads stuck out from the sides of the mount. At the very top of the layer cake mountain, Ruby saw what looked like a tall bracelet of towers linked by bridges. The bridges must have been made of prisms because when the sun hit them, rainbows covered the structure and it looked magical.

The Garda fellas walked with her to the Army barracks. The Garrison was comprised of four buildings placed around a graveled square. On the right side was a two-story block building. To the left there were two more buildings; one contained the dining area. Ruby could smell cooking. She thought the third was probably the soldiers' sleeping quarters. At the back of the square, another building served as the stable. Ruby saw a Garda leading a horse inside. A walled enclosure stood in the center of the open square.

"So, Ruby girl, will ya' kiss us gom-bye then," Carmac asked, grinning at her.

"Don't you be kissing him, I'm the best kisser," Jaime gestured to his lips.

"Are you boys leavin' before taking me to this Maidenstone place?" Ruby's excitement at arriving in the city was gone suddenly and she felt the cool wind hit her face.

Jaime put his arm around her, wanting a kiss good-bye. Surprising herself, Ruby kissed him back. Carmac hit his friend's arm and pointed across the graveled square. A short soldier with medals all over his chest walked toward them and barked out some words. He must have asked for their papers. After looking over the orders, the decorated soldier nodded at Ruby and gestured for the lads to follow him. The fellas looked back at her, a bit ashamed to leave her, but marched after the Lootenant or Captain or whatever he was.

Ruby walked the ancient cobblestone streets toward the market area. She could smell the scent of bread baking. Street musicians played a cheerful tune and children ran toward her carrying small open vessels. She dropped a coin into each leather bowl. The dark eyed little ones were just plain enchanting. There were many shops selling beautiful silks, spices and vegetables. The proprietors bowed to her as she passed. She got up her courage at one shop that sold wool. She entered and touched the yard goods, finding them softer than any she'd felt on the Isle of Viridian A young woman came out of the back and chattered to her. Ruby was delighted she could understand most of her words. Those language lessons Da made her take had paid off.

"I need to go to Maidenstone," Ruby told the clerk. She thought she had said it correctly, but the woman looked confused.

"Maid – en – stone," she said. The girl nodded and pointed to the massive circle of colored towers at the top of the mount. She took hold of Ruby's arm and led her through the confusing array of streets and alleys, until they reached the bottom of an enormous stairway. Ruby had to tip her head back to see the whole of it. Rainbows from the glass bridges came half way down the mountain; truly lovely it was.

"Thank you," Ruby said and reached for her. She took the girl's face in her hands and kissed both the girl's cheeks. It was a customary manner of giving thanks in Viridian. The clerk seemed startled but then smiled. Gesturing to the stairs, the clerk dashed back into the maze of alleys.

Ruby took the steps slowly, feeling the importance of this day, going to this place where her mother had left her sister seventeen years ago. She climbed past beautiful houses covered with flowered vines. Another million steps higher, it seemed, she looked down again seeing a kind of mist that hung around the base of the mountain, solid as a snowdrift.

When she finally reached the top, she saw six colored spires standing in a circle. A taller white tower stood in the center. A web of shining bridges connected them. The rainbows glinting off the structure were blindingly beautiful. Ruby was walking toward the yellow tower when she heard a woman's voice call.

"Sab-ra, my goodness, how is it that you have returned?"

Ruby turned toward a dumpy woman in a pale blue dress. She had a white cap on her gray hair and looked like a grandmother. She was running toward her with outstretched arms.

"Oh," the woman stopped suddenly. "You aren't Sab-ra." She walked up and touched Ruby's hair. Then she said, "I know who you are." She took Ruby's hand and giving her no chance to refuse, led her inside a door in the yellow tower.

Once inside, they walked down beautiful stone-flagged halls until they reached an interior door with a curved top. When the pudgy woman opened it, Ruby saw a beautiful raven-haired woman in a dark blue gown wearing a complex white and ivory braided belt at her waist. The woman stood up and breathed out audibly, her mouth making an "Ah" of astonishment. Together the two women looked at Ruby in amazed silence.

Ruby just stood there, wondering if they were mental. The women talked together but she caught only a word or two. Then the dark haired one spoke to her in her own tongue.

"Ruby?"

"Yes, I am called Ruby." She was feeling irked at this inspection. This place was so far from Viridian. She wondered if these two snotty cows were going to offer her something to eat or drink. It was time for tea, after all.

"I am Falcon, Mistress of Maidenstone. This is An Mali, our Healer. Is your mother Ashlin?"

"Yes, that's me Mum." Ruby felt a stab of homesickness. Why had she ever agreed to leave with her mother in hospital?

"Did you know you have a sister?"

"I came to see her. Mum sent me. As soon as I see this twin, I plan to leave. I'm in bits already from the long journey."

Although they both seemed a bit off, they gestured for her to follow them, leading her to the kitchen where thank heavens, she saw a kettle boiling and smelled clover honey. Ruby sat down at the table, nearly stepping on a small white dog lying on the floor. She reached down and picked him up. "I'm sorry," she told him and he licked her chin. He settled in her lap, unwilling to be put down again.

"His name is Cloudheart," Mistress told her. "He is Sab-ra's dog. He seems to like you." She smiled gently.

After eating their simple meal, Mistress took her up a curving flight of steps to a small room. Inside were two beds with white sheets and blue wool coverlets. From the window, Ruby could see the Garrison and the train station. After the women left, she laid down on one of the beds. She was exhausted and a wave of emotion swamped her. Cloudheart had followed her up the stairs and settled between the beds with a contented sigh. Ruby trailed her hand down to pet him. Just before she fell deeply into a warm river of sleep, she prayed to meet her sister soon, so this wretched trip would be over and she could return to her own country.

Chapter 11 – The Settlement of Rhan Du

As Ruby slept with one hand resting on Cloudheart, Sab-ra begged Rohr to take her west, away from Natil, the King's valley.

I woke early on the second day of our return trip to Natil. When I came out of the dweli, Rohr was loading the horses. Dweli are the portable shelters made of thick felt we take with us on long journeys. Bumpy and Belaro were still sleeping. Seeing the profile of the mountains, I realized that we were very close to Rhan Du, the small settlement near the entrance to the Lost Lake. When I saw the Lost Lake for the first time, I knew the Goddess of the Dhali Ra Mountain had revealed it to the People, to replace the Skygrass valley destroyed by the Avalanche. I had been inside that valley only once. Since then, its unearthly splendor came to me often in dreams.

"Lord Rohr," I called to him, "I've changed my mind. I don't want to return to Natil. I wish to go to the Lost Lake. Rhan Du is close by and there might be an entrance to the Lost Lake near that village."

Rohr glowered. "You have only a short time until you are delivered of the King's son. It is not safe. The Avalanche destroyed your precious Skygrass valley that cost the Kosi so many warriors during the war. There is nothing to return to."

I felt determination rise in my blood, strong as the White River.

"What if the King is alive, Rohr? Say'f could be waiting for us inside that valley unable to get out. Would you deny the Far Seer? Would you deny the call of the King for your service?"

When Rohr and I left after the Avalanche, Say'f stayed behind. He intended to find and kill Captain Grieg, my enemy who had tortured me inside the mountain.

"Do you know he lives? Have you seen him?" Rohr asked me. Although the Kosi prayed to a God of War, they honored and believed in the Far Seer gift.

"In my dreams have seen the Lost Lake where Grieg held me prisoner. In every dream, I see the King's face. He looks sad."

"Then the King is dead. You have seen his revenant," Rohr's voice was adamant.

"You may be correct, Lord Blood Arrow, but I must be sure. I beg you to take me there."

I heard a stirring inside the dweli and Bumpy and Belaro's sleepy voices.

"What will you do with these children?"

"Take them with us. They are forest adepts and could help us find our way."

Rohr grunted and looked at the ground. "Sab-ra, the King is dead. You risk the life of the King's son. I will go alone and kill this soldier, Captain Grieg, who hurt you inside the mountain. This I will do for you, my Queen."

It was the first time he had called me his Queen and it warmed me. My mouth twitched in a smile. I remembered Hodi and the two of us, hardly more than children ourselves, arguing about which of us would kill the Kosi who had abducted his mother, Nyria. It was before we went on our first mission. How very young we were.

"I am sorry, but I cannot let you take this obligation from me. Lord Blood-Arrow. We are bound together to the will of the Kosi King."

Rohr glowered, but turned the horses west.

Three hard days later, we came to the outskirts of Rhan Du, a small wool market village on the western side of the Dhali Ra. The settlement was wet, bedraggled and had been mostly destroyed by the Avalanche. There were only a few homes, inhabited by Bearer Families. The women and children ran into their houses when they saw us. One man came outside and recognizing a Kosi Warrior, nodded his head. The three of us had a fractured conversation, ending with me taking a Skygrass stone from my pouch and holding it up to the rainy skies, pointing in the direction of the Lost Lake.

The Bearer shook his head. I felt a desperate pain pierce me. If the Bearer people, who would guide anyone in the worst winters, would not take us into the high range, the mystic Skygrass valley and its blue diamond mine were truly gone. Our sacred space lived no more.

He took us to a small house. We entered a kitchen that served us a meal of chanry meat and vegetables. The children devoured the food. After we ate, the woman of the house gave us beds for the night. She was not from the Bearer tribe and looked like the women of the Twelve Valleys. I tried to talk with her in my language.

"My name is Sab-ra," I said, "I am from Talin on the other side of the mountain range. Do you know my People?"

She hesitated, but then in a stuttering fashion began to speak my language. It was obvious she had not spoken our tongue in many years. She asked about the children.

"If I gave you two silver parthats, would you keep them until I return?" She nodded and the children looked relieved, but what she said then made my blood run cold.

"Army man, hair yellow. Came here," she said.

My old enemy Captain Grieg who tortured me inside the mountain had been here before me.

"When did he come?" I asked her, my heart frozen.

"Before Crystal Mountain broken," she said, making a smashing motion with her hands. What the Bearers call the Crystal Mountain has the shape of a giant pyramid. The four great rivers of the world begin at its summit. The Green River flows south and brings the blessing of water to my land. The Yellow River flows east to a land of mystery and magic. The Blue River flows from the north side. The Bearers say it travels to the top of the world. The

Red River flows west, but it disappeared inside the mountain after the Avalanche.

"Did a man named En Sun guide this man up the mountain?"

"Yes. Three men went. Only husband returned."

"En Sun is your husband?" I asked. She nodded. "Have you seen the Army man since then? Captain Grieg?" I trembled as I said his name.

When she shook her head, I told myself that he died in the Lost Lake valley, but I could feel him coming—the face of the dire wolf stalked me. Sweat broke out on my forehead.

"The Kosi and I want to enter the Lost Lake valley. We would pay a man of the village to guide us."

She didn't answer my request, but refilled our water containers and gave us more bread and Ghat cheese to take with us. As we were finishing the meal, a man walked into the house. It was En Sun, the Bearer that Captain Grieg ordered to abduct me. He seemed turned to stone when he saw me.

"You," he said, quivering in fear, "Red hair spirit. You died in mountain."

"I lived," I said and looked at him. He was shaking like the waters in the Scry bowl. "You gave me water. You fixed my dislocated shoulder." As I said these words, I could feel him start to relax. "I didn't die."

He reached out to touch me, wondering if I was a ghost, and Rohr growled at him. I put my hand on Rohr's arm and held out my other hand to En Sun. The Bearer thought I blamed him for my kidnapping, but I did not. Grieg alone was responsible for that horror.

"I am not a ghost," I said. He touched me gingerly, as if I might burn his fingers. Once he had calmed, Rohr asked if he would guide us up the mountain.

En sun became extremely agitated and spoke so fast we could understand little. I caught, "Red River, blood, fire," but nothing else. I took some silver parthats from my leather bag and laid them on the table one by one, making a curving silver road.

En Sun's wife kept pointing to the silver, pleading with her husband to give us what we wanted. He left the house, motioning for us to follow him. When we reached our horses, he pointed to the black dweli packed on Rohr's warhorse. Using sign language, he showed me that he wanted the dweli in payment for his services.

"If I give you this, will you take us?"

He nodded. He still looked terribly frightened, but he had agreed.

"Once we arrive at the Lost Lake, you can have the dweli. Not until then."

He nodded again. Later that evening, En Sun brought us circles of leather and long laces, showing us how to tie them to make little boots to protect our horse's feet. The terrain above Rhan Du was rough with broken lava from the volcanic eruption that followed the Avalanche.

We left the village the next morning, after buying an additional pony from the Bearers; a bright roan named Jemma. If we found the King, he would need a mount. We left the children with En Sun's wife. I kissed them good-by, relieved they would be safe and well fed while we were gone. We followed En Sun up the mountain, stopping now and then to check the horses' leather boot covers. In late afternoon, we reached the bottom of the "bite" the Avalanche took from the Crystal Mountain. The remnants of the Red River, trickles of crimson, flowed down its white face but then disappeared into black holes in the mountain. It seemed menacing, red blood flowing across a pure white skeleton. En Sun, visibly shaken, kept raising his clasped hands to the skies, pleading with his gods to keep him safe.

As the sun went down, I noticed Yellowmane limping. It was worrisome. We had been riding continuously for days and I thought she might be going lame. Then I heard a horrible cracking sound and Yellowmane went down on her front legs to her knees. I feared the sound was the crack of a bullet. I looked around in every direction, but saw no glint of metal, no bushes moving. I jumped from her back and tried desperately to find out what was wrong. Rohr came over and together we felt along her right front leg; I saw no external injury, but she wouldn't put any weight on it. Her leg was broken.

Had I tried once again to be the hero? Had I overreached? Was dearest Yellowmane to pay the price for my arrogant pride?

Goddess, forgive me, I begged. Please don't take Yellowmane as the price for my unswerving determination to find Say'f.

En Sun found a small depression nearby and set up the black dweli. The rains had stopped and the shelter dried, steaming in the low sun. Rohr disappeared to hunt. En Sun helped me get Yellowmane's saddle off her back. She was moaning continuously in terrible pain. I held her beautiful face in my hands and crooned to her, making the sounds I made to women in hard labor. I tried to enter her mind, but forests of pain blocked my way.

With En Sun's help, I found some long straight tree branches. Using the leather from her shoes as a bandage, I made a splint by tying the sticks tightly along her broken leg. It seemed to help and her cries quieted. We managed to walk her slowly on three legs to the area where we planned to spend the night.

When Rohr returned, he pulled out his long knife. He made a cutting motion near Yellowmane's neck. He wanted to slit her throat. I burst into tears and begged him not to. I knew it was foolish; ponies with broken legs must always die. I only sought a little more time to see if I could heal her. The men could continue up the mountain on foot, seeking an entrance to the Lost Lake, but I would not take another step. Yellowmane's broken leg told me to go no further on this trip of fools.

I searched the area around our camp for willow bark. It grew along the watercourses but there were few springs in this arid area. With the help of the Goddess, I finally located a seeping spring with a willow bush and cut some branches. The water from the spring was red as blood. Rohr helped me grind the wood into a powder and I fed it to Yellowmane. The clouds hung low above the earth and lightning forked from them. Thunder roared in the distance, but the rains had stopped.

En Sun and Rohr left the next morning. They said they would ascend the trail and return soon to tell me what they had found. After they departed, I searched for food for Yellowmane and the other horses. I carried back armfuls of the yellow sedge grasses. The horses whinnied when they saw my approach and ate eagerly. With some trepidation, I took Rohr's horse, Tye, and Jemma to the blood water spring. They swallowed the water eagerly. I did not give any blood water to Yellowmane. I feared it might take away the power of the willow branch powder. I gave her water from my waterskin.

For a day and a night, I sat near Yellowmane as she rested and put my hands on the break in her leg. I prayed for the healing power to come, but felt only a small tingle. Sitting near her warm body, I drowsed and dreamed of Angelion, the white mooncat of my visions. I had not seen one since I escaped Captain Grieg that fateful day inside the Mountain, but in my mind the mooncat was limping. I thought he felt Yellowmane's pain.

On the third night, my pony seemed more comfortable. I decided I could leave her outside and sleep in the black dweli. In the middle of the night, I heard a horrible rending cry. I stuck my head out of the flap. Moonlight bathed the camp and I saw

Yellowmane rear into the air. As I watched in horror, an enormous black mountain panther attacked her. He sank his teeth into her throat. She fell to the ground and struggled. He roared and she made fearful high-pitched cries. I screamed and ran out of the dweli. He jumped on her back and attacked, biting into her neck repeatedly. I grabbed a stick and poked at his glowing eyes. He gripped her throat more tightly with his teeth. Her cries quieted. Finally, as I screamed in rage and despair, my pony breathed her last.

The panther tore off her back leg and carried it into the mountains. I screamed after him, but it was too late, she was gone. I went to her body and sat weeping for a long time, remembering sweet Yellowmane and all the times she had carried me—on black cutting lava and grassy plains—from the golden fields of Talin to the dreaming spires of Namché.

The next day, weeping continuously, I said the blessing for the dead over her still form. The sand was soft and I buried her in its warmth. I sang the Kosi farewell song and asked the Goddess to take her spirit to the skies so she could run among the clouds. On the day I entered the sky world, I knew she would be waiting.

Chapter 12 – At Maidenstone, in the City of Namché

While Sab-ra sang a final farewell to Yellowmane, the sun coming through the windows at Maidenstone warmed Ruby's face.

Ruby opened her eyes. For a moment, she didn't remember where she was, but then the memory came back. She was at Maidenstone, the ancient school and hospital where she was born and where her mother had left her twin sister behind. She got dressed, went downstairs and arrived in the kitchen, having gotten lost twice. The maze of corridors at Maidenstone was terribly confusing. After breakfast, Mistress said she had several things to tell her. They walked down the hall to her office.

"Ruby, it's unfortunate that Sab-ra is not in Namché at this time. She left here at the end of the Waking Moon, one year ago. A Kosi Warrior took her north to warn her People about the Army attack that was coming to the high country."

"I know about this war. I came to Maidenstone with some soldiers coming to re-supply the Garrison."

"Yes, many soldiers died in the quest for the blue diamonds. Soldiers from other lands are now coming to man the Garrison. I have not heard anything from Sab-ra since she left, but I would know if she died. She lives."

"You considered she might be dead?" Ruby asked. This place was scary and dangerous. She wouldn't stay a minute longer than necessary.

"Many people die during wars," Mistress told her.

"I am not a thicko," Ruby said. She felt irritated at the tone in the woman's voice. When there was no response, Ruby continued, saying, "I have to find Sab-ra. My Mum is very sick and she made me promise."

"It is too cold now to travel to the high range. You will have to stay here until spring is further along. Then you can go north. In order to stay, however, you must contribute. Can you cook? Can you teach? Are you trained as a Healer?"

Ruby tried to control her temper. This poxy female acted as if she was in charge of her life. "If you didn't want me, you only had to say. It's not a bother on me to leave now," Ruby said angrily. She felt her cheeks redden.

"You don't understand. You have to have a guide and none of the Bearers would take you at this time. You will stay here for at least two months."

Ruby thought for a few minutes and sighed. She knew she needed this arrogant woman's help. She took a deep breath and lowered her shoulders. "If it's money you are askin' me for, I have some."

"I would not take money from Ashlin's child," Mistress said coldly. "You insult me."

A short silence ensued while Mistress and Ruby regarded each other, until Ruby's eyes fell.

"I can cook some," she said "But what I do on the Isle of Viridian is go to school or help Mum or go to church. Do you have a church here?"

"We worship the Goddess here, in all her myriad forms. There are many Goddesses in our metaphysics. Some are spirits of water, rocks and plants. Some are spirits of the wind or weather. There is only one Great Goddess, and she is the spirit of the Dhali Ra, the tallest peak in the Blue Mountain range. Do you understand?" Mistress looked at her intently.

Ruby was frowning. "Yes, but in my country the Dar, our spiritual leaders, tell us there is only one God and he is certainly not a woman. If a person believes anything else, they go to the Demon Fires when they die." She felt her face flush as she defended the true religion.

"We believe there are many roads to the afterlife," Mistress' voice was calm and somewhat amused. "Our Priestess, Te Ran, taught Sab-ra the art of the Far-Seer. Your sister can see the future."

Ruby felt her lip curl in disgust. "That is black magic and no good person uses it."

"You may keep your own beliefs, Ruby, but it is discourteous to disparage the beliefs of those living here, especially when we are providing you with a room and food," Mistress said coolly. "Today, you can help Honus and Kieta in the kitchen, but tomorrow I want you to meet Te Ran. Perhaps with her help you could see where your sister is living now."

The next morning, Ruby woke early, dressed and headed directly for the kitchen. Maidenstone House was enormous with its twists, rising staircases and myriad dead ends. Arriving after three false turns, guided by the scent of cooking food, Ruby reached the kitchen and introduced herself to the two cooks, Honus and Kieta. They told her to set the table in the dining room for the students. Apparently, she wasn't allowed to eat with the 'la-di-dah' students. She had to eat in the kitchen with the cooks.

There were only five students studying at Maidenstone; four came from the city of Nam-shay. The war had prevented one from leaving who had arrived before the Occupation. Her name was Deti. She was thirteen, tall and slim as a reed. She was a pretty girl with light brown hair. She often wore an expression of stillness, as if she were listening to someone calling her from far away.

Honus called the girls Novices. Ruby was scandalized. A Novice was a girl called to serve God by becoming a Sor, a female officiate. Mistress Falcon taught these students sorcery. They did at least give thanks for the food, she noticed, but they thanked some Goddess or other. It was all heathen nonsense.

After helping serve the food and clean up the kitchen, Ruby headed down the hall to Mistress Falcon's Office. She finally managed to stumble upon the right corridor, practically by accident and knocked on the door.

"Enter."

Ruby walked into the room, seeing Mistress Falcon seated at her desk. A tall coffee-skinned woman stood beside her, clothed in ivory linen.

"Ruby, it is customary to bow your head to a Priestess."

Ruby clenched her teeth, not wanting to demonstrate respect to this eastern witch, but at Mistress' unflinching gaze, she finally ducked her head.

"This is our Priestess, Te Ran, a talented Supplicant and Far Seer. Te Ran, this is Ruby, she is Sab-ra's twin sister."

"I greet you sister of Sab-ra," the red woman said, looking at her for a long time.

"Starting tomorrow, you will work with Te Ran each day after washing the breakfast dishes. She will test your abilities. This is a gift, Ruby. If the Far Seer permits, you might see Sab-ra in a vision or trance. It is proper and appropriate to thank me, and you will kneel to Te Ran." Her voice was cool and deadly serious.

Ruby felt anger rise inside her. She hadn't wanted to come to this God forsaken country in the first place and now she was supposed to kneel before a coffee-skinned pagan who told the future like a carnival gypsy.

"Ruby," Mistress Falcon's voice commanded, "On your knees."

Ruby shook her head. Te Ran took Ruby's arm and with astonishing strength forced her to the floor. Her knees banged on the cold stone. Ruby got a shock from Te Ran's touch.

"Ouch, you are hurting me," she cried, angrily.

"Next time, I hurt you more," the Priestess said and Ruby felt her breath quicken. The hair lifted on the nape of her neck.

"You are dismissed, Ruby," Mistress said and Ruby fled from the office.

Chapter 13 – The Crystal Steppe above Rhan Du
Vernal Moon, March

As Mistress instructed Ruby in the proper behavior a supplicant uses in thanking a Priestess, Sab-ra began to feel twinges of pain in her lower back.

Ever since Rohr and En Sun departed trying to find an entrance into the Lost Lake, I had felt stabbing pains in my lower back. I didn't know if the pains were true labor, but they frightened me. I lay inside the dweli, afraid even standing up might bring the baby from my womb. In late afternoon, I heard the men returning.

"Come inside the dweli," I called to Rohr.

When he came in and saw me lying in my bedroll, he turned his face away.

"Are you ill, Wife of the King?" Rohr's voice was low and worried.

"Tell me what you and En Sun found?"

"We found a passageway we believe leads into the Lost Lake, but it is hidden in a cleft behind an enormous wall of fallen stones. We worked at removing the stones for a full day, but it would take many moons to move the rockfall. We would need the help of all the Bearers in Rhan Du and they would demand silver parthats in payment," Rohr's voice was low and held a warning.

I thought about the wall of fallen rock and prayed for the strength to make the right decision.

"Where is Yellowmane?" he asked me.

"Gone to the belly of a Mountain Tar," I said, my voice low with sorrow. Tears quickened in my eyes. I sought control and said, "I believe I am in labor, Rohr." He blanched. "I'm very afraid. It is too early for the babe to come."

"You became pregnant the night you married the King," Rohr murmured. "Now the Vernal Moon is ending. The child will come soon. "

"No, Rohr. The baby should not come for three more moons. He will come during the Flowering Moon. The People's women carry their children for nine moons."

"Kosi women deliver after six moons," he told me.

A feeling of doom came across my shoulders. I had not realized Kosi pregnancies were only six months long. The father of my child was Kosi. It could mean my pregnancy would be shorter.

"The Blended ones at the Citadel, how long did the Kosi women carry those babes?"

"Seven moons, sometimes a week or two more."

I felt a little surge of relief. The pain was probably what An Mali called false labor.

"Then I am not in labor," I told him, but fear showed in his face.

"If the baby is very large, sometimes even the Blended ones arrive in six moons," he told me. We looked at each other in dismay.

I looked down at my belly moving as the infant kicked. I pulled my shirt up to below my breasts.

"Do you think this baby is a large one?"

Rohr's eyes opened wide and he looked horrified. "Cover yourself, Wife of the King. No man can look upon the womb of a pregnant woman, save the man who put the seed inside her." His eyes snapped. He was furious at my careless revealing of my body.

"Rohr, you and I have travelled many days and nights together. On the way to the King's Valley after the Avalanche, we slept together in caves of snow. We ate hulion in frigid winter winds. Once you made me eat a worm because you knew I was pregnant, even though I did not know it then. You have been my friend since I met you, but on this day, I do not need a friend. What I need on this day is a midwife."

Rohr looked as horrified as if I had asked him to give birth. "Wife of the King, I cannot do this." He began backing out of the dweli.

"Would you risk the life of the King's son?" I asked. "Rohr, I order you to obey me. Bring the candle lamp so you can see clearly."

"If I look upon you now, I will be unmanned. I will no longer be a Warrior." He was trembling.

"Then I will make En Sun look," I told him and he quivered.

"No," he said fiercely, "En Sun is not from the People and he is not Kosi. He is only a meager Bearer person, not worthy to touch the foot of the wife of the King."

"What shall we do, Rohr?" I asked him in despair. "If the babe comes tonight, you will have to deliver him."

Rohr called out to En Sun. There was a high tense note in his voice.

When En Sun came inside and saw me lying on my sleeping robe, he frowned, looking troubled.

"En Sun, I fear the child comes soon. Do the men of the Bearer Tribe help their wives deliver their children?"

"Never," he said, his eyes opened wide in fright. "If you want your child to breathe the air of the mountains, we must return to Rhan Du."

I lay all night alone in the dweli, fighting the pain and begging the Wind Goddess for her protection. On toward morning, the rain stopped and my pains eased. I walked outside to the fire and woke Rohr.

"We will descend, Lord Blood Arrow. You were correct. I should never have come on this trip."

We reached Rhan Du late in the evening. My pains had not resumed. We spent a comfortable night and I felt much refreshed. En Sun's wife had taken good care of Bumpy and Belaro; they looked well fed. I asked her if she and her husband would adopt them, but she told me they could not. She was pregnant herself and the living they made from the messages her husband carried from valley to valley was paltry.

After dinner, I asked En Sun for some information. "Have you seen Captain Grieg since the Avalanche?"

"No, but he still lives. He is an evil spirit, a djinn that appears and disappears at will."

"Who told you he still lives?"

"A member of the Hakan tribe. They serve the white men who climb the great mountain."

"Where did the Hakan see Grieg?"

"Near the Lost Lake valley during the Hunger Moon of late winter."

A tidal wave of fear paralyzed me. My nemesis and implacable enemy, Captain Grieg, had made it through the winter alive.

"Have you had reports of the Kosi King?"

"None of the Bearers have seen him."

I closed my eyes in pain.

Rohr and I started back toward the Valley of the King at dawn the next day with Belaro and Bumpy riding behind us. As we rode down the Mountain, despair coated me in anguish. How could the Goddess have let Grieg live and taken the life of my King? What kind of deity would permit such horror?

We were two days east of Natil when I felt a warm gush of fluid run down my leg. My heart sank. There was no question this time. My labor had begun.

"Stop," I called to him. "Rohr, I need Wirri-won. The King's son is coming."

Rohr turned away. Sheer terror struck me down like an axe. The baby was two months early and I stood in the middle of an open plain with nobody to help me.

All the color leached from Rohr's face. If he rode straight to the White River, he said, he could make it less than a day, but it would be another day before Wirri-won could return to me. I felt a hard grinding pain in my lower back. I had no idea how long I would be in labor. Rohr and I looked at each other, calculating the time it would take him to reach Wirri-won.

"Would it be faster for you to get my Grandmother in Talin or Wirri-won?"

"If you were not the Wife of the King, I would leave you here to die," he told me, harshly. "You have been foolish. Such arrogant determination is not the way of the Kosi or their Queens."

"You can either ride for help or you can deliver this baby," I threatened him.

"I will get help." His face filled with panic and he whirled his stallion back down the trail. I tried to call him back, but he didn't hear me. The dweli was rolled up on the back of his horse.

I looked around at the nearly barren area we had reached. There was only one small grove of trees lying to the south. I walked slowly toward it with the children following me. It was late afternoon and I had only one slice of bread and two curds of cheese for the three of us. I had been counting on Rohr shooting a chanry bird for dinner.

By the time we reached the grove, the pains were much stronger. I asked the children to make a small shelter by bending birch branches over in an arc and tying them to low shrubs. I pulled my sleeping roll off the pony I had purchased in Rhan Du.

I cursed my own stupidity for leaving nearly all my medicines and supplies with Wirri-Won. In my pocket, I had the small knife Mistress Falcon gave me when I left Maidenstone. I would need it if a mountain lion found us, but could not use it to cut the cord binding baby to mother. Poison could still coat the blade. A single touch would bring the Yellow Water Fever. All night I lay in that small bower as the pain took my lower body in its teeth and shook it as a large cat shakes a mouse.

I knew better than to make any noise. If I cried out, the sound would draw a predator, and I had to protect the children who lay just outside my branched shelter. By early morning, I could stifle my cries no longer. I cried for my mother, the mother who abandoned me, the mother I had never seen. In one brief lucid moment, I promised the Goddess if she let me live to hold my son in my arms, I would never fail him. But as I prayed, I wondered if I would ever see my child alive.

Chapter 14 – At Maidenstone, in the City of Namché

While Sab-ra awaited the birth of the Warrior's Child, Ruby walked slowly down the steps from Maidenstone to the Temple of Light, dreading what lay before her.

Ruby hesitated before entering the tall colonnaded building, but knew she had no choice. Te Ran was waiting for her just inside.

"I greet you, Ruby," Te Ran said. "Come with me into the sanctuary."

Ruby followed her into the large open hall with many seats in rows for the worshippers. That was the only proper thing about the place. It had no true altar. The windows were old and wavy; not one window had been made of stained glass. The place felt alien. The corners of her mouth tightened in distaste, but she tried to suppress her response to this tosspot's wrong-headed religion.

Te Ran walked purposefully to the front of the nave. She was wearing a long ivory robe and veil. It made her look spooky and evil. Suddenly, the sun came out from behind a cloud and all the wavy glass in the windows scattered a thousand crescent moons on the stone floor. It was glorious. Ruby found herself unexpectedly moved by their beauty. She felt a lump in her throat, wondering how long it would be before she knelt in the true church again.

"Come," Te Ran called over her shoulder.

At the front of the great hall, Ruby saw a silver bowl sitting on a translucent rock shelf. Ruby felt her stomach roil but walked slowly forward. Te Ran drizzled oil on the lip of the bowl.

"Watch while I light the rim," she said and struck the flint against a rock. The rim caught fire and flames danced along the edge of the vessel. In the center of the bowl, floating in the clear liquid, Ruby saw a wick.

"You will light the center flame. To do this, you will need to stop the fire from burning your skin."

Ruby had no idea what the gypsy woman meant. She took a white candle and inserted her hand and arm directly through the rim flames. Once the wick ignited, she stepped back. A blue blaze rose high into the air, nearly to the ceiling.

Te Ran looked at her meaningfully and Ruby knelt. She wouldn't wait for Te Ran to drag her down to the stone floor this time, although she felt a qualm. By kneeling in this place, was she being a traitor to her faith? What would Dar. Patrick think?

Suddenly she felt a brush of warm air and the Priestess' body rose in the air. Ruby trembled all over. She desperately wanted to escape, but her body refused to move. The poxy gypsy woman had placed her in some type of supernatural flesh-lock.

Despite herself, her eyes rose to Te Ran's face. It was transcendent with joy. Keeping her eyes locked on Te Ran's face, she swallowed convulsively in fear. Shuddering, Ruby felt a great power inflame her spirit. A few minutes later, Te Ran's body returned to its usual size. She touched Ruby's forehead in blessing.

Feeling the Priestess' touch like a spark, Ruby stood up and raced out of the Temple, desperate to escape the frightening place. Te Ran darted after her and grabbed her shoulder.

"Talk to me," she demanded. "Tell me what you saw?"

Ruby was trembling and could not speak for a moment. "I saw you get larger. I felt something," her voice was grudging with resentment as she said, "I felt the power of transformation."

Te Ran looked at her appraisingly and reached into the pocket of her robe. "This is a Far Seer orb," she said. "Look into it. Tell me what you see."

Ruby looked at her sadly. "Te Ran, I cannot do this. When I knelt in the Temple, I felt I defiled the true religion."

Ruby looked away from the Priestess and up at the sky. To her horror, she saw that it was already dark. She had spent a whole day in the Temple, thinking it had been an hour.

Te Ran gripped her shoulder saying, "I ask you, sister of Sab-ra, please look into the glass. Once you do, you may leave the Temple. Hold the glass in your hand. The moon is already rising.

Twist it back and forth. When the light of the moon falls on the glass, look deeply inside."

"No, this is wrong. It is against God. I should not do this." Ruby felt her back muscles tense and her shoulders hunch up.

"It is only the power of the Goddess," Te Ran told her gently and gazed into her eyes until Ruby's eyes fluttered in trance. Te Ran eased her gently down to sit against the exterior walls of the Temple.

"What do you see?" Te Ran whispered quietly.

Ruby's voice sounded dazed as she whispered, "Red haired female. Big with child. She rides beside a large copper skinned man."

Te Ran snapped her fingers and Ruby returned to the present.

"Did anyone in your family have what the People call the Sight?" Te Ran asked, a curious expression on her face.

"Supposedly, my Great Grandmother had it, but the only thing she could tell was whether a pregnant woman would have a boy or a girl. It was nothing, a cheap con, a carnival trick."

"Be that as it may, Ruby, I think you have the true gift," Te Ran said seriously. "You may go now."

After helping Honus and Kieta with breakfast for the students the next morning, Ruby walked out of Maidenstone's yellow tower. She was still shaken from her encounter in the Temple. She needed to talk with someone from her own country. Standing on the forecourt, she looked down at the hundred steps and saw the Garrison off to the west, near the railroad tracks. It looked as if it would be easy to find, but there was a rat's nest of alleys between the bottom step and the Garrison. When Ruby reached the last step, she turned west and although she had to dodge her way through numerous alleys, after entering many dead ends she chanced upon the Garrison. She walked up to the two-story building and told the soldier on guard she had come to see the two Garda lads from Viridian.

"Their names are Carmac Gifford and Jaime Fitzjohn."

The guard nodded and left. Ruby stood on the stoop enjoying the sounds of street musicians tuning their instruments and the smell of bread baking.

"Hey, Ruby Girl," Carmac called out, running across the open graveled yard from the dining hall. He looked happy and windblown. "Jaime is working in the kitchen, but they told me I had a visitor. Hoped it would be you, I did."

"Can we walk somewhere?"

"Sure we can, Ruby darlin'. What's wrong? You look a bit shook."

"I just need to talk with you a little."

"There's a little park near here where the almond trees are

blooming."

They walked together down the tree-lined streets. Carmac reached for Ruby's hand and she squeezed his fingers. Her hands were cold and his were warm. The scent of the almond trees rode the wind. Their pale pink blossoms looked incongruous on dark leafless trees standing in melting snow.

"How is it going, Ruby?"

"I got to Maidenstone and they gave me a nice room, but the Mistress made me go to this Temple. I didn't want to go. It isn't a proper church and I was afraid Dar. Patrick would be mad, but she said I had to."

Carmac's blue eyes were intent on her face as he listened.

"This woman, Te Ran, they call her a Priestess, but I think she's a gypsy witch, I do. Anyway, she made me light this wick in a bowl filled with oil. When I lit the flame, it rose nearly to the ceiling. Then I saw the Priestess rise in the air, like a balloon."

"What?" Carmac asked. "You saw her floatin?" He frowned.

"That's the only way I can describe it. She made me tell her what I felt."

"What did you feel?"

"Bloody terrified is what. She touched my head and I must have blacked out for a moment, because I saw this twin of mine. I told you that I came here in search of my twin sister, didn't I?

Anyway, my sister was riding in the mountains with a giant copper skinned bloke and she was pregnant. Then this Priestess asks me if I have the Sight."

"Do you have it? One of my old relatives had it, Mum said."

"I'm not sure. Nana said her Gran had it, could see the future like. Carmac, I'm scared of that Temple place."

Ruby was visibly trembling and Carmac put her arm around her shoulders.

"Then ye shouldn't go back to that culchie place."

"You think?"

"Sure, just tell the magic floating woman to fly away somewhere. Tell her you want nothing more to do with her."

Ruby wondered if it could be that easy, as easy as simply refusing. She gave a big sigh and felt the tension in her neck and shoulders ease.

"Thank you, Carmac, I will give it a try," Ruby said, but she had a funny feeling she might not be given a choice in the matter.

"Come give me a kiss then for the good advice," Carmac grinned at her.

Ruby melted into the soldier's embrace. When she pulled back, she had tears in her eyes. She brushed them away and smiled at Carmac.

"Don't tell Jaime," she giggled, "He's the one who boasts he's such the good kisser."

As Ruby walked back up the hundred steps she thought of her boyfriend, Shane, back on Viridian. Carmac was a better kisser than Shane was, for sure. Cuter, too, with his red curls and dark blue eyes; very handsome in his uniform.

Chapter 15 –The Road to Natil, the Valley of the King

While Ruby climbed the hundred steps to Maidenstone after kissing Carmac, Sab-ra's pain rose so high, her spirit left her body

The pain of labor was appalling. I had seen many women in labor, but the intensity of the pain stunned me. Most women experience intermittent pain, with pauses giving them time to catch their breath; but I knew only one continuous screaming agony. I wanted desperately to escape this body, which held me prisoner to the earth.

Abruptly, I found myself rising and floating. I seemed to lay spread out in the air, arms and legs stretched in a star, looking down at the small shelter. The two children sat in the dark, leaning against each other, looking terrified as cries of anguish came from beneath the arched branches. I watched my superfluous body begin to bleed. The red stain spread relentlessly across the sleeping roll, but I felt nothing but a kind of flying peace. At that moment, I knew I could choose to escape. Brother Jun once told me such choices come to everyone who walks the dying road. I only wanted to fly away from the discarded husk on the bed below me.

"I am your mother's spirit," I heard the Angelion speak in strong ringing tones. "She calls you to return, as she promised to return to you one day."

In an instant, I was back in the brutal pain, but the brief respite calmed me. Then the pain stopped abruptly. I had never seen this happen before and feared my son was dead. If he were dead, labor would start again, but hours could pass before that happened.

I crawled out of the shelter. It was morning. The children, Bumpy and Belaro, were hungry, tired and dirty. During my labor, I had forgotten to give them any food or provide them shelter. I gave Bumpy my knife and a simple snare from my pocket.

"Try to trap a ne-ne," I told him. His dark eyes were grave. "We need food, Bumpy. I need food or I will not be able to make milk for the baby."

His face darkened with the importance of the task I set him. He ran off silently in the early morning light, almost a shadow.

"Belaro, will you get water?" I asked, handing her my waterskin. She flashed away like a sprite. Forest-adepts could move so silently among the trees, they seemed magical. Belaro returned an hour later with water. We managed to wash the blood from my sleeping robe, and I enlarged the shelter so all of us could lie down inside its shade. I tried to reach my son in my mind. I felt nothing. He did not move. Dread made me quiver deep inside.

Bumpy returned in late afternoon with two hulion he had trapped. Together we skinned them and stretched their bodies over the fire. Warm after the meal, we cuddled together in the shelter. Eventually, the children slept. My conscience lashed me that I had disregarded Rohr's counsel to return to Natil after we found families for the Blanda. Had my stubbornness killed my baby?

The pain began again at dawn. The fearsome labor-cat bit my lower body relentlessly. I sent the children outside, not wanting them to see a dead baby born. Hours passed and I prayed to the Wind Goddess for deliverance. I begged for the return of Rohr and for Wirri-won. The baby did not come.

In late afternoon, I heard the sounds of hoof beats. Rohr had returned with Wirri-won. I was teary-eyed with gratitude. I got shakily to my feet and hugged him. He looked down at me, still pregnant and smiled. He was immensely pleased with himself.

The Healer expertly tended me. She had brought a plant mixture she said would open my womb and bring the child. A few hours later, I felt the crowning and in a rush of pleasure, I felt my child emerge. I looked down to see a little girl, alive and well. I thanked all the Goddesses in the pantheon as I examined her strong golden body. Her feathery hair was red. She breathed well. A wave of intense love struck me as I looked at her. She opened her eyes and knew me. I felt we had known each other for a thousand years.

Conquin told me I carried a son. She was rarely wrong, but she had been wrong this time. Wirri-won examined the infant carefully and nodded her head in satisfaction. She had brought a blanket, baby clothing and nappies with her. We dressed the small one as she slept. Wirri-won pulled me to my feet. She wrapped her arms around me and together we sang the Kosi Victory song, a lullaby for the birth of a Warrior's child.

But late that night my pains resumed. I wondered if the placenta was still inside me. I lay in silence between the Bumpy and Belaro as the pain rose and rose again. Several hours later, I gave a soft cry. Wirri-won, who slept outside our door near the campfire, moved the foliage of the shelter away and knelt beside me.

"I'm sorry, Wirri-won," I whispered. "It's just the afterbirth."

"No," she said. "Another."

I had no idea what she meant, but when the labor beast seized me again, I knew. I had been pregnant with twins. I remembered Grandmother telling me I had a twin sister. I called my sister in my mind and felt her presence. I gritted my teeth against the pain and fear. I forced myself to stay inside my body. The thought of a second baby gave me strength. Wirri-won held my hand and sang to me.

At dawn, I felt myself open. There was no birth fluid left and this one didn't want to leave my body. Every inch was agony. At last, Wirri-won lifted the miniature baby from between my legs. It was a boy, but he was bright blue. Wirri-won turned away, holding the baby so I couldn't see him. I heard her slap him repeatedly. I cringed, feeling his pain.

"Is he dead?" I cried, agonized, but then I heard the blessed harsh cry of the newborn.

"He lives. You have a son," Wirri-won said proudly and laid my baby beside his sleeping twin. As he breathed, he turned pink. I closed my eyes in pride as the tears of joy came down. The Healer took my waterskin out to the fire. She returned with warmed water and washed the tiny child. She wrapped him tightly in a blanket and showed me his face. He blinked and I saw my husband's golden eyes. My daughter's red hair was already dried and curly. Her skin was lighter than her brother's and her eyes were a shining gray.

"I will name my daughter Crimson," I said. "The boy I shall name Quinn, for my dearest friend, Conquin, who knew all along that he was coming."

I hardly said the last sentence aloud. I was already falling asleep. Wirri-won and Rohr were singing the cadenced rhythms of the song for the birth of a Kosi prince.

Wirri-won left on her small silver mare in the morning. She took Bumpy and Belaro with her saying she could easily find a family for both of them. Rohr and I set off for the King's Valley with tiny Quinn sleeping in a sling around my body and Rohr carrying Crimson on his stallion. Every time he looked at the babes, he couldn't stop smiling. He was as proud as if he had birthed the twins himself.

It took us three days to reach the King's Valley. When she heard our horses, Conquin came running out, screaming in happiness. Thron walked behind her, carrying baby Sab-ri. I felt a sense of profound relief as the fears of the trip washed away. Everything would be all right now. I was with Conquin again.

Chapter 16 – At Maidenstone in the City of Namché

On the same night Sab-ra gave birth to the twins, a piercing belly pain woke Ruby.

Ruby sat up in bed groaning in pain. She looked out the window from her room at Maidenstone. It was the middle of the night. An Mali, the elderly Healer who met her when she arrived, had showed her the clinic at the top of the ancient building the previous day. The Healer said that if a Novice was ill, she came to the Infirmary. Ruby lay watching the moon, forcing back screams as the pain got worse and worse. It was impossible for her to lie still. She got up and paced the room.

Giving up at last, Ruby decided she would find the blasted Infirmary. She felt faint from the pain and terrible nausea. She walked slowly down the hall, clutching her stomach, searching desperately for the circular staircase. By the time she reached it, she was bent double in pain. Walking up the three flights of steps was excruciating. She opened the door to the Clinic, holding her hand over her mouth. She just barely made a sink in time to throw up.

"Who is it," An Mali's sleepy voice asked.

"Help," Ruby cried. She could not stop throwing up and the pain was worse than any she had ever felt before.

An Mali came out of her small room, looking concerned.

"Ruby, what is wrong? Are you sick from food, do you think?"

"This terrible belly pain is beating the living shite out of me," Ruby managed. An Mali put an arm around her and led her to one of the beds. Ruby threw up all over the floor and began to cry.

"I am so sorry, An Mali."

"Show me where it hurts?"

Ruby pointed to her belly. When An Mali touched her stomach, she screamed.

An Mali went to the Medicine table and brought her some poppy pearls. Ruby swallowed them eagerly.

"The pains. They come in waves," she managed. An Mali sat beside her, stroking her forehead. Slowly, as the poppy took her, she slept.

At dawn, the pains were gone. Ruby felt refreshed and calm, happier than she had been since leaving home. She got up, dressed and headed for Mistress Falcon's office. She only took one wrong turn before entering the proper hall and felt proud of herself. She was beginning to learn the crazy layout of Maidenstone. Mistress' door was ajar and Ruby could hear two voices. Mistress was talking with the Priestess, Ten Ran. Ruby slowed down and stopped, knowing she should not listen to their conversation, but unable to prevent herself.

"I believe Ruby has the ability to see using Vision, Mistress," Te Ran said. "I didn't even give her Monkscaul, and still she saw. What is more, she did not see something momentous to come, as I do. The heathen girl saw the present. Ruby found her sister immediately. She rode with a Kosi warrior and Ruby could tell Sab-ra was pregnant."

"Sab-ra is pregnant. Interesting. I wonder if she married. She had a strong connection with the Goddess, perhaps she did not feel the need of a husband," Mistress Falcon said.

Her sister was having a kid and she wasn't even married? Ruby was mortified. Didn't any of these people have morals?

"Did Ruby say anything about our religion?"

"She did. She seemed to consider me little more than a gypsy fortune-teller. However, when I asked her to light the inner flame of the Supplication bowl, she didn't hesitate. She put her hand directly through the fire and lit the wick. She didn't feel the heat of the fire. It took Sab-ra months and months to learn how to do it, and she burned herself repeatedly. When Ruby lit the wick, it rose higher than I have ever seen it. The blue flame nearly reached the ceiling of the Temple. It was staggering."

"I find myself completely perplexed," Mistress said. "Here we have a young woman carrying a commission from her mother, a girl who rejects everything we believe, and yet has enormous talent. It is a puzzling problem."

"It is." Both women were quiet for a few moments and Ruby was about to leave until she heard Mistress speak again.

"I am happy to know that Sab-ra lives and is with a Kosi. I wonder if it is Ghang's child she carries. He took her up into the high range, you will recall."

"I could put Ruby in a trance to find this information, if you wish."

"No, Te Ran, we cannot do this simply to satisfy our curiosity. I was going to wait until summer before sending her into the high range, but I think she must go soon."

"I agree. Will you send Ten-Singh with her? I could go along if you wish."

"No, the high range is alive with wounded and dangerous men. You must remain here, although I would be grateful for anything you see in the Scry."

"The Scry is not for finding an individual's path, it is only to discern the fate of nations," Te Ran's voice was harsh. "I find it astonishing that Ruby could have such a talent, hidden under the layers of her monotheistic religion."

"As do I," Mistress said, deep in thought. "However, when she speaks of her God, I feel her certainty. Although it is very different from our beliefs, there is power in her faith."

Ruby turned and ran down the hall. She didn't want this so-called Vision talent. It shook her down to her boots. Mistress said the mountain was alive with dangerous men and yet she planned to send Ruby there? She quivered and clenched her hands. They were sweaty.

Ruby and Sab-ra's small dog Cloudheart were sitting in the grass near the fishpond that afternoon when the young Novice Deti opened the door and came outside. According to Mistress Falcon, Deti was from an unknown valley in the Blue Mountains. While Deti was away at school one day, Harn soldiers attacked and burned her village to the ground. The shock of finding her family all dead and her home smoldering in ashes had rendered her mute. When he arrived at Maidenstone, the Monks worked with her for some time, eventually learning that she had been in training as an artist. They had encouraged Mistress to foster Deti's artistic talent. Ruby watched her draw one day, impressed by her ability to capture the essence of a person in a few strokes of a paintbrush.

"Mistress said to give you this," Deti handed Ruby a letter. The stamps were from Viridian and Ruby knew it was a letter from her Da. Ruby walked up to her room and sat on the bed opening the envelope slowly.

Dear Ruby,

I hope this letter reaches you. Your Mum is not doing well. The pneumonia has spread and right now, she is in surgery. I am sitting outside in the spring sunshine trying to think good thoughts for her recovery, but I fear being left alone with your Mum gone and you so terribly far away. I talked with Mum last night. She knew the surgery would be dangerous and it might not succeed. She told me to say for you not to come home unless you can bring your sister with you.

I am of two minds about this business. Your Mum wants you to fulfill your promise to her, but I want you here. I am terrible afraid of how you would feel if we lost your Mum and you didn't get to say good-bye. But I'm being morbid, sure I am. She'll be grand.

Your Mum also said that you were to tell your sister that Mum is desperate with remorse about leaving her. If she had it to do again, she said she would have taken her too. She's also suffering that she kept the secret from you so long. She asks you to forgive you. She says she won't go easy into that good night until she knows you and Sab-ra are together and you have seen the Lion Baba. For some reason she says once you see him, you will understand why she married Dani, and why she left Sab-ra behind.

I'll write again when I know more. Your Lovin' Da

Ruby felt a sick desperation and her heart twisted inside her. She felt a wave of homesickness for her Mum, her Da, her dog and the lovely isle of Viridian. She trembled, thinking that she might not have a mother now. She paced the room, trying frantically to think of what she should do. She took her small purse and checked the money inside. She had enough to send a telegram.

Running fast down the hundred steps, Sab-ra went directly to the Garrison. She was panting hard when she arrived. Her red hair blew across her face and she brushed it away impatiently.

"I need Carmac," she told the guard and he nodded.

A few minute later, both Carmac and Jaime came walking across the gravel.

"So how ya' today, Ruby?" Jaime asked. Carmac reached out and gave her a hug.

"Boys, I have had a terrible letter from me Da. Mum has been in hospital and a surgeon was called to do an operation. Da says I should not come home. Ma doesn't want it, but I am frantic to know if she made it through the surgery. I want to send a telegram to me Da and ask him to send one right back here. Can you help me?"

"Sure we can, come with us."

The three of them set off walking through a haze of scents from the spice merchants, to a tiny dark stall in the Market district. A thin man bowed repeatedly to all three of them. It took some time, but he sent Ruby's telegram at last. She used as few words as possible.

"Is Mum alive? Twin not here. Want to come home."

They waited for several hours. At one point Jaime went to a food stall and brought them all something to eat. Ruby was ravenous. The sun was setting when the bowing man gave her the return telegram.

"Mum better. Stay. Find twin."

Chapter 17 – In Natil, the Valley of the King
Planting Moon, May

While Ruby resigned herself to a longer stay at Maidenstone, Sab-ra, now safely back in the King's valley, watched her babies grow.

Every day I could see my babies growing stronger. They were both astonishing in their physical abilities. Quinn could pull himself up to a sitting position at only three months. Crimson could speak in words by then. At four months, both of them could crawl. They knew Conquin's name, Sab-ri's, Kim-li's and Kensing's. I thought the babies' coordination and skills came from their Kosi father. I missed their father dreadfully, but my children's amazing spirit and total lack of fear entranced me.

Late one evening I heard the jingling of a horse's harness and a man's voice. I walked out to the step. It was a warm evening. My dear friend Justyn had returned.

"Sab-ra," he said and took me in his arms. "I have come to ask you again to marry me. My Grandmother said you married the Kosi King in the Skygrass valley and that you were expecting a child. I am sorry to give you this news, but the Bearer people tell me the Kosi King rides the skies. Your child needs a father. I would be that man."

His declaration brought tears to my eyes. He seemed to confirm the fears I had about Say'f but his generosity of spirit gave me a wondrous gift, his willingness to serve as father to my children.

"I had twins," I told him and his openhearted smile warmed me, reminding me of my lost spy partner, Hodi. He took my hand and we walked into my apartment. He looked down on Quinn and Crimson, sleeping so quietly. They lay curled around each other. Sometimes at night, they even sucked each other's thumbs.

"Sab-ra, they are perfect," he said, "Absolutely flawless."

Tears stung in my eyes and I reached for Justyn's embrace.

Over the next few weeks, Justyn stayed in rooms near mine. He took little Quinn's hands and held him as he learned to stand. He told Crimson stories of the People. Soon Quinn called him "Soama," a word for father in the language of the People. Crimson just called him Justyn. If Justyn became the twins' father, their Kosi heritage would die. Still, I treasured Justyn's love for my children. I told myself I should marry him.

One sunny afternoon, Justyn and I sat together watching Quinn and Crimson crawling through the lilies in the King's garden.

"Sab-ra, we have become a family," Justyn said, his eyes crinkled with warmth, "Marry me, sweetheart, be my wife and my love," his voice was plangent with adoration.

I looked down at the grass, trying to gather my thoughts. I didn't want to hurt this wonderful man, but I was not ready.

""I cannot marry you, Justyn." I felt my stomach clench. "I love you, but not as I love the Kosi King."

"Is it something I've done, Sab-ra?" The wrinkles around his eyes deepened and his voice was sad.

I took a deep breath. "When I entered the Kosi King's chamber at the Citadel and saw Say'f for the first time, I felt my body had entered the warm waters of a running river. The current of his life pulled me toward him irrevocably as if we were destined to be together. I am sorry, Justyn," I held out my hand to him, but he would not take it. His face was dark with pain. His lips tightened with anger.

"I remember when Say'f named you Wind Woman, and called you wayward. He was right. Even now, when I know he is dead, you vacillate between us," anger tinged Justyn's voice.

"Against my culture, against a hundred years of Kosi predation, against all of nature it seems, I longed for the Kosi King. Living or dead, I want him still," my voice was bleak.

"But he is gone," Justyn said gently. I reached for his hand and felt him tremble.

"Dear friend, I must have proof. Until I see for myself that he no longer walks the earth, I am a married woman. I cannot have another." My voice filled with unshed tears.

"Then I will be Quinn and Crimson's father until their mother is ready," Justyn said reaching out his arms for me. We embraced and I felt my sorrows ease.

"If Say'f is still alive, what will you do, Justyn?"

"I will return to Namché and wait for you."

"But I don't plan to ever return to the city."

"Someday you will return to Maidenstone and I will be waiting." When he said those words I wondered if he too had the ability to see the future.

On a beautiful evening several weeks later, as the fireflies danced in the trees, I carried my children to see Conquin. Her husband Thron greeted me warmly. Kim-li and Kensing lived with them. I played with the girls a little while and they asked to hold their baby brother and sister. Crimson said their names quietly. Conquin brought me tea and cookies warm from the oven, scented with cinnamon.

"I have been thinking about my future," I told her. "I could stay here in the King's Valley. If I stayed, Quinn and Crimson would grow up with their sisters, Kim-li and Kensing. Little Sab-ri could become my daughter's best friend. I would be able to be with you," I smiled at her.

"What else have you considered?" Conquin asked.

"If Say'f is dead, I know I should marry Justyn. I could return to Namché and become midwife to the women of the city. Or, I could study with Te Ran and enter the secret world of the

Priestess. I could also return to my own valley of Talin. In any case, I should go for a visit soon. My grandparents have never seen my children."

"Do you believe Say'f gone?" she asked me. Her eyes probed my soul.

"I see him often in dreams, fighting with someone in the blue snows. It could be the fight I see is his last." I looked down, fighting tears.

"What about your children's Kosi heritage?"

"I think about it often," I told her. "They carry the blood of the People, the blood of my red haired mother and the blood of the Kosi. I want them to know their whole lineage."

"If Say'f is gone, Quinn is King of the Kosi," she said softly.

Struck by Conquin's insight, I felt a stab of guilt. Since arriving back in the King's Valley, I had not thought of Quinn as a future King. The night Say'f and I were married, he told everyone that our son would be the next King. I should have remembered.

"What do you think I should do, Conquin?"

"Well, I want you here, but I think you should visit Talin. Then, perhaps you and Justyn might go to the Kosi Citadel at the Springs of Natrun. Didn't Lord Sta'g tell you it was time for the Kosi to choose a new King? It wouldn't hurt for the Kosi to see that the son of the Kosi King lives. If you go, would you want to take Kim-li and Kensing with you?"

I hesitated. Kensing was still just a baby, less than three. I thought a long time about Kim-li. She missed the Citadel and described it to me often. She needed her Kosi heritage too, especially if both her parents were dead. I explained to her that I was taking Quinn and Crimson only because they were still nursing; I could not leave them behind. I promised to return soon with news of her father. I had hoped Rohr would come with us, but when I asked him, he said his duty had been fulfilled. If I left Natil, he planned to return to the Citadel.

I bade him farewell on a bright windy morning, tears brimming. We had not been apart since we escaped together after the Avalanche took the People's Skygrass valley.

"Farewell, my friend. I hope we will meet again in this life."

"I will await the day," he said confidently, "But I told you before, Warriors are not allowed to have women as friends."

"Then farewell, my Hero and my Guardian," I told him and the corners of his mouth curved up in a smile. When he cantered out of the King's Valley, he raised his arm in a Kosi salute. How I would miss him.

I returned to my apartment to pack for my long delayed visit to Talin, my childhood home.

Chapter 18 – At Maidenstone in the City of Namché

As Sab-ra bade her Guardian Lord Rohr farewell, Mistress waited in the forecourt of Maidenstone, tapping her foot and watching Ruby ascend the hundred steps.

"Where were you?" Mistress asked Ruby angrily. She looked tall and imposing with her black robe swirling in the wind.

"I went to send a telegram to me Da. Ma is still sick, but she survived the surgery."

Ruby knew her voice sounded sulky. She resented having to tell Mistress why she left or what she did. It was no business of hers, snobby cow.

"Te Ran told me that you saw Sab-ra pregnant in the Temple and An Mali said you had severe abdominal pains last night. Do you think your pains might be connected with Sab-ra?"

"I did wonder if it was because my sister was having her baby. Me Nana would call it sympathetic suffering," Ruby admitted reluctantly.

"I planned to try to get you to Talin before Sab-ra delivered, but if you think it's too late, perhaps you should stay here longer. The white tresses of snow still lie upon the foothills of the Dhali Ra. It is very cold in the high range. Before I make a final decision, I would like you to talk with Brother Jun."

Another one of the fey people, Ruby thought resentfully. Her mouth twisted.

They walked back to the Yellow Tower together.

"Go now and help Honus and Kieta in the kitchen," Mistress said.

She's using me like a galley slave, Ruby thought sourly, although she admitted to herself she was in no hurry to leave. If she stayed at Maidenstone, she could see the Garda from time to time, especially Carmac, and if Da sent a telegram about her Mum, they would bring it to her. Once she left the city to go higher in the mountains, she might never get word of Ma's condition.

A young looking monk in a red robe was waiting for Ruby outside the kitchen when she finished washing the breakfast dishes the following morning.

"I am Brother Jun," he told her calmly. "Will you walk with me?"

As if I have a choice in the matter, Ruby thought sullenly. She followed the monk with little Cloudheart pattering behind them. Jun heard the click of Cloudheart's toenails and looked over his shoulder. Ruby thought the Monk might send the little dog packing, but what he did instead was startling.

"Cloudheart, I greet you," he said quietly and actually bowed to the white dog.

This place completely baffled Ruby. Who bowed to a dog?

They left the Yellow Tower and walked across the lawn to a Green tower. Jun opened the door and ushered her inside. They proceeded across an open stone-flagged space and climbed a circular staircase. It went up many stories until they reached an eight-sided room at the top of the spire with windows on all sides. The view of the Blue Mountain range was stunning.

Jun looked at her with a gentle smile. "Te Ran tells me you have the Sight," he said.

"No. I don't. It's just that culchie Te Ran who says so," Ruby heard the crankiness in her own voice.

"Do you fear the Sight?" Jun asked.

"T'would be a silly thing to be afraid of something I don't have," Ruby said defiantly.

"I want you to talk with Brother Marzun," Brother Jun said. "Would you let him see into your mind?"

Ruby felt an immense frustration. She hated all this nonsense, seeing into People's minds. It was ridiculous. She took a deep breath and said, "I am only here because I have a twin sister. Sab-ra is her name."

"I know her well," Jun said, his eyes sparkling.

"Once I see her, I plan to return home. My Mum is sick and I would go back now, but she made me promise I would see Sab-ra before I returned. I hoped Sab-ra would be here in Nam-shay, but she left a year ago. Mistress is keeping me here until it is warmer and then I have to go up into the mountains to find her." Ruby felt peevish and reached down to pet Cloudheart. Petting him always made her feel better and eased her longing for her own red dog.

"Would a weapon help you on this journey?"

"Yes, it would. Could you give me a gun or at least a knife?"

"No. I meant a mind weapon. Brother Marzun could give you a weapon of the mind."

Better than nothing, I suppose, Ruby thought, exasperated.

The following morning Jun was waiting in the hall when Ruby left the kitchen. This time, he took her to the turquoise tower. After walking the circular staircase up several flights, Jun opened a door to the outdoor bridge. The wind blew fiercely and his red robe whipped around his slim ankles.

Ruby looked down at the wide arched bridge in the air that led from the turquoise spire to a white tower. Floating tendrils of rising mist wrapped the bridge. Brother Jun stepped forward into mist that rose to his waist. Ruby took a step into the fog and felt it pull her forward gently. When they reached the white tower, Jun looked back at Ruby.

"Don't the glass steps with no hand rails frighten you?" he asked, with a perplexed expression on his face.

"I don't see glass steps. What I see is a broad white bridge made of glistening icy stone. It is wide enough that a team of horses could have ridden across it."

Brother Jun looked at her in amazement and murmured, "This girl sees beyond the spells we put upon the bridges."

Inside the White Tower, they walked up more flights of stairs. These, Ruby could tell were made of yellow glass. The sun hit them and yellow prisms were everywhere. Ruby's resentment left. She was entranced by the beauty of tiny rainbows floating up the walls.

"I will leave you here. Brother Marzun will come."

Soon a door opened and a fat little monk entered the room. His head was bald and his small eyes were dark. They twinkled.

"I am Brother Marzun," he told her. "When you look out at the beautiful Blue Mountains, what do you see?"

"A bunch of little valleys, running along a river." Ruby's voice sounded bored.

"You can see that far?" Brother Marzun seemed amazed. "The Twelve Valleys country is ten days ride above Namché."

"Does Sab-ra live there?"

"If you count the valleys from west to east, Talin is the third valley. That's where Sab-ra came from."

"They are so beautiful, like a necklace of golden jewels strung along a green river," Ruby said, wistfully. This place was astonishing in its loveliness.

"Like a necklace, indeed," Brother Marzun said.

"When I go up into the Blue Mountains, will I take a train?"

"No, Ruby, there are no trains above Namché."

"Then how do I get there?"

"On horseback. It's about a ten day trip."

Ruby was devastated. A ten-day trip in the mountains on a horse would be a nightmare. She hated this whole thing. Why couldn't her mother have gone to find this sister by herself? Ruby gritted her teeth. She felt guilty when she realized she actually resented her mother's dire illness. She felt a headache coming on.

"I dread this trip," she admitted, looking down, "But I promised me Ma I would find my sister, so find her I shall. If I were on Viridian, I would ask Dar. Patrick to bless my journey." She felt a sadness that made her chest feel heavy.

"Then I shall do so in his name," Brother Marzun told her gently. He drew a circle in the air above Ruby's bright curls.

"I have a question for you," Brother Marzun said. "It may seem odd, but I want to know if you know me?"

What kind of a question was that, Ruby wondered, irritated.

"No, I don't know you. How could I? I only just met you," Ruby found herself increasingly frustrated by Brother Marzun's gentle demeanor.

"Look into my eyes," the monk's voice was soothing.

Ruby gazed into his dark eyes. They were like small pools and after a moment or two, she gasped.

"What do you see?"

Ruby's voice was low and sounded tranced, "Why, you are my Grandfather." Soft amazement filled her voice.

"Yes," he smiled at her. "I was once married and had a beautiful wife. She died giving birth to our second son. The midwife who attended her felt terrible remorse over her death. I could not work and take care of two young children, so I asked the midwife and her husband to adopt the infant. I named him Dani. I am your Grandfather."

Ruby's face filled with amazement.

"A year after the midwife and her husband adopted my infant son, I felt the Universe nudge me and heard the call to enter the Monastery. I took my older son to the Valley of Talin. They adopted him also. The two boys grew up together in Talin.

My eldest son was named Hent; my youngest son was named Dani." As Brother Marzun spoke these words, Ruby felt her eyes grow heavy. "Tell me what you see," he said.

Her voice had a singsong quality as she spoke. "Mum sits in fields of flowers and a dark haired boy. They play with a wee white lion."

"Would you like to stay and work with me?" Brother Marzun asked her kindly. "There are many things I could show you." He snapped his fingers.

"Yes," she breathed out a long sigh of relief, coming back to the present.

"This trip will be a journey of great import," he said. "For both of us."

Chapter 19 – Leaving the King's valley for Talin
Flowering Moon, June

The day Ruby agreed to work with Brother Marzun, Sab-ra and Justyn left the King's Valley, travelling west toward her home valley of Talin.

In Rohr's absence, Thron, Conquin's husband and Norgay, the King's Horse Captain, were assigned to escort me and my children to Talin. Justyn was coming with us. The King had his carpenters make a small wagon for the babies. The leather workers made a harness to attach the wagon to Jemma, the roan mare I bought in Rhan Du. Conquin and I padded the bottom and sides of the wagon with pashmin wool. We put Quinn and Crimson in the wagon and had Jemma pull them around the castle garden, accustoming them to riding.

The morning was bright with sunshine and the small ones were bouncing happily in the cart the day we rode straight up and out of the caldera. Less than an hour later I heard Quinn call me saying, "Crim-mee, Crim-mee."

I turned around to see that somehow my daughter had managed to climb out of the wagon. She fell, landing on the road. She scraped her knee and at the sight of her blood, Quinn wept. I had noticed this before. Whenever Crimson got hurt, which was often, Quinn cried. When Quinn injured himself, he had the stoicism of a tiny warrior.

"Stop, Justyn," I told him. I dismounted, grabbed my intrepid small daughter and sat her in front of my saddle. Enthralled by everything she saw, she was completely still, her eyes wide open. There was no fear in my daughter's heart. Holding her was like having a small falcon in your hand or a lion cub in your lap.

Less than half an hour later, Crimson cried out, "Whin, Whin." It was her baby name for her brother. We stopped. Looking back, I saw Quinn hanging on the outside of the wagon, about to let go. I gave Crimson to Justyn climbed down and grabbed Quinn.

As we rode east, I pointed out some flying raptors, telling my son their burning eyes sought the nest of the ne-ne. He seemed compelled by the sight of them and raised his voice calling, "Sky Dogs, down," moving his arm downward. I remembered the enormous eagle in the King's sleeping space at the Citadel. If Say'f were dead, that eagle would belong to Quinn.

At the King's command, Justyn and I announced the Peace Accord to the Elders in each of the Twelve Valleys as we rode across the folded earth. The King's scribe had made twelve copies of the treaty between the Kosi and the People. The Accord had been drafted at my instigation and bound the Kosi to take no more women against their will from the Twelve Valleys. Kosi women, to their unending sorrow, were infertile. Kosi men who desired a wife that could conceive a child, would come and court her as was the usual practice among my People. A marriage could not take place without the woman's consent.

We were welcomed everywhere, although many of the men asked difficult questions. We met at evening around the Communal Flame. I spoke as an Elder then, a married woman with children. I told them about the importance of the Accord. I brought Quinn and Crimson with me to the Flame. My son sat beside me unmoving; held rapt by the night, the flames and the stars. When the men asked to hold him, he shook his head, holding my fingers tightly. Crimson had no such reservations. The men passed her from hand to hand. She sat so quietly, erect and proud. Everyone was entranced. I spoke of Quinn as the future for our People. He became the honorary son or grandson of everyone there. Crimson had many offers of marriage before the night was over. I obtained the names of the People's women the Shunned took from each valley. I had Say'f's promise they would have a choice about whether to return to their home valleys.

Although they welcomed my visit, most of the Elders looked at me with doubt in their eyes and shook their heads. They said Say'f was dead and doubted a piece of paper would control murderous Kosi warriors with no one to enforce their obedience. I felt the loss of Say'f urgently then. His life was my destiny. Without him, I could never bridge our cultures and find true peace for the high country. After the Flame ceremony, I slept in the Headman's house with my babes. I lay awake a long time, trying to reach my husband with my mind; across the hills and valleys of the pleated Blue Mountains.

We rode into Talin in the early evening. The news that we were coming preceded us. The People had erected festival tents and the food smelled wonderful. The scent of the distinctive cuisine of Talin rode out to meet us. I smelled the fragrance of mingled herbs, warm tsampa bread and Ghat cheeses. Grandfather and Uncle Hent rode down toward us, calling out welcoming greetings. I remembered the first time I rode into Talin with the Kosi, it seemed an eternity ago when I first brought Say'f to Talin. That day Grandfather was furious and ordered the Kosi King and his warriors away. Only by invoking the Wind Goddess, was I able to convince grandfather to let Say'f speak to the Elders. This time the air resounded with songs and happy cries.

"How beautiful they are," Grandmother said, taking Quinn in her arms. Grandfather took Crimson and showed her to everyone in the village.

"They both are amazing," I told them, "Quinn can already take a few steps on his own and Crimson is talking so much. I am so proud of my children."

"Sab-ra," Quinn said, laughing. He already knew how to tease me. He knew I didn't like him to call me by my first name.

"You must not call me Sab-ra, Quinn," I said for the hundredth time. You should call me Bah-ma," the Kosi word for mother.

"He probably should call you Queen Sab-ra," Grandfather said quietly. "Quinn is the future King, but you are Queen of the Kosi now."

Shaken by my responsibilities that hit me like a hailstorm, I realized this trip was about far more than presenting Quinn to the Kosi at the Citadel. I felt the crux of time and the absolute necessity of getting to the Springs of Natrun. How would I preserve my son's kingship? Where are you Say'f, I cried in my mind.

Chapter 20 – At Maidenstone in the City of Namché
May

The day Sab-ra's grandparents met Sab-ra's babies; Ruby realized that spring had come to Maidenstone. Two months had gone by and she was horrified to realize she had no memory of those days.

It seemed to Ruby only a few days had passed since she began working with Brother Marzun when one day she noticed that all the snow was gone. Small yellow sativa flowers were blooming in the Kitchen Garden and all the trees were topped by a cumulous of green leaves.

"What month is it now?" she asked Honus.

"The Planting Moon has begun," she answered. "You have been here two moons already."

Ruby frowned. She had started working Brother Marzun only a week after arriving in Nam-shay. Horrorstruck, she realized she had no memories since she began spending her days with the old monk. She walked to Brother Marzun's turquoise tower and ascended the circular staircase. When she reached the top room, he was sitting in his chair looking out as the green plants of spring climbed the Blue Mountains.

"According to Honus, I have been coming here every day for over two months, although it only feels like we began days ago," Ruby's voice shook with her words. "I remember nothing."

Brother Marzun's serene countenance wore a sudden frown.

"Did you hear me? I don't have any memories since we began," Ruby wailed.

"I will get Brother Jun," he said. When he came back, he asked her to tell Brother Jun what she had told him.

"I remember meeting Brother Marzun and realizing he was my Grandfather. Other than that I remember only a few times helping in the kitchen and one day with Cloudheart in the garden."

Brother Marzun said, "Ruby, I fear you have the Far Seer disease." His face creased in sympathy.

Ruby was disgusted. Working with the old monk had given her a disease? What had happened to her Ma in the last two months? Was she even alive? Had she received any letters or telegrams? She was about to ask, but Brother Jun spoke, breaking her chain of thought.

"The Far Seer disease is not a true disease, Ruby. It is what happens to extremely talented Far Seers who cannot control the Sight."

"Exactly," Brother Marzun said calmly. "You have a rare form of the Sight called the Vision. Most of the acolytes that study with Te Ran learn to scry; to see momentous events in the future. You have the ability to see what is happening to others in the present." Ruby looked at the men, feeling panic starting to rise inside her. Her breathing quickened.

"When Te Ran took you to the Temple, I understand she asked you to look into her crystal orb and tell her what you saw. She said you entered a light trance and spoke in a singsong voice. You saw a pregnant red haired woman who rode with a dark Kosi warrior."

"I remember that," Ruby said tentatively, seeking desperately to understand what had happened to her.

"The Far Seer disease comes because the Seer actually enters the consciousness of the person she sees. For the last two months, you have been inside Sab-ra's mind."

Ruby felt her cheeks redden and tears of rage begin to form. "This Vision thing took my life," she wailed. "When I agreed to work with you, nobody told me that a huge block of my memories would vanish. I never would have agreed to you probing around in my mind if I knew this would happen."

"None of us knew it would happen," Brother Jun told her gently. "We have not had this happen before to any of our acolytes."

"What matters is what you do from this time forward," Brother Marzun said crisply. "Listen carefully, Ruby, this is important. You need to control this. You must never seek the Vision again, unless your own life is in danger. Are we agreed?"

"Yes," Ruby told him firmly. She feared this awful Vision business. Avoiding it would not be a loss. Crazy fey stuff. She wished fervently that she had never come to Maidenstone. Walking back to the Yellow tower, Ruby paused to see the changes warm weather had brought to the land. The Garda lads must have missed me, she thought.

Mistress Falcon was waiting when Ruby reached the Yellow door. She said there was no need to delay her trip to the Mountains any longer.

"Who is going to take me up into the Mountains," Ruby asked, suspiciously.

"One of the Bearer people who works for me. Ten Singh is his name."

"I cannot leave Maidenstone on a trip alone with a man," Ruby wailed in horror. "My Da would be scandalized."

"Deti will be going with you also. I would like you to take Cloudheart along, but I am not sure he will leave Maidenstone. Call him and I will ask him to choose."

What nonsense, Ruby thought, giving the dog a choice. "Come to me, Cloudheart," she said. He ran to her. She lifted him up in her arms.

"Set him down now," Mistress said. "Cloudheart, come here," she called, but he would not leave Ruby. He sat at her feet, fixing his eyes on hers lovingly.

"My true companion," Ruby murmured. Cloudheart's loyalty had helped her not miss Maeve so much.

"Then you may go with Ruby, Cloudheart," Mistress said, looking at the dog.

"Mistress Falcon, have I heard from my father in the last two months?"

"Yes, child. Your mother has recovered enough to leave the hospital. She and your father are together at home. You may write them, if you wish. I will send the letter."

That evening Ruby wrote a long letter to her parents, telling them she was going up into the high range. She described Brother Marzun and told her mother that he was Dani's father. She said she missed them terribly, told them to kiss her Nana, hug her dog and say hello to Shane for her.

It was late afternoon when the small cavalcade got underway. Ten Singh, Deti and Ruby walked down Maidenstone's staircase with little Cloudheart trotting beside them. It was a warm breezy day; the sky was blue and cloudless.

Ten Singh was a slim man with intelligent brownish green eyes. Mistress told Ruby he was one of the high range Bearer people who took messages from one settlement to another. Ruby wondered if he could defend her from wild beasts. Then she noticed how his muscles bulged and how easily he lifted her from the last step on the staircase to the ground. Three ponies stood tied to a post nearby. One had a dark woolen roll on the back of his saddle. All three animals looked around wildly, jerking on their laces. Their eyes showed white whenever sound came from inside the tunnel.

"This is your pony, Ruby. She is a gentle sort, named Star."

"She doesn't look very gentle right now," Ruby said, fear filling her stomach. "Do we have to go into that dark tunnel?" She gestured to a circular opening, filled with a boiling mist.

"Yes, but Star will be fine once we get inside. Have you ridden much in your country?"

"Once or twice," Ruby said, noticing a look of dismay on Ten Singh's face. "They have small ponies at the parks and kids can ride them. Mum took me sometimes when I was a wee little thing."

Ten Singh's mouth twisted and he frowned.

"I will keep our pace as slow as I can, but Mistress said there was some urgency about getting you to Talin. This first day we will ride only for about four hours. I am going to lead all three of the ponies into the tunnel. I will hold your hand until we get through. If you are frightened, close your eyes. Deti, will you be all right walking beside me?"

"I will be fine," Deti told him. "I'm excited to go on this trip. I haven't been out of Maidenstone since I came here before the War." Holding Cloudheart's leash, Deti skipped ahead in clear delight.

White fog boiled out of the tunnel entrance, but once they were inside, it was completely dark. Ruby felt cool air wetting her eyelashes and found the thick white vapor hard to breathe.

"Keep your eyes shut," Ten Singh reminded her.

When they were out in the bright day again, Ruby sighed in relief.

"Don't turn around," Ten Singh commanded her brusquely.

"Why?" She had almost turned back.

"The Leopard Gate frightens most people."

"Not me," Deti said, bravely, but Ruby noticed she didn't look back either.

In front of them, a guard was checking people leaving the city. Past the checkpoint there was a multi-arched stone bridge spanning a water barrier. Beyond the bridge, Ruby saw a huge wall. It wavered in the sunlight and seemed made of fabric.

"What is the wall made of, Ten Singh?" she asked. "It looks like cloth."

"It is a kind of magic mesh and no arrow or even bullet can penetrate it. When the Harn Army came, we could have defended the city, if enough citizens had joined the Resistance." His voice sounded bitter. "Instead, we opened the gates." His face was disgusted.

Beyond the wall, Ruby was relieved to see a road. The ponies clopped along slowly, leaving dusty hoof prints behind them. Soon, she would see Sab-ra. What would she feel when she saw her sister, she wondered. She was anxious to get this trip over with so she could return to her parents and her friends, but knew she would be sad to leave Cloudheart.

Chapter 21 – At the Citadel, near the Springs of Natrun

While Ruby rode north toward Talin with Ten Singh and Deti, Sab-ra told Justyn she planned to journey south, to the Citadel. The sisters were coming close to each other.

"I have to return to the Kosi Citadel at the Springs of Natrun, Justyn," I told him after spending a few days with my grandparents in Talin.

"I don't think you should," Justyn said. "You are the wife of the dead King. They will not want you there. And you are a mother now. You must think of your children before yourself."

I felt a wash of shame, but it didn't stop my burning intent to visit the Kosi stronghold.

Over the next few days I begged Justyn to accompany me to the Citadel, hoping against hope that Say'f would be there. Grandmother cried and urged me to stay longer, but dried her tears when I said I would leave Quinn and Crimson in Talin. I would be back in a few weeks, I told her. Justyn shook his head in despair at my stubbornness.

"Why can't we all go to Namché? We could be married there. Since the Harn Army is gone now, I could get a position translating for the Headman of the city. You could resume your Healer work. We would be a real family." Justyn's eyes pleaded for my consent.

My heart crunched a bit for Justyn and in truth for myself, although I found my mind turning away from the vision of the four of us living in Namché. I could not stop thinking about the Kosi. What would I be to the Warriors? Would I be their Queen, as Grandmother said? Or, would I be an irritant, a problem to be disposed of, as Justyn feared. My old dread of the Kosi woke inside me as Justyn and I rode south on the Wool Road toward the great Kosi grasslands.

We entered the side trail leading to the Springs of Natrun at evening four days later. We travelled among tall green bamboo that caught the evening light. The Citadel was several hours ride south of the springs. I began to feel nakedly vulnerable. I was angry with myself for allowing Norgay and Thron to return to the King's Valley after they left us in Talin. Norgay was the Kosi captain of the King's horses. If Norgay were with us now, the Shunned would have to show him respect. Justyn didn't even have a knife. I brought my old knife from Maidenstone, its blade still coated with the deadly poison. With a shock, I realized I couldn't use poison on a Kosi; they were my People now.

We camped near the Springs of Natrun, in a valley filled with tall green grasses and white windflowers. The springs were full of turquoise water, warm as summer sun. I soaked my tired body in its warmth. Later, we lay on our sleeping bags on the grass floor, looking up at the skies through a frame of waving bamboo. The grasshoppers flew high that night and the Firebrand bees looked like stars. For the first time, I seemed to see my sister's face. I wondered if she had come to my land from the far place that was her home. She seemed very close and I sent her my love on the wings of bees.

"We should talk about what you are going to say to the Warriors at the Citadel," Justyn said, interrupting my thoughts about my twin. I smiled at him, thinking how much he really was like Hodi.

"Yes, I agree. I brought a white gown with me, made of the finest pashmin wool. I plan to enter the Citadel dressed as their Queen. I will claim the right to sleep in the King's Alcove. Do you remember, Justyn, it was by the round viewing window."

"You might find someone else has taken that place," Justyn said, looking at me from narrowed eyes in an anxious countenance.

"Who would have the temerity to do such a thing?"

"Sab-ra, sweetheart, the Bearers told me the Kosi King was dead. They probably told the Kosi that also. All the Kosi who survived the war have by now returned to the Citadel. They will pledge loyalty to the strongest warrior. I suspect many battles have taken place since you left there, battles over who is King now."

This whole trip seemed suddenly perilous and despite the beautiful evening, I felt dread inside me. Without the King, what would happen to the Accord? How would I accomplish my goals of healing the wounds that still festered between the People and the Kosi? I had been so proud presenting the velum copies of the Accord to each Headman in the Twelve Valleys. Now my dream of peace between the People and the Kosi could die. Goddess of the

Winds, please guide me, I prayed, but a cold breeze swept us that night as we slept by the fire—the night before the beginning of the death mission.

We rode into the Citadel at midday. Everything seemed too quiet. I heard a crow calling and a dog fox bark in the distance. The odd stillness brought to mind memories of why I was sent to Maidenstone. For many years the Kosi tribe kidnapped our fertile young women. Their own birthrate had been eclipsed by the sterility of their females. As a child, I was trained as a spy. I watched the Kosi and warned the Elders of planned attacks. Hodi was my spy partner, my spirit brother, my only friend. Tears brushed my eyelashes as I remembered him.

On our first spy mission, Hodi and I were sent to the Green River Camp. Our objective was to liberate the People's women who had been abducted by the Shunned Kosi. I escaped because Hodi distracted a Kosi guard. Although I tried desperately to save him, he was killed and his body placed in a garbage pit. My stomach still roiled then I remembered that horror. When I returned to Talin to tell the Elders what had happened, they were furious and pronounced my punishment. I would be sent away to school at Maidenstone, the ancient Lamasery in Namché. Although banishment to Maidenstone was to be a punishment, I learned to love the slow beautiful pace of meditation and service.

No one came out of the Citadel to greet us. We dismounted and tethered our mounts. I walked to a nearby grove, dressed myself and combed my hair in the high braided Kosi style. Justyn and I walked side by side to the sliding rock that concealed the main door to the stronghold. It seemed to swing open of its own accord and we walked into revulsion.

The stench was overwhelming. I turned aside and vomited in the nearby grasses. When I could make myself stand upright, I peered into the Citadel. In the dim light, we could see bodies of men and even women stabbed, beaten, killed. We saw two children and one pregnant woman among the corpses. No one seemed alive in that charnel house.

I was horrified to be stepping over Kosi bodies, but Justyn insisted that I see if anyone might still be breathing. I knelt by each body and took pulses. I found no one alive. The dark metal colored feathers of the King's golden eagle lay on the ground. The eagle was missing. I prayed he had escaped.

We found a young female gazehound hiding in the bedchamber of the King. She was starving and desperately thirsty. She made the sound of the feral lynx when she heard us. I picked her up, crooning to her. Justyn searched the area around the Citadel and located a cold spring. At the bottom, he saw a container, partially covered by waterweed and rocks. He pulled it to the surface and we were elated to find good chanry meat inside; so was the little gazehound. She ate it raw, rapturously.

The next morning, working like slaves in the hot sun Justyn and I began burying all the Kosi. There were thirty-one men, three women and two children. It took us many days. The earth was hard as granite. We had no choice but to cover their bodies with rocks and pronounce the blessing for the dead. I had learned the Kosi song for those who had passed away from little Kim-li and sang it. The notes rang in the evening darkness. I didn't know what the words meant, but it was an eerie lament to the lost beauty and glowing warmth of the Citadel. The ancestral home of the Kosi was gone, like the great Skygrass valley. Darkness filled my soul. I found it hard to breathe.

Late that day, we opened every door, every smoke hole and every hidden exit to the stronghold. We rode back and forth to the Springs of Natrun, returning with many containers of hot water. I scrubbed the stone floor of the fortress on my hands and knees using soap grass. I was determined to leave the bastion empty and clean, in case any Kosi who escaped might return. I left the beautiful furs of the King untouched, adorned with the bright feathers of his eagle. If I stopped working for any reason, the little gazehound came and sat directly at my feet. She looked intensely at me and crooned a high-pitched anxious sound. She was trying to tell me something, but I was too busy to listen.

Justyn and I began to argue about what we should do next. He wanted to proceed directly to Namché, saying Grandfather could bring Quinn and Crimson to us when he came to the city during the Harvest Moon to sell his wool. He feared if I returned to Talin, I would want to stay there permanently. My own intent grew slowly during those days. I knew I did not want to return to Namché. I did not intend to return to Talin either, but I missed my children desperately. Before I could do anything else, I needed to see them again.

"We must return to Talin. The little ones wait for both of us," I told him. At last, Justyn agreed. I did not tell him that I intended to stay in Talin only briefly. I would go north from there, alone if necessary. Since I had been at the Citadel, I found myself believing my King still lived. I knew there must be a reason he hadn't returned. It was my destiny to find him.

Chapter 22 – Toward the Valley of Talin

While Sab-ra and Justyn cleaned the Citadel of the smell of death, Ruby proceeded north toward Talin.

The rain began toward the end of the first day of Ruby's trip to Talin. It pelted down and Ruby's travelling cloak was soaked. Her shoes squished against the flanks of her pony. Her red curls were plastered to her forehead.

"Ten Singh, can we stop soon. I am perishin' for me tea."

They arrived at a poor farmstead about an hour later. A peasant dressed in rags told them to dismount. Deti jumped down and dashed around exploring the farm with Cloudheart. He found a hen and barked at her. The chicken was sitting on some eggs on the muddy ground. Ruby looked around in dismay. Was this dirty farmhouse where they were going to sleep? Even though they had ridden only about four hours, her bottom was terribly sore. Dismounting from Star, Ruby was unsteady on her feet.

The farmer gestured and they followed him into the dank wooden structure. There were only three rooms, and none of them had doors. Ruby shivered, thinking about sleeping in this dark place with two grown men.

"Where do we wash, Ten Singh?" she whispered.

"There is a spring behind the house, use that."

"Won't the water be cold?"

"Of course," Ten Singh said looking at her with a wry expression, partly amused, partly irritated.

"I am sore," she whispered and patted herself on the bottom.

"I will ask the farmer for some milk-bag unguent."

Something from a cow's dirty udder? Ruby thought uncomfortably about what the farmer would bring her to use on her sores. When Ten Singh returned, he had a piece of what looked like cowhide folded into a packet. Opening it, he showed her a dollop of black tar. Although Ruby dreaded applying the sticky substance, and the cowhide smelled disgusting, she forced herself to rub the gel into her skin. Revolting it was, but she had to admit it helped.

Ten Singh took the dark wool roll from the back of his pony. It was some kind of tent, Ruby thought, watching him erect the shelter. Inside it was very dark, but clean and warm. Ten Singh spread some furs on the floor saying it was where she and Deti would sleep. Cloudheart settled himself between them with a sigh. Ten Singh said he would sleep in the farmer's house. Ruby was relieved.

When the farmer pressed Ruby to take the rest of the unguent the next morning, she thanked him and took it. Despite it coming from a common dirty cow, she knew she would use it. They faced many more days on the road.

The following afternoon, the sun came out and they entered an area of harsh black sand and enormous boulders. Ten Singh called it the Garden of the Gods. Ruby looked around for any type of house or inn. There was nothing but wind and raw nature. At sunset, Ten Singh called a halt, started a campfire and told Deti to get some water from a nearby stream. He asked Ruby if she would be able to sit on a rock near the fire. She did, with difficulty. She was sure her bum was bleeding. Deti and Cloudheart bounced over to them and sat nearby. Ten Singh handed them some bread. He had spread cheese on it and warmed it over the fire. It was a long way from a proper tea, but Ruby was grateful. The bread was delicious.

"I was near to havin' a weakness," she told Ten Singh. He shook his head, unused to guiding girls who complained as much as Ruby.

After dinner, Ten Singh led her away from the campfire to a small spring bubbling out of the ground. The water was icy cold.

"I will leave you. Remove your pants and sit down in the water. It will help."

Ruby practically screamed when she lowered herself into the water. She jumped out several times, but made herself get back in. The water did help and after applying the black unguent again, she found herself more comfortable. She walked back to the campfire and asked Ten Singh where he was going to set up the black tent.

"It's called a dweli, Ruby, but tonight we sleeping beneath the stars," he grinned at her startled expression. He led both girls away from the enormous boulders, deeper into the grass that encircled the gray guardian stones. They followed a slim little trail, hardly visible in the fading light. At first the grass only reached up to her waist, but deeper into the green scrim, it towered above her head. The grasses parted and Ruby saw a large circle of flattened green rushes. It looked as if something had stomped them down. Ten Singh spread their sleeping robes on the grass and went back for the ponies.

"This is a Ghat bed," Deti whispered, sitting down.

"What are Ghat?" Ruby asked, still standing.

"Wild oxen."

"Will they come back?" Ruby heard terror in her voice. She envisioned cattle running in the night, stepping on them with their cloven hooves. How she wished she had never left the civilization of Viridian. She wondered if her parents were sitting down to tea and ached to be with them.

"Ten Singh wouldn't have us camp here if the Ghat were coming back. You are a silly girl, Ruby," Deti said.

Cloudheart kept leaving them to run into the tall blades and Ruby called him back several times before trapping him and setting a big stone on his leash. He tugged against the rope and looked at them, pleadingly. Both girls shook their heads. Cloudheart sat with his head hanging down. It was unusual behavior for the little dog.

Lying on furs, looking up at the stars through the moving circle of the grasses, Ruby saw a dark vee formation in the colored sky of sunset.

"Are those birds, Deti?"

"Grasshoppers. They are as long as your arm. They are all black, except for one. The lead hopper is yellow. They are carnivorous, but they only attack bee hives and wasp nests."

"Look at the stars," Ruby marveled. "They look so close."

"Those aren't stars, they are called Firebrand," Deti told her. "They are as big as birds, but are bees. They bumble through the air like small fuzzy puppies."

Ruby thought about her mother's notations in the green book. Ma had written about grasses taller than her head and grasshoppers longer than her forearm. My Mum was here before me, Ruby told herself. She wouldn't have sent me if she didn't know I'd be safe. Lying back on the furs, she saw herself walking in the steps of her small red-haired mother from decades ago. Suddenly she saw her sister's face. They smiled at each other.

"Perhaps it wouldn't be so bad to have a sister after all," she murmured.

The next day, Ruby noticed that the great grass plains were changing. The earth had begun to roll up and gently down. The hills grew larger, becoming a wave of rising curves before they cascaded against the great Blue Mountains. By late afternoon, the land changed again. They rode through enormous ferns and white barked trees. At sunset, they reached a cluster of gigantic boulders with water cascading down their stone faces. Green mosses covered the gray granite. At the base of the stones, a pool had formed from the spring water. The water was turquoise blue and so clear they could see all the way to the white sandy bottom.

"We have reached the Springs of Natrun," Ten Singh announced. "We will camp here tonight."

Ruby took off her boots and put a toe in the water, expecting it to be frigid. To her delight, the water was warm, almost hot. It smelled like sulphur. She wrinkled her nose.

Ten Singh said he would leave so they could bathe and the girls happily dove into the water. When they emerged, their bodies were red as strawberries. Ruby applied the last of the black oozy ointment to her bum, but she hardly needed it any more. Later, they ate some sort of chicken bird that Ten Singh cooked over the fire. To her surprise, Ruby was beginning to enjoy the trip.

I'm changing, she thought. I am actually enjoying this wild country of my sister's.

"We are more than half-way to Talin now," Ten Singh told them. "Soon you will see your sister and your family from the Twelve Valleys."

Ruby had not thought about having family in Talin. It was a pleasant notion. But every day carried her further from Viridian. She wondered if she would ever see it again.

Chapter 23 – The Citadel, near the Springs of Natrun

While Ruby and Deti bathed in the Springs of Natrun, Sabra and Justyn prepared to leave the Citadel. At that point, they were only two hours south of the Springs of Natrun.

Desperate to wash the dust from my body, I sought a nearby hot spring. I took the little gazehound with me. As we walked, I noticed whenever I glanced down, her intense eyes locked on mine. When I found a small warmed pool, I stripped off my clothes and dove in. After I finished my bath and sat on a sun-warmed boulder combing my hair, the little gazehound closed her teeth on my comb and pulled. She wanted to take me somewhere. I finally had time to heed her wishes.

We walked through several meadows until I heard the Lakt. It was a huge swarm of the half-bird half-serpent creatures; they were buzzing in excitement. A dark cloud of them circled overhead. The gazehound led me up a high ridge. When I looked down at the fallen rocks below, I saw hundreds of Lakt feeding on more dark bodies. I felt faint with the terrible smell, but the gazehound kept urging me on. Then I heard a scream of rage. Below us I saw a Kosi warrior. He was alive and throwing stones to keep the Lakt from ripping skin off his dark companions.

Stepping carefully down through sand and rocks, I made it to the bottom. There were four Kosi—three men and one woman, all barely alive. One called out to me. I ran to his side and was elated to find my dear friend and guardian, Lord Rohr. Beside him was the unconscious body of Ghang, my guard when I left Maidenstone to warn my people of the Army plan to invade the Skygrass valley. I didn't recognize the other man, but the female was the Kosi woman who brought me soup when I first came to the Citadel. Rohr could hardly speak. His body stank from shed blood and the infection from his wounds. I managed to get him upright and he leaned heavily on me as we walked to a creek nearby where he drank his fill. I refilled my water skin and left it with him to share with the other Kosi. I said I would get help and return. The gazehound, gratified at finally getting her message through to me, trotted at my heels, obedient as the rest of her kind.

When I reached the Citadel, Justyn stood up, holding out his hands.

"Sab-ra, I've been so worried about you. You were gone a long time. The spirits of the Kosi call out for justice. I can hear them. This is no place to linger. We should leave for Talin now."

I was out of breath, but managed to say I had found Ghang and Lord Rohr alive as well as two other Kosi who might yet live. Justyn was clearly disheartened at the thought of additional delays before leaving for Talin, but we mounted our ponies and returned to the stream. Rohr had washed himself in the creek.

He called out when he saw me, "Queen of the Kosi, I salute you."

I felt a shiver, a soft stroke as if a feather waved across my forehead. The crown of a regent had descended on me.

Lord Rohr said he could walk. Justyn managed to get Ghang on his pony and I lifted the woman on to sturdy Jemma. We left the last man with more water, telling him we would return. Justyn made a rapid round trip and brought the last Kosi to the Citadel. When they reached the stronghold, I tended their wounds. Lord Rohr roasted the rest of the chanry. Like the gazehound, all the Kosi were grateful for the hot red meat.

Lord Rohr spoke my language well by then and told us that it was Hozro, the leader of the Shunned, who had attacked the Citadel. He had waited until all the Kosi returned after the Avalanche struck Skygrass. He killed any Kosi who would not swear allegiance to him. The few who would swear fealty, all women and children, he took with him. Lord Rohr said they travelled to the camp by the Green River. He and Ghang escaped just before the end of the battle. They had been trying to reach me.

I was enormously grateful to both of them. I didn't need to extract an oath of loyalty from Lord Rohr, First of the Blood Arrows. He had saved me after the Avalanche. Ghang had demonstrated his devotion to me on the trip from Maidenstone to Talin. Both these men were steadfast to the bone. The woman's name was Niffa and she immediately swore to be my servant, but I was leery of the last man, Argo. Rohr told me he was the tribe's assassin.

His eyes were proud and he had a haughty look. He appraised me disdainfully, narrowing his light gray eyes. I took out my knife and with Justyn's help forced him on to his back. We probably could not have overcome his resistance, but he was very weak from his time in the Lakt feeding grounds. I put my knife to his throat telling him even a single prick would give him the Yellow Water fever.

"I am wife to Say'f, King of the Kosi. I am your Queen," I told him fiercely.

"You are not a Queen," he hissed. "Among the Kosi, there is no Queen without a King."

"You will obey me," I commanded him fiercely. "Say it now or I will have Justyn cut you. You will die the death of a loathsome serpent. You will not be able to piss. At the end you will drown in your own fluids."

He looked at me a long time, but finally bent his head in submission saying, "I will obey," but I caught his murmured words later whisper, "While I live, you will never be Queen of the Kosi."

I glared at him, knowing I would have to watch him carefully.

I decided to sleep in the King's alcove on our final night. The Citadel smelled warm and clean by then. Justyn walked me down the long hall. When he said good night, he wouldn't meet my eyes. He was blinking back tears.

"What is it, Justyn?" I asked. My voice was low in pity. My heart clenched for what I had done to this loyal friend.

"Sab-ra, I sense you have come to a decision. You have chosen a life I can't be part of, haven't you?" He was trying hard to control his despair. "You have decided to reign as Queen of the Kosi. I don't understand what could make you give up a life of love and comfort in Namché with your children and me, for these few remaining warriors." Justyn's eyes were dark with pain and I felt my heart clench. How I hated hurting him.

"It is because there are so few Kosi that they need me, Justyn," I pleaded, wanting him to understand. The small number of Kosi still alive had hit me with a terrible force. The Warrior King said I cost him his Kingdom in the fight to save Skygrass. I owed him the lives of these people. It was the same fierce intensity I experienced when I realized my People were going extinct. The Kosi now faced the same fate.

"Sab-ra, you are no warrior," Justyn shook his head. "If you try to lure the rest of the Kosi from the leader of the Shunned, he will take you as his wife or kill you."

I remained stubbornly silent, but the Goddess of Fear crept into my heart.

"Sab-ra, if you cannot speak the truth to me, at least don't lie to yourself. You are risking your life and probably the lives of your children in this quixotic task. What you want could be the death of them. If you lost Quinn, it would be like Hodi all over again. I cannot imagine your pain if you lost Crimson."

Fear slid down inside me, cold and wet. Justyn was right. Both children needed protection, but I knew what I owed the King of the Kosi, even if he no longer lived. For me, there was no turning back. I was in the grip of the Goddess; she would not let me abandon his people. I hated saying farewell to Justyn, but I had become one with my adopted Kosi. Despite Argo's disdainful assertion that I was not the Kosi Queen, I felt the dark mantle of a regent descend around my shoulders.

Looking at my face, Justyn grimaced. "There is no need for me to return with you to Talin. Rohr will take you." Pain crossed his features. "Do you plan to try to look for the Kosi King's body?" he asked, struggling for control.

"Yes, I do. Justyn, when the Bearer People told you Say'f was dead, what made you believe them?"

"They found one of his boots," he said. "Say'f had carved twelve arrows tipped with red stones, into the leather. A large predator had chewed it, but there was no doubt. It was his boot."

I felt cold despair and my jaw clenched. When a man in the high range begins to shed his clothing, there is no hope. The People do not know the reason, but when a person begins to die in the heights, the thin air tells them to remove all their garments. The Wind Goddess takes them naked into the skies. Finding his boot was a terrible sign. Say'f knew the dangers. He would never remove his boots unless he walked the dying road.

"The life of a warrior is uncertain," Justyn called back to me as he walked down the central hall of the Kosi Citadel. I looked at his slender body and felt his pain inside me. "Your children may still need a father. When you find the Kosi King's body, remember I will be waiting in Namché."

"I'm sorry, Justyn," I called out to him, but he didn't turn around and left early the next morning without speaking to me again. I shivered, wondering if the path I had chosen would mean my death.

I decided I would leave the Citadel the following morning, riding north past the Springs of Natrun.

Chapter 24 – In the Grasslands, near the Springs of Natrun

As Sab-ra bade a sad farewell to Justyn, Ten Singh heard the wails of the captives taken by the Shunned.

Horrible life-ending screams rode the air the next morning as Ruby, Ten Singh and Deti prepared to leave their campsite near the Springs of Natrun.

"What is that ghastly sound, Ten Singh?" Ruby felt an awful trepidation. Her heart beat faster and her breath caught.

"I don't know, but my grandfather told me that the Kosi had a stronghold near the springs. We must avoid them at all costs. They take young women." His voice was low and ominous.

The cries continued the entire time Ruby and Deti gathered up their things and packed them on their ponies. Cloudheart stayed so close to Ruby she tripped over him several times. Her fingers kept fumbling with the horse's saddle girth. Drops of sweat formed on her forehead.

"Hurry," Ten Singh commanded. The horrible shrieks ceased for a moment and they all stopped working, wondering why the heart-rending sounds had stopped. Then they heard a whip crack, a long howling ululation, followed by the sounds of men yelling and children screaming again.

"I'm going to see what is making those cries," Ten Singh said. "Stay here." He rode off. Half an hour later, he returned.

"It's the Kosi Shunned. They are driving a group of women and children in front of them. You two must ride south or risk capture from scouts. I will find you later today or tomorrow," his voice was dark with dread.

The girls mounted up. Ruby had trouble getting back on Star with Cloudheart in her arms. He was struggling and fell to the earth, flipped over and ran after Deti. Ruby followed, feeling her throat close in suppressed panic. When she and Deti had ridden for several hours and Ruby could see Cloudheart was completely tuckered out, they stopped.

"We can stay here until Ten Singh comes," Deti said. They hobbled the horses. The weather worsened, storm clouds rode the skies.

"We better set up the dweli," Deti told Ruby. "We will be here all night."

They struggled to set up the dark round structure. The wind became their enemy, blowing the dweli down every time they almost had it secured. Finally, they succeeded, crawled inside panting and yelled for Cloudheart to come in. He did not appear.

"I'm afraid Cloudheart has run away. He probably believes he can find Sab-ra somewhere." Ruby's voice was flat and discouraged. She sensed Sab-ra was nearby. Maybe Cloudheart sensed it too.

"I am going to ride north a little ways, maybe I can find Cloudheart," Deti said. Her words were confident, but Ruby knew she was frightened too.

"Deti, please don't leave me," Ruby pleaded. Her heart thudded against her ribs.

"I told Sab-ra when she left Maidenstone that I would keep Cloudheart safe," Deti's mouth was set in a stubborn line. "Just stay in the dweli."

Deti opened the slit door and peered out. Rain was beginning to fall. Her slim body was a shadow as she disappeared into the grayness. Ruby wailed, but Deti did not return. Ruby opened the flap a hundred times until the moon rose. There was no sign of Deti or Cloudheart. Finally, exhausted from fear, she fell to the furs on the floor of the dweli, sobbing. All night she waited, sleeping on and off until dawn came in—pink and golden.

She walked outside, saw Star hobbled nearby and took some food from her packs for herself and the pony. Star was struggling against her restraints and Ruby wondered if she was thirsty. She untied the hobbles and fumbled with Star's packs, trying to reach her waterskin. As she did so, the neck rein slipped from her hand. When she turned back to offer water to the pony,

Star whirled and disappeared into the grasses. In seconds, they swallowed her whole.

"No," she screamed, but it was useless. It was as if the pony had never existed. The grass muffled even her clopping feet. The only sound Ruby could hear was a low keening wind. Now she was completely alone. Deti, Cloudheart, Ten-Singh; all of them gone, like the world she came from.

Deti came upon Cloudheart in late afternoon, still running north toward Talin. Grabbing him, she hugged him hard.

"You stay with me, you little monster," she told him. He struggled and growled quietly. She was unmoved. She put a thin rope around Cloudheart's neck and told him to find Ten Singh. Following Cloudheart's lead, she came upon him late in the day.

"The mob rode off," Ten Singh told her in relief. "The party was going northeast. Only the Kosi warriors were mounted; the women and children were walking. Where is Ruby?"

"I left her at the dweli, straight south of here."

They rode knee to knee until it was too dark to see the trail. Ten Singh found a small grove of stunted trees and they tethered the horses. A light drizzling rain began. They didn't make a fire, worried the Kosi would spot the smoke. In the misty light, they ate their cold food, rolled themselves in furs and slept.

Around the same time that Deti found Cloudheart, Ruby thought she heard the faint sounds of horses. She jumped to her feet and walked outside screaming, "Ten Singh, Deti, I am here." But when the blades of grass parted, it was not Ten Singh. It was not Deti. It was an enormous dark-skinned savage riding a black horse. He was bare-chested and his face was narrow and linear. His nose curved like a hawk's beak. He had a longbow on his back and a quiver of arrows. He wore a serrated silver knife in his belt. His eyes snapped when he saw her. He uttered a few guttural words.

"Mother of God help me," Ruby entreated and fell to her knees. She kept her eyes on the ground, praying he would ride off, but he didn't. She saw his leather boots come closer. He grabbed her by the hair and lifted her up.

"Let me go, you are hurting me," she screamed, twisting away from him.

He put his arm around her waist, pulled a piece of leather from his long braided hair and gagged her. He tied her hands together and lifted her on to his horse. He saw her backpack and tied it to his saddlebag. He gave a piercing whistle and a tall rangy dog came out of the reeds. He mounted behind her and they rode northeast.

The next morning Deti and Ten Singh continued south. The weather had improved and both were in better spirits.

"We should reach the dweli in another hour," Deti told Ten Singh cheerfully. "I told Ruby to stay there. She's such an easily frightened little thing. Not brave like Sab-ra at all."

The dweli had a funny abandoned look when they spotted it. They tied their ponies to bundles of tall grass. Abruptly, the reeds parted and Star trotted into the clearing. Ten Singh grabbed her, holding the reins until she stood quietly. He petted her gently, calming her fears. Deti pulled open the dweli door calling Ruby's name, but the dweli was empty.

"Ten Singh, she's gone," Deti said, despair rang in her voice.

Together they read the signs of broken grasses and trampled foliage.

"Did she leave any message?" Ten Singh asked. "Where is her little diary book?"

"Her pack is missing. The book was in her pack. I feel terrible; I should not have left her."

"One of the Shunned Kosi scouts took her," Ten Singh told Deti. He looked away in shame.

"Oh Goddess, no," Deti wailed.

"From the pattern in the grasses, I see that he rode northeast when he left. He travelled in the same direction as the captives." His voice was old as death.

"What should we do?" Deti's face was white.

"I will take you to Talin. I can get help there to go after the Kosi who kidnapped Ruby."

Chapter 25 – At the Citadel near the Springs of Natrun

As Ruby rode northwest with the Shunned warrior and Ten Singh and Deti rode straight north toward Talin, Sab-ra prayed for help from the Wind Goddess.

I spent a long night begging for the guidance of the Wind Goddess as I struggled with my decision. I woke, knowing what I had to do. I walked the length of the Citadel, calling Ghang and Argo. I stood tall before them.

"I hereby command you both to go the Green River Camp and find Hozro. I want him captured and brought alive to Talin."

Hozro had killed more than thirty Kosi. I would make him stand trial for his crimes. The Elder Council would determine his guilt. Although the People had walked the path of peace for a thousand years, after the War the Guildmasters passed a law permitting a death penalty in the case of mass murder. At Hozro's trial I would argue for beheading. I would see the demon slain. I wondered as these thoughts crossed my mind, where the easily terrified girl I once was had gone.

"Don't kill you dare kill Hozro, Argo," I told him sternly. "I want to see his face when the Guildmasters sentence him to death."

Argo nodded, but his sly eyes still mocked me.

"Do as I say," I commanded him. "Do not fail me."

Turning to Ghang, I said, "Rohr and I are going north to Talin and from there on to Halfhigh, the mid-point between Talin and the entrance to the Lost Lake. Once you have taken Hozro captive, bring him and any Kosi warriors who would swear allegiance to King Say'f to Halfhigh. If any refuse, say I banish them and their descendants forever from the Twelve Valley's country." I was the Queen Incarnate then, and she wore a dark crown.

I said a silent good-bye to the Citadel, remembering its glowing presence when I first arrived from Maidenstone, trying to banish the memories of the slaughter. The Shunned left no horses behind. We had only little Jemma and Rohr was far too heavy for her. He and Niffa walked beside me as I rode. I named the little gazehound, Dusk. She joined us, running for hours, never winded. Watching her, I missed Cloudheart terribly.

The sounds of screams and whip cracks rose from the great grass plains. Rohr scouted ahead while Niffa and I hid in the deep grass. When he returned his face was dark with rage.

"It is some of Hozro's Shunned Warriors. They are Kosi by blood, but have no honor. They are driving a stolen group of women and children ahead of them," Rohr said.

"Women and children? Is that the sound of their cries we heard?"

He nodded.

"How many were there?" I asked him, trying to still my horror.

"I think five or six women and a few children. The men are on horseback, but the women are walking, carrying the younger children."

"Which way are they going?"

"They are headed northwest in the direction of the Green River."

My heart filled up with despair, like a cup of hemlock. I knew that camp; it was the place where the Kosi Wolf took the life of my spy partner, Hodi. I still felt a stabbing pain in my heart remembering the night Hodi made the dire wolf's cry to lure the Kosi's eyes away from me. Hodi saved my life that night, but lost his own. I shuddered at the fate of anyone who defied the Kosi Wolf.

We passed a small spring late that evening. Its waters were cold and pure. I stopped to fill my scry bowl. We set up camp near the bubbling artesian well. When the ringed moon rose that night, I walked to the nearest hill, tipped the bowl to catch the moonlight and watched while the waters pleated, folding over repeatedly. Nausea gripped me, but I held on. The bowl itself quivered and grew hot. It almost burned my hands, but I would not let go. At last, the waters cleared and I saw the face of a woman with long red hair. I thought at first it was me, but when I looked more carefully, it was my sister. My twin rode in front of a large Kosi Warrior on a dark horse. The man had a red feather in his hair. The Shunned had killed Hodi and now they had captured my sister.

Time swept around in a great circle and I keened, shrieking my rage to the heavens.

Then the waters rolled again and I saw the Lost Lake valley. In that place of transcendent beauty, I saw a dark skinned man. He climbed the massif toward an Angelion who lay bleeding among broken stones. I closed my eyes, shaking. Did the image mean my Say'f lived? Would I find him only to discover Sumulus lying dead in splintered rocks?

Two days later, we spotted a herd of wild horses. A stallion stood in front of his group of mares on the top of a hill. Seeing him, Rohr quivered like a gazehound on point. He whistled through two fingers and the stallion lifted his head abruptly. The warhorse saw us and charged. I backed my mount, Jemma, away and gestured to Niffa to stand back. The stallion came on like a screaming hurricane. When he reached Rohr he reared, his front feet striking the air. Rohr gave an enormous cry and darted underneath the upraised stallion. He grabbed him around the chest and they stood together for a moment. Then the horse slowly lowered his body, and Rohr slipped from under him. The stallion extended his head toward his master. It was Tye, Lord Rohr's warhorse. There was a dark cut on his neck. His bridle was gone, but he knew his master. Lord Rohr mounted him with ease. He offered a hand to Niffa and swung her up behind him. Dusk kept pace with us as we rode on toward Talin.

"Why was Tye with the wild ones?" I asked Rohr.

"He refused to allow Hozro and or either of his scouts to mount him even after they cut his neck. He escaped after the battle at the Citadel," Rohr smiled in pleasure remembering the loyalty of his warhorse.

We reached the rising road to Talin at dusk. Although we were allies now, I knew the People might fear the Kosi who rode with me. I asked Rohr and Niffa to wait at the bottom of the trail for my signal. Jemma galloped at top speed to the village. She reared in the air suddenly, as a small white ball hurtled toward me. Total joy flooded my body. I jumped from Jemma's back.

"Cloudheart, oh my precious Cloudheart, how did you get to Talin?" I murmured. I had left him at Maidenstone when I escaped the city after the Occupation. Cloudheart pelted toward me like an arrow from the bow, flung himself into my arms, and I staggered backward with the force of his love. I held him in my arms, laughing down at his shining eyes, our hearts beating in the same rhythm. A slim young girl emerged from the stable. Seeing me, she dropped the reins of the pony she was leading and dashed toward us.

"Deti?" I asked, astonished as she came to a dusty stop before me. "How did you come here?"

"With Ten Singh," she blurted out. "Sab-ra, something terrible has happened. Your twin sister, Ruby, came to Maidenstone to find you. We were on our way here, but a Kosi kidnapped her."

"I know. I saw her with the Shunned in the Scry." My voice was choked with pain. We walked to the stable. I refused to set Cloudheart down. I kept hugging him and looking into his happy eyes. I felt enormous relief he was alive. It clashed against my despair about my sister's fate and my fears about Say'f and Sumulus, the white lion of the high range.

"Let's go to the house and you can tell me everything, Deti."

Grandmother opened the door and reached to hug me. "I am so relieved you are back, Sab-ra."

After hearing all Deti could recall, I told my grandparents that only four people were alive when Justyn and I reached the Kosi stronghold.

"Your husband was not at the Citadel then?" Grandmother asked.

"No. Neither the living King nor his body were there," I said and tears came into my eyes. Grandmother reached out to touch me gently on the shoulder.

"Where is Justyn?"

"He returned to Namché when I told him once again that I would not marry him." My chest got tight and pain stabbed me behind my eyes.

"Should you not have waited until you knew the King's fate?" Grandmother asked kindly. "Justyn loves you so much, Sab-ra." Her eyes were sad.

"I know, but when I learned Hozro had killed most of the Kosi, the Goddess called me. I must make one more attempt to reach the Lost Lake. If Say'f survived the winter, I believe he will be there. Seeking Say'f would mean travelling north, but my sister is at the Green River camp, west of here. I don't know which way I should go."

"Ten-Singh already left to rescue your sister," Grandmother said. "I think you should wait until you know the outcome of their efforts."

"Perhaps you are right, Grandmother. Ghang and Argo are also going to the camp of the Shunned. Hopefully, the three of them will bring my sister to Talin."

Turning toward Grandfather I said, "Please go to the edge of the plateau and welcome the Kosi woman who rode here with me; she is called Niffa. Lord Rohr is also waiting at the base of the mesa. You remember Lord Rohr, I'm sure, Grandfather. He brought me safely to the valley of Natil after the Avalanche. Both these Kosi are trustworthy. They have a gazehound with them and Rohr's warhorse."

"While your grandfather sees to the Kosi, let's go and see your babies," Grandmother smiled and the Goddess of Grace descended upon me, bringing joy.

Chapter 26 – At the Green River Camp

As Sab-ra reunited with Cloudheart and her babies, Hozro's scout took Ruby to the Green River Camp of the Shunned.

On the second day the barbarian removed the leather strap that tied Ruby's hands and the gag from her mouth. He gave her some inedible food that she threw fiercely into the fire, looking at him in contempt. Later he gave her water, which she gulped down, although bitterness still waved across her features.

The man spoke seldom and when he did talk, Ruby didn't understand a word. She was outraged at her abduction. She wanted to stab the savage with a knife, but the idiots at Maidenstone had sent her on this journey unarmed.

Late on the third day, they approached a river. Ruby saw the flashing light of the rippling water running through the forest. Across the waterway, she spotted twenty or more hide tents and many dark-skinned people. The savage aimed his horse straight down the vertical slope from a high ridge and splashed through the lime green water to the edge of the encampment.

Women ran toward them with loud cries of excitement. The men surrounded the warrior's horse. One savage pulled Ruby off the horse and she stumbled, her feet unsteady on the white sand. Many of the women were bare-breasted and Ruby was horrified. All of these women were filthy pagans, she supposed.

A Kosi woman led her into the largest tent. There were no men inside, for which Ruby was grateful. Then she noticed an ivory-skinned woman sitting quietly in one corner. The woman had black eyes and hair. Her whole being seemed flat, like a black and white picture in a school book. Ruby fastened her eyes on the woman's face and caught a tiny blink of recognition.

"Who are you?" the woman asked.

For a moment, Ruby was unable to respond. The kidnapping, terror and hatred had reduced her to almost an animal state. She sank to the floor, shaking. Finally she said, "I am Ruby." The woman rose slowly and walked over to stand beside her.

"I thought you were Sab-ra, but now I see I was wrong," she said.

"You know Sab-ra?" Ruby found it unbelievable that here in this camp of savages she found a person who knew her sister.

"Yes. I am from Talin and I have known her since she was a child. My name is Nyria," the woman said. Her voice was flat. "I have been with the Kosi tribe for many years now. Where were you captured?"

"I was travelling through the grasslands on my way to Talin to find Sab-ra when the beast took me." Ruby felt disgust curl her lips.

"The great grass plains belong to the Kosi. They take anyone who travels it without their permission." Nyria's voice was dull and matter-of-fact. She showed no emotion at all. Living here had sapped her vitality. She seemed a ghost of a woman, half-alive, half-dead.

"Have you ever attempted to escape?"

Nyria flicked her eyes toward a cluster of Kosi women and shook her head. She put a finger to her lips and whispered, "Later. Some understand."

A muscular Kosi woman approached and motioned for Ruby to follow her. They left the tent and walked down toward the river. The women tugged on Ruby's shirt, trying to pull it over her head.

"Stop," Ruby cried frowning at the woman and pulling her shirt back down.

The woman stepped back and in a single graceful movement, drew her long dark dress over her head. She wore nothing beneath it. Ruby was scandalized. A group of Kosi Warriors stood by a smoldering bonfire, laughing. Ruby was horrified at the woman's calm nudity, outside no less, and in full view of the men. Did the woman have no pride at all?

"No," she said again, when the woman tugged at her shirt, her voice rising in panic.

The Kosi woman called others and together the women ripped all Ruby's clothes off. They pushed her down into the river. It was stingingly cold, brutal on her skin. They scrubbed her all over to the delighted amusement of the men who came closer to watch. Ruby was furious. Once released, she stomped up the bank and stood with her hands on her wet hips glaring at the men. Nyria came up with a dark red gown and helped her dress.

Ruby and Nyria returned to the large tent and sat together in the back corner, watching through an open tent flap as the Kosi women prepared the evening meal by the campfire.

"Why did they drag me to the river, Nyria?"

"You have to be clean for the wedding."

"What are you saying? I'm not staying for a wedding. Somehow we have got to escape," Ruby's voice was low and frightened.

"He has decided to marry you," Nyria said. "They washed you so that you would be clean for the ceremony," she said.

"What?"

"The Chief of the Shunned Kosi is going to marry you. I pretend I can't understand the language, but I can."

"I would never marry a dirty savage. I shall unequivocally refuse. I came here from an island far away and have a Ma and Da there. They would have to give permission and I am going to get married in a church in a long white dress…" Her voice trailed off. She realized she was babbling. She heard the sounds of the foreign Kosi tongue from outside and her stomach roiled. She exhaled sharply, realizing she was a long way from becoming a bride in a pure white dress.

"The Kosi don't ask a woman's permission," Nyria said flatly. "'He thinks you are Sab-ra and that you married his rival, a man named Say'f. They say Say'f is dead and has no claim on you now. He wants to be King of the Kosi Warriors and has decided on you as his Queen."

"Would he force me, then?" Ruby asked. She felt the blood drain from her face.

Nyria looked at Ruby and nodded sadly.

Ruby felt faint and put her head between her knees.

"We have to get out of here," she said.

"Who travelled with you to the land of grass as tall as men?"

"A man named Ten Singh from the Bearer People and a little girl named Deti."

"Would they come after you?"

Ruby exhaled in relief. "You are right, Nyria. They will come after me. All we need to do is wait until they arrive. I'm sure they will come." Her heart was beating fast, but she made herself calm down. Terror would be of no help.

A Kosi woman entered the tent and motioned for them to come out to the campfire. They walked outside and smelled meat turning on a spit, browning, sizzling.

"Which one is the Chief of the Shunned?" Ruby asked Nyria in a whisper.

Nyria pointed to a large muscular man. As he turned toward them, Ruby saw he had a white eye.

"His name is Hozro," Nyria said. "He is the beast who killed my son. My little boy's name was Hodi." Her face seemed carved in stone and even her chilling words produced no expression on her face.

Late that night as Ruby lay in the Kosi women's tent Nyria whispered, "I don't think a lone Bearer person could take us out of here."

Ruby felt fear come over her like a cold rain.

"Then we should try to escape before they get here. If we travelled south, we might find Ten Singh," Ruby's voice sounded small and unconvincing. This country was so vast. Finding him would be like spotting a tiny light in an endless forest of darkness.

"I think we would be re-captured before we got very far. When Hozro heard the rumors that Say'f was dead, he went to the Citadel and forced the Kosi who were waiting for Say'f to swear allegiance to him. Those who wouldn't, he killed. Many women died there too, but he took a few with him to this camp. He is a vicious brute."

"Did he truly murder your son?" Ruby's whisper was shocked.

"Yes. My son came here to find me. Hozro killed my little boy and put his body in the garbage," her gentle voice was so soft Ruby could hardly hear her words.

"Dear God, Nyria, I am so sorry."

"The Bearer People brought his remains back to Talin. I have two younger children living with their father there."

"So, you were kidnapped from Sab-ra's village in Talin?"

"Yes, it was many years ago, but unlike many of the captive women of the Twelve Valley's country, I never stopped hating this ugly, brutal culture. Now I am ill and fear I will die here, never seeing my children again."

"We won't let that happen," Ruby's voice was sibilant with ferocity. "We will escape." Her rage at the death of Nyria's son took away her despair.

I have the Vision, she told herself. Brother Marzun said so. I see can what is happening in the lives of others. It was time to chance the Far-Readers disease. Ruby asked Nyria for something that would reflect the light.

At midnight, Nyria crept from the tent, disturbing a sleeping Kosi guard. He asked her what she wanted.

"Brin," she said and the Warrior laughed. It was an intoxicating liquid the Warriors drank to blur the harsh outlines of their lives. He found it amusing that a woman would want it. He pulled his waterskin from his belt and gave her a sip. They sat together drinking companionably for a while.

When she returned, Nyria had a small bowl filled with amber liquid. They waited for another hour to be sure all the women were sleeping. Then they lit a tiny candle. The light from its flame spread across the golden brew.

"What can you see, Ruby?"

Ruby didn't respond. She had entered a dream state in which she voyaged to the grass plains. Hours later Ruby's voice, sounding drugged and slow, woke Nyria.

"Four people are coming to the Green River camp. Two dark warriors, one Bearer, one old woman with long white hair. Singing she comes."

"Ruby," Nyria nudged her awake. "Wake up. You said that four people are coming here. Are they going to save us?"

It took a moment for Ruby to understand the question. She was still partly in a trance. "All we can do now is wait and pray. Pray as hard as you can to your Goddess and I will pray to the one Lord who rules us all."

Hearing Nyria whisper her prayers, Ruby asked God for deliverance from the Green River Camp but shivered knowing how very far away she was from the lush Isle of Viridian. She wondered if God could even hear her prayers in this savage country.

Chapter 27 – Leaving the Valley of Talin for Halfhigh

While Ruby prayed for rescue, Sab-ra began preparations for a trip to the Lost Lake.

When I told my Grandparents and the Elders I planned to go to the Lost Lake valley with Lord Rohr, they unanimously opposed the idea. They said Say'f was dead and thought if I stayed in Talin, I could protect them from marauding Kosi. I reminded them gently that I didn't need their permission any longer. I was an Elder myself and sought only the blessing of the Wind Goddess. Rohr, first of the Kosi Blood Arrows, would be more than enough protection from the evil deeds of men.

It had been a difficult decision. I longed to remain in Talin with the babies. I ached to know my sister's fate, but the image of the Lost Lake from the scry bowl pulled me north to the Lost Lake valley. The Scry had given me hope that Say'f still lived. With Lord Rohr for protection, I would ride north in search of my King.

Although I missed them terribly while Justyn and I were at the Citadel, I couldn't take my babies with me. Quinn had already progressed from taking steps while holding my hand to running. Grandmother didn't think he ever walked. Crimson was chattering continuously, most of which I couldn't understand, but she was so serious and intent I knew it was important.

When I brought the little gazehound, Dusk, to see my children, they were captivated. Quinn ran to the pup and Crimson began to cry. She couldn't walk yet and was jealous of Quinn's skill. Tears came into Quinn's eyes when he heard her sobs. Any sadness in his twin brought him to tears. He stood on his toes to pull on the gazehound's ears. The dog followed Quinn and lay down at Crimson's feet. She used her chubby little hands to wipe away her tears. She whispered her intense serious words to Dusk. He lifted his almond shaped eyes to hers; the gazehound was a good listener.

Quinn was empathic, I realized. His body looked exactly like his father's, but his mind belonged to me. I wondered if he could hear the thoughts of dogs. I remembered him calling to the eagles with their flaming eyes. Perhaps he could communicate with them too.

This will be the last trip, I promised myself. With or without my husband, I would rule in the Citadel until Quinn became King and Crimson found her destiny. Both my babies were changing so rapidly and I didn't want to miss any stage of their lives. If there was any disobedient prideful child left in me, the birth of the twins erased her. I cared only that the twins would grow up alive and well, so when it was time, Quinn could assume his Kingship.

If they lived to reach adulthood, I would be satisfied I told myself, but oh how I lied. Goddess forgive me, I lied. Having the twins reach adulthood was not enough. I wanted the man who made them. All my hopes for the Kosi, who were now my People and for peace between our cultures would turn to dust without him.

Lord Rohr and I left Talin a few days later for Halfhigh. Halfhigh stands on a flat-topped butte and is a semi-permanent camp part way to the remnants of the mythic Skygrass Valley. The Lost Lake valley was unknown until the evil Captain Grieg discovered it. It lies in a gorge behind the Skygrass valley, tucked between the folded ranges of the Dhali Ra Mountain. Halfhigh was also a strategic location during the war, a first aid camp where I tended the wounded. I had already sent a message to En Sun asking him to meet us at Halfhigh and to bring a guide to take us to the Lost Lake. We knew a wall of rocks blocked the original passage, but I hoped En Sun would know a different route.

I wept that whole first day of the trip aching for my children. Lord Rohr refused to comment. He looked at me askance several times, but didn't speak. When we stopped for the night, he vanished into the trees. He was hunting. He would return triumphant and I would be grateful. It was still cold in the high range; hot food would raise my spirits. After roasting the chanry on a split over the campfire, Rohr spoke.

"Have you seen the King in the Scry, Queen of the Kosi?"

"Only brief scenes of him fighting in the blue snows, but whether he lives or rides the skies, I must know."

He nodded, grunting in agreement. "Wife of the King, I will find him without you. Return to Talin. The King's children need a mother."

"This is an old argument between us, my friend. I will not go back. We will find him together."

"You should not call me friend. A Warrior may not have female friends," he said, frowning. "I have told you this before. A Warrior is bound to his fellow Blood Arrows, owes fealty to his King and loves only his wife and children. He may not have a woman who is not his wife too near him, or he will be tempted to take her for himself."

"Lord Rohr," I cried out delighted, "Do you desire me for yourself?"

"Any man but a Blood-Arrow, sworn to the King, would have taken you long ago," he told me gruffly.

"Even if the King lies dead, I will never marry Justyn," I told him suddenly aware that my ambivalence had vanished. "I know my destiny now. I will raise the twins. I will rule the Kosi."

"If the King lies dead, by our tradition the Queen of the Kosi must name a new King from among the Blood Arrows. A Queen may not rule Warriors alone. If that day comes, I will stand and offer myself to you."

"And I would have no other," I told him gently. I felt my cheeks color slightly and looked down, embarrassed. "In the time coming to be, if I must name a new King, I would be honored to choose you, Lord Rohr."

His gaze rested passionately upon me. I felt its warmth like the sun, but when I reached out to touch his hand, he pulled it away, as if my touch seared.

"Do not touch me, my Queen," Rohr said, "Lest I be tempted beyond my ability to resist."

When we reached Halfhigh, the first thing I did was to check the Aid Station we used during the war as a clinic. It was still standing, as were the two houses of stone; one was used as a stable and had a haymow. There was also a boma corral to contain the horses. After we ate, I made myself a bed of the soft plants called bedstraw. I entered the Aid Station, lay down and drifted off to sleep, fragrant straw for my pillow. The next morning, I heard the jingling of horse harnesses and looking over the rim saw En Sun riding up the butte with a male companion.

"En Sun," I cried when they reached the top. "I am happy to see you."

He smiled and told me his friend's name was Kilby.

"I greet you, Kilby," I said. "What tribe do you come from?"

"He is from the Hakan, Mistress," En Sun told me. "He can't speak your language.

"Ask him if the Hakan have a new Queen."

The men exchanged a few words.

"Yes, they do. Her name is Verde."

I felt satisfaction, remembering my role in Queen Verde's banishment. Verde was a bitter woman, hating King Ruisenor's young Consort because Ion'li was able to conceive a child with the King of the Twelve Valleys and Verde could not. Although it cost me the blue Cord of the Empath that I had earned at Maidenstone, I was proud I had prevented Ion'li's murder.

"Tomorrow we must find a way into the Lost Lake," I told the men.

"It will not be easy," En Sun warned. "Many have died seeking that paradise."

"It is not my time to die," I told him confidently.

"Nor is it the day for me to die," Rohr said. We smiled at each other.

En Sun and Kilby talked for a while. Then En Sun turned to me.

"An enormous rockfall blocks the old route to the Lost Lake. Kilby knows another way into the hidden vale."

The Hakan would tell us nothing more. He turned away when I pressed En Sun for details. I regarded Kilby with caution. The Hakan had long been allies of the Mongols, ancient enemies of all who lived in the high country. He was a short, squat man with a proud carriage. His eyes were sly and furtive. Something about him reminded me of Argo, the Kosi assassin who swore I would never rule his tribe.

"Why won't Kilby tell us where we are going?" I asked, bothered by the man's silence.

"He says the White Snake will kill him if he does."

"What is this White Snake he fears? Is it a true snake?"

"He says it is a man, but immortal. Humans cannot kill him. He saw the marks on his body, marks of stones, snakebites, cuts from a knife. Yet still he lives."

"What does this man look like?" I asked, shock overtaking my mind.

"He is tall with yellow hair."

I turned toward Rohr, horrified. "Lord Rohr, the Hakan is describing Captain Grieg." I could hardly speak the words. Captain Grieg, the head of the Army Garrison was my mortal enemy. He was the man who sought my death in the depths of the mountain. I felt the old dread rise inside me. My stomach lurched, threatening to bring up my dinner. I ran from the campfire, retching into the brush. After I had regained some composure and washed the sick taste from my mouth, I returned to the men.

"When we find the Kosi King, he will tear the guts from inside the body of the White Snake," I told them fiercely, but none of the men would meet my eyes.

Chapter 28 – The Green River Camp

As Sab-ra sought an entrance to the Lost Lake, praying her husband would be there, Ruby wrote what she believed would be her final entry in her diary.

Dear Diary;

I don't know if anyone will ever read this. I've been captured and sit on the sand near a green river while bunches of filthy half-naked copper skinned Kosi savages work around me. Some of the women wear long gowns, but nothing beneath. No knickers at all! Apparently, those are the married women. The unmarried women wear trousers like the men, but walk around bare-breasted. They have no shame. I am blushing myself scarlet being so scandalized.

A man named Ten Singh brought me into this god-forsaken wilderness, but he and Deti left me alone and a dark skinned warrior kidnapped me. Nana, I know you would be pleased to hear that I have reluctantly admitted to myself that I have the Sight. Last night, in a Sight Dream, I saw Ten Singh returning. I don't feel very encouraged though, he's probably a prisoner too.

If anyone finds this little book after my death, I beg you to send it to Viridian. I want Ma to know that I forgave her for keeping the secret of my sister from me. My Da needs no assurances; he knows I love him dearly. Nana, I say farewell to you with the greatest sorrow.

I met a woman here whose name is Nyria. She actually knows my sister, Sab-ra. She told me that the Chief of the Shunned plans to marry me—without my consent, I must add. The brute's name is Hozro. He thinks I am Sab-ra who married another Kosi Chief. At least my sister got married before having her babies. I was glad to hear she had some morals. What could have made her marry a filthy savage I have no idea. Maybe she had no choice.

Hozro is a big ugly buck with a white eye. Nyria told me he killed her son, a boy named Hodi. My heart goes out to her. This place has taken all the juice, all the sap from her personality. It's like talking to the walking dead. Every time I look at Hozro, he is looking back at me. I'm like a juicy goose he is waiting to cook and eat.

Nobody can read here, so I can put me plans down on paper. After talking myself blue, I have finally convinced Nyria to try to escape. We are going to make a break for it after dark. She has been making friends with a horse, bringing him little crab apples and such. She thinks we can both ride him. Without a saddle, I have me doubts, but we have to try.

We are going to wait until the camp sleeps. Then I will swim through the river to the other side. Nyria will bring the horse later, leading him through the water. She thinks the sounds of saddling could wake some of the men, but since the horse is the fastest mount they have, she says if we don't fall off, we will be able to get away. It sounds all well and good, but I just found out she has never ridden a horse, and he is a big stallion. I pray hourly for deliverance.

I won't be able to write again and I will have to leave this book here. I've made my last amends and prayed for my soul to join the heavens.

Signed, Ruby's Final Entry

At moonrise, the women went down to the river to bathe. Ruby and Nyria went with them, talking quietly as they walked a sand path through whispering shrubbery.

"Should I try to get across the river now?" Ruby asked.

"Yes. The mist is rising already. When the Kosi women swim out deeper into the water, get across the river and wait for me. I will come later with the horse."

"If I remove my clothing to swim, I won't have anything to wear except my knickers once I get to the other side."

"It isn't that deep, you can walk. Make your gown into a bundle and hold it on your head or pull it up above your waist. Wait until the moon slides behind the clouds."

As the Kosi women stripped and walked laughing out into the moonlit water, Ruby looked carefully around. She and Nyria were alone. The mist was already up to their knees. Ruby pulled her gown over her head and tied it into a roll. She whispered good-bye and walked down to the river. She sat on the bank and slid down with a splash. The water was icy cold and the bottom of the river slippery with clay. She forced herself to walk deeper into the current, keeping one hand on her rolled dress. She turned back once, but it was too dark to see Nyria. She kept on, fighting against the muscular cold water that wanted to pull her under. As Ruby approached the other side, the water grew warmer. She sensed her sister beside her, pulling her across the water to safety.

She emerged dripping and ice cold on the other side. Reeds and marshy ground rose slowly all the way to the bottom of the ridge. Ruby stood and pulled the dark red gown over her head, covering herself. Shivering convulsively, she began to make her way to the base of the escarpment. Once she almost slipped into a tiny spring. It was colder than the river. She put one foot into the water, testing to see if it had a solid bottom. Icy swirling sand pulled at her foot. It was quicksand. She pulled her foot up out of the water frantically. Fear gave her legs strength and she pelted through the reeds and emerged onto solid ground.

Panting, she sat down near the base of a silvery shrub. She was too cold to sleep, but sat shivering, resting off and on until nearly dawn when she fell into a light doze. When she opened her eyes, she saw the back of a Kosi Warrior. He was squatting on the ground in front of her, starting a fire. When he turned around, his white eye burned her. It was Hozro.

He pulled her up beside him by one arm. Ruby struggled. Hozro looked deeply into her eyes.

"Saah-brah," he said and satisfaction showed in the brutal lines in his face

Ruby screamed.

Chapter 29 – The Crystal Steppes

While Ruby despaired at the Camp of the Shunned, Kilby gestured for Sab-ra and Rohr to follow him.

Lord Rohr and I left Halfhigh the next morning following En Sun and Kilby. For the first few hours we rode the flat plains below the mesas but by afternoon we entered the middle reaches of the Blue Mountains; a region called the Crystal Steppes. Feeling the small body of Jemma beneath me, I missed Yellowmane constantly. Jemma was a sturdy plodder but lacked the smooth gait of Yellowmane. In the days when Yellowmane and I were comrades, I rode the wind. Now she paced the clouds without me. My heart was low with grief. Kilby led us up and down on tiny mountain paths. Most were only as wide as my arm. The enormous massif of the Dhali Ra, the mountain home of the Great Goddess, rose like a giant thunderhead beyond the Crystal Steppe.

Despite all my efforts to dig information out of Kilby, he continued silent as a captured prisoner. I hated not knowing where we were headed, trusting a man I didn't know to take me to the Lost Lake. I sensed that he might be a traitor, leading me straight to Captain Grieg.

"Rohr," I whispered at one point when we were able to ride side by side, "Do you trust this man?"

Rohr looked at me thoughtfully. "No," he said, with a thoughtful glance, but still we rode behind him.

In late afternoon, we entered a narrow valley leading deep into the Blue Mountains. The area was heavily wooded, crowded with sentinel pines and the yellow trunks of syce trees. Their scent lay across us, practically visible in its intensity. I felt uneasy in this closed-off space. It awoke memories of my capture by Captain Grieg and my imprisonment in the mountain. En Sun and Kilby talked together in whispers. I kept my eyes on Rohr. He was as irritated as I was fearful. Both of us felt Kilby was leading us into a bad situation.

"Where are we, En Sun?" I asked.

"This is where the Hakan found the Kosi King's boot," he responded. I felt my spirits sink lower.

"Show me," I commanded.

The little Hakan led me over to an area at the end of a box canyon, directly below a ledge high on the mountain's face.

"He says he found the boot on that outcropping," En Sun said, pointing up to the ledge.

"Did he leave it there?" I asked En Sun. He said something and Kilby nodded. I turned back to the Blood Arrow. "Rohr, can you climb up to that ledge and see if the King's boot is still there?

Rohr surveyed the terrain and pulled a rope from his saddle packs. He tied a loop at the end of the rope and threw it upwards. It landed near a yellow syce tree that grew nearly straight out of the rock. He threw the rope again and again until it caught. Using his phenomenal strength and pulling against the rope, he climbed upward through the trees. When he reached the ledge, he peered into a large dark hole.

"What do you see?" I called up to him.

"The lair of a cave leopard," he called down. He entered the cave and after a few tense moments, during which I worried that En sun and Kilby might take the opportunity to run off or take me prisoner, Rohr came out again. He held something in his hands.

He descended slowly—hand over hand. My breath caught as I watched. Although Rohr would not name himself as my friend, I cared deeply about him. If he fell, I feared I could do nothing to help. At last, he reached my side and pulled the King's boot from under his chest strap. I wondered the cave leopard had killed my husband.

I was in despair that Grieg still lived. I had willed a snake to bite him, I had stabbed him with my poisoned knife; I had pelted him with rocks. Goddess of the Winds, how had I failed? A superstitious fear made my heart shudder. I worried that Kilby was right when he called Grieg immortal. Perhaps no living person could kill the fiend. I shivered in dread. Rohr took my arm and led me to an area where we could not be overheard.

"I think the White Snake has not lived in that cave for a long time," his voice was low, "I saw no campfire or supplies. If he is still alive, he has probably gone deeper into the mountain."

Rohr looked apprehensive saying this. He feared the dark tunnels that riddled the Dhali Ra, as did I.

"What do you think we should do?" I asked.

"I think the Hakan will desert us soon," Rohr said philosophically. "En Sun may leave too. He has the look of fear on his face. I would go deeper into the mountain, but I didn't want to leave you alone with them. I sense treachery."

A rising tide of blood lust rose in me, fierce as the burning frenzy I felt seeing the dead Kosi at the Citadel. Like Hozro, Grieg's deeds demanded his life in payment. I glimpsed Brother Jun's gentle face, but pushed away his counsel. Captain Grieg was mine.

"If the King lives no longer, I demand the blood right to avenge him. If we come upon Captain Grieg in the tunnels, you must stay your hand. Hold back, I beg you, Lord Rohr and permit me to deliver the final blow."

We were silent for a moment, considering our next steps.

"I would ride the rope with you Lord Rohr," I said. He started to protest, but seeing the look on my face, he nodded.

We walked together to the trailing rope. Rohr tied it around his waist and began to climb with me on his back. His tremendous strength was tested to the limit but we rose, hand over hand to the ledge. We stopped there, although the ledge we stood on was only as wide as my foot. While Rohr's breathing returned to normal and he threw the rope again upwards to the ledge outside the cave leopard's lair, I said I would climb the last part by myself.

He didn't respond, looking down a hundred thent to the men at the bottom.

"They ride," he said and I saw En sun and Kilby leaving, pulling Jemma behind them. They fled the canyon as if the dogs of hell ran after them. As Rohr screamed all the things he would do to them if they took our supplies, I grabbed the rope and began to walk straight up the mountain.

"No," Rohr yelled, but I was already above his reach.

It was far more difficult than it looked. My shoulder began to hurt. It had never completely healed since Grieg dislocated it when he held me prisoner. My breath came faster and my heart thudded in my ears. Twenty feet below the upper ledge, I felt my shoulder give way and I screamed as I dove down. With tremendous force, Rohr grabbed me from the skies and hauled me back onto the tiny landing.

"You stay here," he said fiercely, breathing hard, "Or I will beat you, Queen of the Kosi or not." I could not meet his eyes. He climbed upward to the ledge, looked down to see me sitting meekly beside the syce tree and vanished into the darkness.

Once Rohr entered the tunnel, I looked about to see if there was any other way to reach the upper ledge. Finally, I spotted a possible approach through the sentinel pines. I crawled hanging on to trees that grew straight out of the mountain. It was difficult and I poured all my concentration into not falling. When I finally pulled myself on to the ledge, the pain from my arm was intense. My foot was hurting too, and I sat down and pulled off my sueded boot. There was a hole in the seaming; a stone had worked its way inside. I leaned back against the warm rock, resting my sore shoulder. Rohr had gone deep into the tunnels. I looked up at the rounded clouds seeing the pink of late afternoon gild their undersides. I closed my eyes and drifted into the world of sleep.

In my dream, I was mending leather slippers with a silver needle. The world grew dark and an enormous weight pinned me to the mountain. I heard the voice of my nightmares.

"You returned to me," Grieg said and laughed aloud.

I screamed, twisting with all my might, trying to escape. I opened my eyes and saw his eyes bore into mine. With all my strength, I forced my needle into his eye. He screamed and vanished. I opened my eyes and saw my friend Rohr's amused face above me.

"It was a dream, my Queen," he told me gently, "I only wished to wake you. You tried to kill a dream."

"No, no it was Grieg. I forced a needle into his eye," my voice trailed off.

"There is no one here except the two of us," Rohr told me. "It was your knife that stabbed the air, although I had to dodge to keep you from injuring me. Of course, it would take more than a small white woman's knife to kill a Kosi Warrior." He was clearly amused.

I kept shaking for a long time. My chest felt so tight I could hardly breathe. At last, I was able to ask, "What else did you find in the cave?" My voice was thin and high with stress.

"The cave ends in a wall. There is no way in, save from the front. It is the lair of a man-killing leopard; the stalking kind, like the black and white birds who take sparkling things. It was probably the leopard that brought the King's boot there; a totem of his kill."

I took a deep quivering breath. My voice when it came from my throat was resonant with grief. "Then I fear the King lives no more," I said, as if pronouncing a blessing on the dead.

"If the King is dead, so is Captain Grieg," Rohr said, trying to comfort me. "The Warrior King would not succumb to his wounds until he first took the life of your enemy."

I nodded.

"It is almost sundown. We must descend my Queen."

He strapped me to him, breast to breast, heartbeat to heartbeat.

"Put your arms around my neck," he told me, "And wrap your legs around my waist."

"If we fall, we will both die," I warned him.

"Then we will both ride with the King," he said, smiling. He looked deeply into my eyes.

It was a brutal, terrifying trip. We bumped and lurched down the cliff-face, but arrived finally at the bottom, bruised and cut from rocks, but alive. Wrapped so tightly against Rohr, I felt his great heart beat with mine. I saw the two of us ruling as King and Queen of the Kosi. His body and his loyalty warmed me. Then guilt stabbed me. It was wrong, thinking of naming Lord Rohr as the Kosi King. Even if Say'f rode the clouds, allowing myself to feel such feelings for another man, I had betrayed my husband.

When we stood on level ground, I told him, "We must return to the great rock wall. It is possible that Say'f escaped the beast. Perhaps the leopard only took Grieg's life. Perhaps the King still lives."

"My Queen, you see what you want to see. This is a foolish chanry's errand," Rohr told me softly, his eyes warm.

"He might still be alive," I said. A sob escaped my lips. I burned Rohr's eyes with mine. "I must know, Rohr." Unable to avoid my unbreakable resolve, at last he nodded. "When we conquer the rock wall that hides the Lost Lake, we will walk into the valley shoulder to shoulder," I told my Guardian.

"As you command, Queen of the Kosi," Rohr said, a tiny twitch of bemusement on his lips.

Chapter 30 – The Green River Camp

As Sab-ra sought an entrance to the Lost Lake valley, Ghang and Argo approached the Green River Camp.

Hozro tied Ruby's hands behind her back and marched her across the river into the Shunned camp. She looked for Nyria but didn't see her. The horse she and Nyria planned to use stood calmly in the circle of thorn bushes the Kosi used to contain their mounts. Nyria had never even gotten him out of the corral. Ruby closed her eyes in despair as tears dripped down her dusty cheeks.

One of Hozro's women came up to him and said something in the Kosi language. He handed Ruby to the woman. She took Ruby by the upper arm, leading her to the women's tent. In a back corner of the shelter, Ruby met Nyria's eyes. Her face was covered in bruises. Nyria pointed at her foot and Ruby was horrified to see that a broken bone stuck out through the skin. Revulsion came over her. The Kosi had maimed her only friend. Ruby shoved the hand of the Kosi woman off and ran to Nyria. Her eyes were dull; she looked half-dead.

"Did they break your foot?" Ruby asked in shock.

"Yes."

"Can you feel your toes?"

Nyria shook her head.

"Was it because we tried to escape?" Ruby asked, repulsed by the Kosi violence.

"Yes," Nyria mouthed, "But Wirri-won is coming."

"Who is Wirri-won?"

"Kosi Healer."

The few words seemed to have tired Nyria even further.

Later that day, the tent flat opened and a woman who looked a hundred years old strode in. She was tall and commanding in appearance. Her face was white as soap. The top of her head was bald as an egg, but long white plaits grew from the back of her head, nearly reaching her waist. Each plait had a silver ring at the end; they clinked together as she walked. She wore a long gown made of a yellow fabric. Many silver rings shone on her fingers. Tattoos decorated her upper arms. Ruby recognized her; it was the singing woman she had seen in the Vision.

"Sab-ra," the old woman called out and strode to their corner.

"No, my name is Ruby," she replied, stunned to find this wild ancient woman knew her sister.

""She is the great Kosi Healer, Ruby, bow your head." Nyria managed to say. Wirri-won knelt and examined Nyria's leg carefully. She removed the binding with a single cut of her knife and shouted at the Kosi women in a rage. She knelt by Nyria and aligned the bones in her foot, holding them tight until there was a snapping sound. Then she rubbed some green plant mixture into the place where the bone had protruded.

"If foot bone snaps again, you will die," Wirri-won said philosophically to Nyria. "Don't stand on it." Then she turned to Ruby and said, "Hozro wants to marry you."

"No, Wirri-won," Ruby pleaded. "I can't marry." She thought desperately for a reason the woman might understand. A sudden insight made her say, "I am pledged to the Church."

Wirri-won turned back to the lead Kosi woman and they talked in low tones.

"Hozro will fight other husband, this man named Church," Wirri-won told her.

"No, pledged to Temple. To Te Ran, to Goddess," Ruby said prevaricating wildly, desperate for anything to keep from falling into the hands of this brutal criminal.

"Then no marriage," Wirri-won said and Ruby nearly fainted in relief.

"Beg her to take you to Talin," Nyria whispered. "Do you have any silver parthats?"

Ruby walked over to her bag and pulled out all the money she had left. She held it out in her cupped hand.

"Wirri-won, please take us to Talin."

The Healer looked at her scornfully. She grabbed Ruby's bag and upended it on the floor. After scrabbling around on the ground for a bit, Wirri-won rose triumphantly with Ruby's mother's little green book. Ruby shook her head.

"Let her have it," Nyria hissed.

"No," Ruby said and held out her right hand on which she wore a small silver ring with a rounded garnet stone. It was Da's gift to her when she left for Namché. Reluctantly, she drew the ring from her finger and held it out to Wirri-won. Her stomach clenched as she offered this ancient woman the last vestige of a world that seemed to spin further and further away.

Wirri-won took the ring and nodded but continued to go through the items from Ruby's pack, at last finding a small bottle of pain reliever Ruby brought with her from Viridian. She took two pills and gave them to Nyria, pocketing the rest. Wirri-won strode from the tent, her robe swirling around her bare feet.

That evening, the Kosi put on a kind of savage celebratory dance. Everyone sat around the fire and an old man wearing only a dirty orange loincloth beat a large metal pot in a complicated rhythm. Two young boys had finger drums that echoed to the rhythm of the larger drum. Three naked Kosi warriors with white painted patterns on their skin, walked into the circle of light. They began to dance, slowly and then faster. The Kosi women began to sing a hauntingly sweet melody.

Another warrior marched three women, bound together with leather thongs, into the firelight. The men circled around the captive women in their dance. A more highly decorated warrior entered the dancer's circle. He slashed downward with his knife, cutting the leather thongs that bound the women to each other. He cut one woman's dress from the neckline to the base and she stood naked in the moonlight. The Kosi roared and their women shrieked in glee. The Warrior seized the woman and ran from the firelight with the woman lying across his shoulders, screaming.

The dance resumed. Over the course of the night, warriors stripped the other two women and carried them away, leaving only Hozro dancing to the drums. The tempo beat faster and Hozro spun in circles, his white eye left a circle of light in the air, following the speed of his spin. Suddenly, the music stopped and Hozro strode over to Ruby and pulled her to her feet.

"Wirri-won," Ruby screamed and the ancient healer came forward. Wirri-won raised her hand in the air, palm forward and put it on Hozro's chest. He and Wirri-won argued loudly. Ruby stepped back to stand beside Nyria; she was leaning against a tree and Ruby bent down to hear her whispered translation.

"Wirri-won is telling him you are Sab-ra's sister. She says you cannot marry. You are pledged to a Temple in Namché."

Hozro took out his knife, gesturing with it, touching the blade to Wirri-won's breast. Then he drew it along her jawbone leaving a long thin cut that seeped red. She remained as still as if she had been carved from ice.

Nyria whispered, "Hozro thinks Te Ran is the name of another man. Wirri-won is explaining that Te Ran is a Priestess and that you have given your word to enter the Temple. He does not believe her."

Chapter 31 – The Crystal Steppe near the Lost Lake Valley
Thunder Moon, August

As Ruby prayed for deliverance, Rohr rode his stallion to the rock wall. Sab-ra sat behind him, her arms wrapped around his chest. She found herself comforted by his large warm body.

Lord Rohr and I rode the trails of the Crystal Steppe all the next day. We were headed to the enormous rock wall that sealed the Lost Lake valley. It was cold and misty. Kilby and En Sun had taken Jemma, so I sat behind the Blood Arrow. Rohr's horse, Tye, seemed undeterred by walking along the extremely narrow trails cut into the mountainside. Even dense fog didn't seem to bother him. On my right, the mountain fell a thousand thent straight down into a misty nothingness.

In the afternoon of the second day, the fog lifted and we entered an area of the mountainside covered in trees. We walked through dappled light that fell on us in a beautiful tapestry of shadows. Limbs of trees made a delicious shaded canopy over our heads. I asked Rohr to stop so I could dismount. I wanted to walk for a bit and to stretch my legs. Rohr said he would scout the trail ahead. The trail jogged to the right and I lost sight of him.

Hiking around the bend, I heard an animal scream so terrifying for a second I could not move. Then I ran in the direction of the scream. I saw an enormous spotted yellow and black streak propel itself from a large branch down on top of Rohr and Tye. The warhorse bucked and yelped in pain. The mountain leopard clung to the horse's side. Rohr kicked at it, desperate to save his mount. The leopard fell to the rocky trail. Rohr jumped from Tye's back and pulled out his knife, slashing at the leopard who roared again. The enraged leopard struck—a blur in the dying light. Rohr fell to the ground. I ran to him, my small poisoned knife in my hand.

The leopard whirled around and stood up on its back legs. He was twice my size. He had injured my Blood Arrow, and I felt a rage of blood lust. I stuck him deeply again and again in the belly. He fell down on top of me. His weight crushed my lungs. I smelled the stench of death. Then he struggled to his feet and disappeared into the higher range.

"Rohr," I called as I managed to stand. The leopard had clawed me when he fell and I was bleeding in several places. "Rohr, can you speak?" He didn't answer. I walked closer to his fallen body. "Rohr," I whispered.

"My Queen," he murmured and closed his eyes again.

"Don't sleep," I told him. I managed to pull him to a sitting position. "You have a head injury." Rohr kept falling backwards. I shoved a large rock behind his back, propping him into a sitting position. He lolled forward.

Tye had run down the trail, but I called him back. Obedient as the gazehound, I heard him returning. I checked him over carefully, seeing several deep puncture wounds in his chest and withers. I tied him to a small tree and pulled Brin from Rohr's saddlebags.

I forced Rohr's mouth open and dribbled the Brin down his throat. He struggled, pushing my hand away.

"Wake up," I demanded fiercely.

"Stop," he managed. His eyes cleared and for a moment he was fully conscious. "Give Brin to Tye," he managed. Then his eyes rolled back and he returned to the land of unconsciousness.

I sat beside him, resting on the trail, our backs to the warmed mountain. There was no water this high in the range either for drinking or to wash our wounds. We faced a desperate problem. Spotted mountain leopards prey on Lakt. When they sink their talons into the Lakt, their claws pick up filth and disease. I had nothing with which to wash the deep punctures on Tye's body, except a few swallows of Brin.

"Rohr, can you ride?" I asked, poking him awake.

"No," he told me and fell asleep again.

Both of us were feverish the next morning. Rohr was raving in delirium. Tye stood to the side of the trail, head hanging, breathing hard. I was in the best shape of the three of us and knew I would have to go for help. I used the last of the Brin on my puncture wounds, cursing mountain leopards in every language I knew.

I am such a stupid girl, I thought suddenly. Although the Wind Goddess rarely came to me while I was pregnant, I was not pregnant now.

"Rain," I begged her. "Send rain to the least of your worshippers. Send rain to the Kosi and his horse. Send rain to the mountain country."

Late that afternoon, I heard the crackle of lightening. The aptly named Thunder Moon gave us its blessing. Lightening split the clouds that boomed back together. I smiled to myself as I fell asleep. The rain was coming. I smelled trees. I smelled fire. I woke to Rohr bending over me in the dark.

"The mountain burns," he said. I looked up and saw a vee of fire racing down the mountain. A high wind had whipped the fire into frenzy. The deep sound of the fire terrified me.

"We have to leave," I said. It was horridly difficult for Rohr to mount Tye, but we managed and left everything behind. The horse bolted, running straight down the mountain, away from the searing, burning, throat-closing heat. When we stopped to give Tye some rest, the rain began in earnest. I caught as much water as I could in my leather canteen, found soap grasses and washed Rohr's wounds. I poured more into my punctured sores and used the rest on Tye. I touched Rohr's chest to see how far the infection had spread. My heart fell when I saw red streaks running from the punctures toward his heart. He had blood poisoning.

"Your skin is warm, Lord Rohr," I told him. "The infection is spreading."

"Today is not my day to die," he said gruffly and despite our desperate situation, I found myself warmed by Rohr's unstinting confidence.

"Nor is it mine," I said unhesitatingly. Our interchange raised my spirits, but we were far from any settlement and had a long way to go for help.

When I woke the following morning, I felt better although my sores were stiff. Rohr was sleeping. I checked on Tye and he seemed better. I had kept about half the water from the rainstorm the previous night, and I gave Tye a drink. Then I led him down the mountain, looking for a meadow where he might graze. I found one about an hour later, spread like a green embroidered carpet between rising pale gray peaks. One small tree stood on the edge of the meadow. I tied Tye there and returned to Rohr.

"Lord Rohr, you need to wake." I pulled him to sitting position. He shook his head and bared his teeth at me, growling. I poured water into his mouth. He shook his head and sputtered. His eyes cleared and he knew me.

"Tye is better and I took him to an area where he could graze. We need to leave here so I can get help for you," I touched his forehead. His eyes were already closing. "Stay awake," I ordered him fiercely. "You are my Guardian and I need you. We need to decide what to do together."

He murmured some blurry words, nothing I could understand. I looked around to see where we were in relation to the sun and the mountain. It had been dark the night before when we stopped our headlong flight down the mountain. Looking up into the fastness, I saw a huge swath of blackened trees. Tendrils of smoke rose from it still, curling. We were only about a day's ride from the settlement at Rhan Du but before I could go for help, I had to see if the fire was completely out.

I climbed back up the mountain. Most of the smaller branches on every tree were gone. Only one or two limbs stuck out from the sides of blackened trunks. They seemed to hold out their dark arms for help and rain. When I reached the devastated area, some embers were still smoldering. One little burning coal rolled out of the ashes and hit some dead leaves. They caught fire lazily. Rohr lay a hundred thent directly below me. I couldn't leave him in the path of the fire, but he was at least twice as heavy as I was. We were out of food and water now. I was a poor shot with a bow and already felt the rumble of hunger. Fear rode my mind, whipping it into a blaze brighter than the forest fire.

Descending, I tried again to wake him. He had slipped into a fever coma. I went down to the field where Tye was grazing. It was a beautiful day, with high blue skies and a light warm breeze. The meadow itself was a floor of flowers, some pink, some purple. I took Tye's tether and led him back up to Rohr. I was going to try to get the Kosi on his horse.

After struggling with Rohr's limp heavy body for several hours, I wept with despair and frustration. I could not lift him. He was far too heavy. I was going to have to ride to Rhan Du by myself. I managed to roll Lord Rohr under a rocky shelf beneath a sheltering tree. I left the rest of the water in his waterskin. I pulled his bow from the leather strap across his back, removed the arrow points from his belt and mounted them on the shafts. I pulled his knife from his pants pocket and laid it carefully in his right hand. I would not leave my Guardian unarmed.

"Lord Rohr," I told his recumbent form. "I am riding to Rhan Du. I will be back as soon as I can." He did not respond. His skin was darker than ever and he lay so still. I was deeply afraid. I knelt beside him, leaned forward and kissed him gently on the lips. His eyes opened just a crack. "Do you know who I am?" I asked him, low and quiet.

"I would never forget you, my Queen," he whispered and said no more.

"Farewell dear Guardian and friend," I called as I mounted Tye. The stallion was huge, much bigger than anything I had ever ridden. I hoped I was going to be able to control him.

"Run," I said in Kosi and although I'm sure he thought my accent funny, Tye bolted forward. We raced down the mountain, far too fast for the little trail. I leaned forward on his enormous neck and whispered encouragement to him. "You are a mirror of your master. He is First Blood Arrow; you are First Stallion. We have to save Lord Rohr. Run!"

Chapter 32 - The Green River Camp

While Sab-ra ran thundered down the mountain to Rhan Du, Ghang and Argo rode into the Green River camp.

A sudden hush stilled the camp as everyone heard the thudding sounds of horses running fast down the ridge. Two men rode into the clearing; both were Kosi warriors. The women screamed and ran into the tents, except for Ruby and Nyria, who stayed where they were. Nyria could not walk without help. Fear held Ruby motionless. The Vision had proved true; she had seen these two warriors coming in her trance.

The smaller of the Kosi warriors dismounted and pulled out his knife. He charged toward Hozro, his knife raised. Men ran from the circle to grab bows and knives. Hozro held up one hand and all the men stopped moving. He and the small Kosi warrior began circling each other. Both had knives and jabbed them forward into the air. Hozro's warriors called out death threats, vowing to destroy the small Kosi.

Hozro sliced into the side of the small Kosi man. He grunted in surprise. Blood ran down his dark skin in a red curtain. The knives flashed so quickly it was hard to see what was happening. Then Hozro gave a cry and went down on one knee. The smaller Kosi stood back, giving him time to rise. Hozro's warriors began to surge forward, but Hozro held up his hand again and slowly got to his feet. He lunged forward with his knife outstretched but stumbled and fell. With a single stroke, the smaller Kosi stabbed his knife into the back of Hozro's neck. Hozro fell to the ground without another sound.

The warriors moved forward warily toward the killer. He raised his arms in the air, screaming triumphantly. Wirri-won stepped between the small warrior and the others. She uttered some fierce words.

"What is she saying?" Ruby asked Nyria.

"She says the man who killed Hozro is called Argo. He is the Kosi assassin. Wirri-won says the group must now adhere to the old Kosi ways. If Say'f lives, he has one moon to come forward. If he is dead, his Queen must name and then mate with the next King."

"Who is this Queen," Ruby asked.

"Sab-ra," Nyria said. "Your sister is Queen of the Kosi."

Good Lord, Ruby thought, how on earth had her sister become Queen of this dirty tribe. Was she the only civilized person in this God forsaken country?

Argo hacked viciously at Hozro's neck until he severed his head from his body. He grabbed the head by its long greasy hair; showing Hozro's face to each warrior. Several blanched. The women of the Kosi screamed. Hozro's white-eye was open, horrifying even in death. Argo walked to his horse, grabbed a leather bag and put Hozro's head inside it.

Ghang walked to stand beside Wirri-won. "I am Ghang," he told the group. "I serve the Queen of the Kosi. I call upon you, Green River Kosi, to return to the service of King Say'f. Come forward and kneel before me. I will take you to Halfhigh. The true King will be waiting."

One old warrior walked slowly forward to Ghang. His chest showed evidence of many scars. He knelt before him saying he would pledge to serve the King. One by one, the rest came forward and knelt. Each warrior threw his knife into the fire as he knelt. In the end, there were only three women who refused. One was Horzro's chief wife. Her flashing topaz eyes looked contemptuously at Ruby and Nyria.

The women who would not swear loyalty to Say'f and their children followed Wirri-won to the horse enclosure. They all mounted up. The Healer mounted her elegant silver mare and led the small band away.

By late afternoon the camp was packed and the Kosi who swore to obey Say'f were mounted. Ruby and Nyria, her foot still unable to bear her weight were bundled into a wagon with raw red meat and the bodies of dead chanry birds. Ghang and Argo led the cavalcade splashing across the bright river and up to a trail at the top of a high ridge. Ruby's heart pounded as the Kosi mares pulled the wagon up a near-vertical incline. When it hunched over the edge between the trees, she sighed in relief.

When the caravan stopped at evening, Ruby climbed out of the wagon and stretched her arms above her head. Then she helped Nyria down. Supporting her weight by an arm around her waist, Ruby took her to a nearby tree. They sat underneath its welcome shade. Ruby noticed a bad odor coming from Nyria's foot. She feared it was infected. Watching the Kosi women assemble a meal for everyone, Ruby asked Nyria to translate their conversation.

"The women don't believe Say'f is still alive. The Kosi King was lost in an Avalanche last year. He and Sab-ra were in the Skygrass valley, the location of Talin's blue diamond mine, when the Avalanche struck. Many People and Kosi lost their lives that day."

"What happens now?" Ruby asked.

"When a new King is crowned, he chooses twelve Blood Arrows as guards. They must offer to give their lives to protect him. Most of the Blood Arrows for King Say'f met the soil during the war with the Army or later in the Avalanche. According to Kosi law, Sab-ra must marry one of the surviving Blood Arrows."

"Perhaps Ghang thinks by bringing all the warriors to Halfhigh, Sab-ra will name him King and marry him."

"You could be right, Ruby. Hozro killed many Kosi. When Hozro's killing spree ended only Ghang, another Blood Arrow named Rohr and Argo, the Kosi assassin still lived. Your sister ordered Ghang and Argo come here and kill Hozro. She and Rohr have gone to Talin."

"We owe her our lives," Ruby murmured softly.

The caravan trekked on. Nyria knew the countryside and told Ruby they followed a trail above the Twelve Valleys. Once a young boy on a pony rode up to see who was passing through. When he saw the Kosi, he darted away. Later Ghang sent a Kosi Warrior ahead of the caravan to scout the trail. When he returned he spoke to Ghang.

"Stop the caravan," Ghang shouted and the Warriors stopped. Several Warriors dismounted and followed Ghang on foot. They walked up a small hill and lay down, looking northeast, bows at their sides.

Argo ran forward, joining the men on the hill, preparing to ambush the person coming, but Ghang put out his arm to hold the assassin back. Ruby caught the word, "Bearer." Nyria told her the Bearer people were neutral in the tribe conflicts that plagued the country. They were allowed safe passage everywhere. She felt her body ease. Ten Singh had arrived.

When Ten Singh reached the caravan, he ran over to Ruby.

"I am so happy to see you alive," he whispered. "I feared you dead."

"I knew you would come. Please take us to Talin, Ten-Singh. Nyria has a husband and children there. She is afraid she is dying and wants to see them once more. Her only hope would be to amputate her foot and only Wirri-won could do that."

Ten Singh and Ruby walked over to the wagon where Nyria lay. In the last half day she had lapsed in a coma. He knelt beside her and looked carefully at her foot.

"She wouldn't live through the long trip to Talin, Ruby," Ten Singh whispered sadly. "I am sorry. She is dying." He looked down at the ground and then off toward the sun falling behind the mountain. Ruby felt warm tears run down her face.

"Could you go after Wirri-won? Bring her back her to help Nyria?"

"No, Ruby. I cannot find this Wirri-won person. She left here days ago travelling east. Mistress hired me to bring you and Deti to Talin. Deti is already there. We will go tomorrow."

Ruby saw his fixed expression and knew he would not budge. "When do we ride?"

"In the morning."

"Can't we take Nyria with us?"

"No, Ruby," he shook his head, his eyes full of pity. "She floats the Black River already. She is too close to the entrance of the world beyond. We cannot save her. All you can do is tell her husband and children in Talin that she never stopped loving them or trying to escape."

"May God have mercy on her soul," Ruby whispered, wondering if she would survive long enough to ever make her way back to the green Island of Viridian and the true Church.

Chapter 33 – The Settlement at Rhan Du

While Ruby despaired over leaving the dying Nyria behind, Sab-ra went for help. All that desperate run down the mountain, she feared Lord Rohr lay dying from the cave leopard's infected talons.

I thundered into Rhan Du in late afternoon. I jumped from the saddle and ran toward En Sun's house. I thundered my fists on his door. When he came cautiously to the door and opened it, fury ran down my arms. He turned pale. He was clearly appalled to see me.

"You are a liar and a cheat," I told him furiously. "You promised to take me to the Lost Lake, but you and the traitorous Hakan waited until you could steal all our supplies. You ran from the box canyon. You are a yellow coward."

En Sun backed away as my rage flamed over him.

"I am sorry, Mistress. The Hakan made me leave you. He said the White Snake was coming. The Hakan threatened to kill my wife and unborn child if I would not go with him. When we reached the lower mountain, he left and I rode home. My wife was near to her time. She delivered the baby the day I returned. I wanted to come back for you, but dared not leave her."

"Your betrayal may have caused Lord Rohr's death," I told him, coldly. "We were attacked by the spotted leopard on the way down. The Blood Arrow lies on the trail in a fever coma. You and two more men will come with me to bring him down the mountain."

When he hesitated, wavering, I screamed at him, "Now you idiot, now!" En Sun and two others brought a stretcher. While they assembled their gear for the ride, I searched the area for plants with medicinal properties.

No feverfew grows in the high range. Nor do poppies grow there. Luckily, En Sun's wife had poppy pearls and dried feverfew. I found osier wands growing by the creek and took several dozen. I smashed them with a rock until they opened and I cut their marrow out. Osier takes fever away.

We rode from Rhan Du at a furious pace as the sun set. Tye easily outpaced the Bearers' small ponies, anxious to return to his master. We rode most of the night as the moon rose. We reached Rohr's resting place as the sun came up. I dismounted, feeling a horrid trepidation. My heart pounded so loud I felt it in my temples.

The First of the Blood Arrows lay where I had left him. I fell to my knees. Beside him lay the dead body of a huge spotted leopard. Rohr's knife was imbedded in the beast's chest. Desperate to find a pulse, I checked Rohr's throat, wrists and ankles, but the Guardian of my body, the Defender of my King rode the sky worlds. I led Tye over to see his master's body. He sniffed him tentatively, shying away from the leopard's reek. Dying Kosi Warriors killed their stallions so they would have their mounts with them to ride the clouds, but I could not take this beautiful animal's life.

"Lord Rohr lies dead," I told En Sun and the Bearers, coldly. "Place his body gently on the stretcher. We are taking him down the mountain until we find a cave large enough to contain his great spirit."

"Please Mistress," En Sun pleaded. "Lord Rohr is huge. We won't be able to lift him on to the stretcher. We will cover his body with rocks and leave him here."

"It was because of your treachery that he died," I told him viciously. "Even in his death throes, the valiant Blood Arrow took the life of a mountain leopard larger than himself. His courage shames you all. How dare you plead and whine that he is too large a man for you three weaklings to lift." I clenched my jaw together to control my fury. I wanted to sink my teeth into these cowards.

It took all three of them, but they managed to get Rohr's body on the travois. While they struggled and cursed, I sat down on the trail beside the leopard's dead body. I sought some appropriate way to honor the memory of Lord Rohr. Taking out my knife, I began cutting off the leopard's head. When I held the great head in my hands, I put it in Tye's pack. The stallion shied away, fearful of the leopard's smell. I stripped the leopard's organs from his spotted pelt, threw them into the brush and rolled his skin into a cylinder. Tye reared and protested at the scent but I forced him to stillness while I tied it to the back of his saddle.

"Now we will descend," I told them, my voice chilled with the contempt I felt for their spinelessness.

None of the Bearers' ponies was strong enough to pull the travois with Lord Rohr's body on it very long. One after the other the ponies began to wheeze and cough. Finally I acceded to En Sun's request and we made camp. We would rest for a few hours.

Later, we transferred the travois harness to Tye. He had difficulty standing still for the harnessing, but ultimately it was accomplished. As we descended the mountain, I sang the song for the Death of a Blood Arrow, blessing Kim-li for teaching me so many Kosi songs before I left Natil. We reached a tiny mountain valley lying right up next to the high peaks. The Bearers knew this part of the mountain well.

"We have reached the Crystal Cave," En Sun told me.

"You will bring Lord Rohr's body here," I ordered them, "And we will seal the opening with rocks. No leopard will ever mutilate his body."

They grumbled, but did it. Once they almost let him fall and I pulled my knife. I had to scream at them before they would try again. By the time the light left, Lord Rohr's body was lying peacefully on the white sands inside Crystal Cave.

"You," I ordered pointing my finger at each of them in turn, "You find food. You start a campfire. You find water." They fled from my wrath.

I walked into the cave carrying the head of the leopard. I placed its head on my Guardian's chest. The screaming leopard in full roar faced my Blood Arrow whose face was contorted in a grimace. I was in the grip of a dark passion, as if I walked in waist deep water. Trembling, I took my knife and made a long slice in my arm. Then I took one of Rohr's arrows and dipped the feathers in my blood until every pinion was scarlet. I pushed the arrow deep into one of Rohr's wounds and then forced myself to stick the point of the arrow deep into my palm, screaming in pain. I closed Rohr's cold fingers over the arrow that dripped red with my blood and his.

"From this moment, I take your place as First Blood Arrow for the King, my Guardian," I whispered. The finality of his death hit me and I began to shudder. I wailed my sorrow across the mountain valley in a harsh ululation. When my sobs slowly quieted, I knelt and kissed his forehead.

"I have buried you with honor, Lord Rohr. We are one blood now. I would have named you King of the Kosi, lain with you and conceived strong sons for you, had I not believed the true King still lives. I will always grieve for you. Even in death, you were the Heart of the Leopard."

No one spoke to me when I came to the flame. They handed me food and water but averted their eyes from my despair.

The next morning I told the morose Bearers they had to find enough rocks to brick up the entrance to the cave. One had already deserted. I could tell En Sun and the last Bearer felt unequal to the task and sliced their faces with my eyes.

"We are already very tired, Mistress," En Sun told me.

"En Sun of the Bearer People, unless you close the door of the Blood Arrow's Crystal Cave, I will have the Kosi Assassin cut off your feet when he returns."

Without feet, no Bearer could make a living. En Sun straightened his shoulders, signaled to the other laborer and they began to build a wall of rocks at the cave's entrance. I worked with them.

We left the valley in late afternoon. When the sun set and the world cooled, I pulled the leopard skin from Tye's saddle and wrapped it around my shoulders. In the fading light, I murmured to my dead Guardian, "I will carry the skin of the leopard to the King of the Kosi, Lord Blood Arrow. I will tell him of your faultless courage. I will tell him of our epic journey across the high range in winter. I will tell him how you brought Wirri-Won to coax our babies from my womb. I cannot take the life of your stallion, but I will groom and exercise him each day until baby Quinn is old enough to ride him into battle."

Chapter 34 – Leaving the Green River Camp for Talin

While Sab-ra grieved for Lord Rohr, Ruby prayed that Ten Singh would let them take Nyria to Talin.

The next morning, Ten Singh told Ghang that he and Ruby were leaving the caravan. He explained that he had been commissioned by the Mistress of Maidenstone to take Ruby to Talin. They would be leaving shortly. Ruby walked into the Women's tent slowly. Nyria had slipped ever more deeply into a coma. Her breathing was slow and ragged. Ruby sensed Nyria would probably be dead by the end of the day.

When Ruby mounted Star and she and Ten Singh rode from the camp, she heard a high ululation ring horridly from behind her. It sounded like Nyria's voice, she looked beseechingly at Ten Singh, but he shook his head. Ruby's face was a mask of regret and the tracks of tears.

By evening the following day, Ten Singh pointed out Talin's high plateau lit by moonlight. Ruby had dreamed the previous night of Nyria, smiling in the arms of her husband while her small children danced at their feet, but even asleep, she knew it was a dream and not the Vision. Ten Singh cantered up the slope into the village with Ruby behind him. The moon was rising.

The whole village lay asleep. No one came from their houses to greet them.

"Come," Ten Singh whispered. He dismounted and led his pony toward a small wooden building behind the crescent of white stone houses that encircled the plateau. Ruby followed him to the stable. The warm scent of hay and horses drifted out toward them as Ten Singh slid the stable door open. He lit a candle lamp and they walked inside; the sound of their ponies' hooves deadened by the straw on the floor.

"Look," he whispered pointing into a stall.

A bright yellow mare tossed her head when she saw them. A small male colt nursed at her side.

"How beautiful he is," Ruby whispered and a tiny smile came to her face. "A right perfect little dote."

They climbed the ladder into the hayloft and bedded down there. For the first time since the night with Deti and Ten Singh on the great grass plains Ruby felt calm.

"Why didn't anyone come out to greet us?" she asked Ten Singh.

"It's probably too late and they are sleeping, but usually someone is on guard," his voice was thoughtful.

Deep in the night, Ten Singh woke her, shaking her by the shoulder.

"Ruby, wake up. You are having a bad dream." He could not rouse her and she continued talking in a tranced voice.

"Nyria rides the black sailed boat, her eyelids closed."

"Ruby," Ten Singh called, but she had slipped back into sleep.

When Ten Singh woke in the morning, he saw Ruby standing in the doorway to the stable. The rising sun outlined her body. She turned back to him, centuries of sadness coating her young face in shadow.

"Nyria's gone," she said and Ten Singh nodded.

Later they heard a voice calling from the grass outside the stable. Ruby walked down the ladder and opened the door.

"Ruby, is that you?" Deti's eyes widened at seeing Ruby and her voice rang across the open paddock.

"Deti, I am so happy to see you." A warm rush of pleasure ran through Ruby's veins. "Is Sab-ra here? Is everything all right?"

"No. Sab-ra left Talin a few days ago to go to a place called Halfhigh. Since she left, a terrible disease has struck Talin. The People get large rounded purple growths on their skin and die. It's awful. Nobody knows how to cure it. Your grandmother went up the mountains searching for plants that might help."

Ruby climbed down the ladder and took Deti in her arms, kissing both her cheeks.

"No, don't touch me," Deti said, twisting awkwardly away.

"Why?" Ruby's voice sounded hurt.

"We don't know how a person gets the Mottled Sickness, but we are afraid it comes from getting to close, or kissing someone. Hello, Ten Singh," she greeted him.

"Are you well, Deti?" Ten Singh asked.

"I am. According to Ruby and Sab-ra's Grandmother, I have already had this disease. They found a small purple welt from years ago on my body. Apparently, you can't get it more than once, but I could still carry the infection. That is why I fear touching you. I can't let you come inside the house. I'll make you some tea and bring it to the stables."

"Can't I meet Sab-ra's grandparents?" Ruby asked, sounding troubled. She thought Talin would be a safe harbor, but once again tragedy had demolished her hopes.

"They will come to see you when they can. I will bring blankets and food. I'm sorry, but until Grandmother returns, I am afraid to let you leave the stable."

Deti turned and ran back to the semi-circle of houses. She returned shortly with tea, blankets and hot bread. She climbed the ladder up to the haymow and the two girls sat together in the opening, dangling their legs in the sunlight, careful not to touch.

"Why does Sab-ra want to reach this Lost Lake valley?" Ruby asked.

"She thinks the King of the Kosi, the father of her children, is sealed inside the valley, unable to escape."

"I saw her pregnant in the Sight, but you said children. Did she have more than one baby?"

"She had twins and they are so beautiful. Grandmother says Quinn, that's her little boy's name, is the future King of the Kosi. And little Crimson, we call her Crimee, is a Kosi princess."

"I would love to see them," Ruby's voice was warm.

"You won't be able to hold them or touch them, but I will bring them to the stable so you can see them."

"Have any People of Talin died from the Mottled Sickness?"

"Almost a third of the village is already gone," Deti's voice was low. "Luckily, Ambe, the woman who is nursing the twins, is unaffected so far. She and her husband may leave Talin with the babies until the illness runs its course."

The following day Ruby stood watching from the second floor haymow window as a tall elderly man helped bring supplies out to a wagon. A young couple with a toddler were getting ready to depart. After the woman finished saddling her pony and filling his packs with supplies, she walked off toward one of the houses. When she returned, she had two papooses wrapped up in her arms. She walked over to the stable so Ruby could see the babies. Both of them had sparkles in their eyes.

"Hello, Ruby. My name is Ambe. These two are Quinn and Crimson. I wish I could bring them up to you, but my husband and I have decided we need to leave Talin for Halfhigh."

The elderly man walked down toward the stable. "I am Silo'am, your ...Grandfather," his voice hesitated before saying the word. "We are afraid for Sab-ra's babies. My son Hent and his wife Ambe are taking them and their own son, Manny, away from Talin. We think they would be safer in the upper range."

"Could I go with them?" Ruby asked, hopefully

He frowned, as if he hadn't thought of this possibility. "No, I don't think so. Ellani, your Grandmother, will be back today. She will want to meet you and will be awfully disappointed if I sent you north."

Ten Singh came up behind Ruby. "Silo'am, I am Ten Singh. I am leaving Talin soon to return to Maidenstone. Are you sure Ruby is safe here? I could take her back to Namché with me. I could take Deti also."

Deti was walking toward the stable, leading a pony.

"Deti, do you wish to return to Maidenstone?" Ten Singh asked.

Deti hesitated a moment, but seeing Ruby's expression of dismay, said, "No, I like it here. Flashes of my former life come to me and I have been drawing every day."

Ten Singh nodded, disturbed at the thought of leaving both girls in the center of a deadly disease. Then he took a deep breath and said, "I understand."

Silo'am returned to assisting Hent and Ambe with their packing. When the pair rode off the rim of Talin's plateau, Ambe held two little papooses and her husband carried their toddler. Deti ran to the rim, watching them leave and drawing little circle blessings in the air.

Ruby felt a deep sadness. Everything in this pagan land seemed to conspire against her seeing Sab-ra. And until she saw her sister, she would never be able to return to Viridian.

Chapter 35 – The Settlement of Rhan Du

While Ambe and Hent rode off the butte with Sab-ra's babies, Sab-ra herself rode west to Rhan Du, more determined than ever to enter the Lost Lake valley.

After a night in Rhan Du, I called for all the male Bearers in the village to come to En Sun's house to hear my plea for laborers. Even the death of my Guardian, Rohr, had not dissuaded me from trying to enter the Lost Lake valley. I stood on En Sun's raised porch looking toward the little straggle of houses clinging to life on the flanks of the Great Dhali Ra. Eight men assembled grudgingly below me.

"Do you all know the great fall of rocks that separates the lands we know from the lands inside the mountain?"

There were murmurs of assent and several nods.

"I want the wall removed." The men turned to each other and I saw them shaking their heads. "I see eight strong men here, but I also see your women and children. They are thin and weak. The village needs money to buy food. Winter is coming."

The men looked at each other uneasily. One of the women came out of the house with two little children.

"If you will remove the rocks that block the passage into the Lost Lake, I will give you three parthats for every day you work." At the word "parthats," I saw the woman's face light up.

She took her husband by the sleeve and talked with him earnestly. Several more women came outside, including En Sun's wife who carried their newborn.

"I ask for your help, Bearers of Rhan Du. Who among you is willing to work for silver parthats to save your women and children from the winter wolves of starvation?"

When no one responded, I called "Women of Rhan Du, for the sake of your children, compel your men to work for me. Summer is ending already; white men who need guides to take them up the mountain will not return until spring. If your men will not work for me, who will feed the hungry mouths of Rhan Du?"

One man walked forward. Slowly, all the rest joined him.

"We begin tomorrow. Bring wagons and carts to haul the stones away from the bottom of the rockfall. Each man who comes must work a full day from sunrise to sunset. Only then will I give him the promised silver."

As the gathering began to break up, I pulled En Sun aside. "What have you heard about the White Snake?"

En sun looked uneasily at me.

"Tell me," I ordered fiercely. "I must know what we face on the other side of the rock wall."

"A Bearer from fourth valley told a man of my village he saw the djinn earlier this moon. He stood on the mountain face not far from where the blue diamond mine was before the Avalanche took the Skygrass valley."

I felt the earth sway under my feet and my fears rose into my throat choking my breathing. It took me a few moments to get myself under control.

"Have any of the Bearers reported seeing a Kosi Warrior on the mountain?"

"One man saw a Kosi warrior. However, it was last winter and he was on foot in the high range."

The next day all the men, ponies and wagons from Rhan Du trekked across the lower range until we came to the rockfall. I felt a dreadful qualm when I saw it. The fall of stones was enormous, almost as big as Maidenstone. The Bearers stood quietly as I gazed upwards. When I looked at them, I saw the same look of shock on their faces.

"Make camp," I ordered. I couldn't let the men know how afraid I was that the rock wall would prove too much for us. The men assembled the one black dweli I had given En Sun when I was pregnant with the twins. Other men set up small leather flap tents. En Sun's wife and several of the other women had sent stew with us in olla pots. We started a fire and put the pots on the flames. The air was soon redolent with the scent of chanry meat and root vegetables.

Around the campfire that night, I asked if any of them had climbed the rockfall. One man, a short Bearer that resembled the Hakan traitor Kilby, said he had.

"What did you find?" I asked him.

"An opening, Queen of the Kosi. It was only as large as a dog, but I looked inside and it went on forever."

"That is a good sign," I told him. "What is your name, Bearer of Rhan Du?"

"My name is Ra Khat," he told me.

"Before we begin to carry away the rocks, you will climb up again, Ra Khat," I told him. "A Hakan traitor told me he had seen the White Snake on the Mountain. He is an Army soldier. Have you seen him also?"

"He came out of the opening one moon ago," he told me. "I rode my pony below this level. I saw his yellow hair when he emerged."

"Tomorrow, you will see if you can wiggle into the White Snake's opening."

Ra Khat shuddered and looked away. I had to do something to compel his obedience.

"Five parthats to enter the Snake's hole," I forced myself to calmness. The fact that Grieg was still alive had shaken me badly, but I could not let them see my fears.

"One hundred," he said softly. A fine tremor shook his hands. "It would take a hundred parthats to tempt me into the Snake's nest, Mistress," he said. I saw sweat on his forehead.

"Twenty," I said calmly, looking off in the distance.

"Fifty," he said, but I saw the corners of his mouth twitch. He was starting to enjoy the bargaining. The rest of the men began laughing, shoving each other and placing bets on the final price.

"I will crawl into the hole myself, before I give even forty parthats of the People to a cowardly Bearer who is afraid of tiny white snakes," I said, narrowing my eyes. His eyes sparkled, knowing I was teasing him.

"Thirty," he said. "And not a parthat less will I take."

"Twenty five," I said, grinning at him.

"What is money, when we are all family?" he asked, laughing.

"That is right, little brother, I need pay you nothing. Family obligation should compel you to do my bidding."

"No true sister would endanger her brother's life in such a quest," he told me. "Only twenty five parthats and we are forever blood."

I stood and walked to him, held out my hand and he took it.

"Blood," I said.

"Twenty five," he said.

Smiling, we each pricked our palms with knives and pressed them together.

"Now I would see these twenty five parthats," he said, still amused.

"And I would see your bottom enter the snake's nest before I show them to you," I said and neither of us could stop laughing.

The next morning, he climbed the Crystal Steppe and entered the black hole. It was so small from the ground it looked like the pupil in the eye of a Goddess.

Chapter 36 – In the Valley of Talin

While Sab-ra watched Ra Khat enter the black hole, Ruby and Ten-Singh talked in the haymow of the stable at Talin.

"I urge you to reconsider, Ruby," Ten Singh said. "I think both you and Deti should come with me. I can bring you back to Talin after this sickness has passed."

"No," Ruby said slowly, considering his offer. "I must stay. I want to meet my Grandmother who raised Sab-ra. If I leave with you, by the time we get back here both my Grandparents could be dead. And I have yet to meet my sister."

"I will wait another day, in hopes that your Grandmother returns by then. I do not wish to leave you here. You are in grave danger from the disease."

"I will not change my mind." Ruby's voice was firm. Although Ten Singh asked her three more times, Ruby steadfastly refused.

Ten Singh rode off the rim the next morning. The following day a messenger rode into Talin. Ruby watched from the haymow door as Grandfather Silo'am walked out to meet the man. She heard him say he had encountered Ten Singh at the Springs of Natrun and showed him a letter from the Mistress of Maidenstone. Ten Singh directed him to the Valley of Talin.

"The People have the Mottled Sickness," Grandfather told the man. All the color drained from his face. Trembling, he handed Grandfather the letter. Forgoing tea or a meal, he left immediately. Grandfather brought the letter to the stable shortly thereafter. The letter was sealed with the silver crest of Maidenstone.

Grandfather was starting to look better, Ruby noticed. His raised sores were fading and his cough was less persistent. Deti lowered a rope and Grandfather attached the letter to it.

Ruby opened the message with quivering hands. She scanned it twice before Deti who was tapping her foot said, "Ruby, I can't stand the suspense. What did Mistress say?"

"A telegram came from me Da. It said Mum was steadily improving and should be able to go home in another week. He reminded me that I am to find Sab-ra and if she is willing to come, bring her back with me to Viridian. Do you think that is possible, Deti?"

Deti frowned, clearly deep in thought. "I have known Sab-ra for many moons now, and I don't think she will leave the high country whether she finds her husband or not. I believe she will stay and rule the Kosi."

"I thought the King of the Kosi was dead. Are you saying she will stay here and try to rule that filthy savage tribe alone?"

"I believe so," Deti said, solemnly.

Ruby gave Deti an "are you mental" stare and shook her head. "We are so different. I only want to do what God says is right and to find peace for myself. Sab-ra must be a cheeky little wagon to think she could do such a thing without even a husband."

"It's not so much that she is arrogant," Deti said, quietly. "She only wants her life to mean something. She wants to be remembered after she is dead."

"Seems to me she is getting above herself with such notions. She should be preparing her soul for the day she stands before God," Ruby said.

"In her own way that's exactly what she is doing," Deti's voice was so soft it was nearly inaudible.

Two days later, Grandmother returned to Talin and came to the stable. She stood in the grass below the haymow and called. Ruby came to the doorway and looked down.

"I am pleased to see you at last, Ruby," Ellani said, profound pleasure in her face.

"I am happy to meet you," Ruby replied. "I have come a long way."

"The Mottled sickness is going away. Both you girls can leave the barn and come up to the house now." Ruby and Deti hugged each other in happiness.

When they entered the beamed kitchen, they saw a large tub of steaming water. "You may bathe," Ellani told them.

Both girls were grateful for the hot water and soft linen rags Ellani brought them. Once they were out of the water, Grandmother took all their clothes and washed them in the tub. She gave the girls long nightshirts, soft things of Sab-ra's, and sent them to hang their clothes out to dry.

Once outside hanging up their clothes in the clean wind, Ruby said, "Deti, I am not going to stay in Talin much longer. It has already taken months, this trip. I am becoming desperate I am, to see my Mum and Da. I have decided to go to Halfhigh. Since the Babas are there, Sab-ra will come to them in time. I can see her and my promise to me Ma will be kept."

"It's a five day trip to Halfhigh. You don't know the way."

"Will you go with me, Deti?" Ruby felt her breathing quicken.

Deti stood hanging the last piece of their clothing with the wind and bright sunshine all around them. "Yes. I will. And I want to show you something before we go."

Ruby and Deti returned to the stable and Deti scooted up the ladder into the haymow. She returned with a rolled sheaf of drawings. They walked back up to Grandmother's house. Once inside, Deti unrolled the ant'l hide parchments on the table. The drawings were of Ruby, Sabra with her babies, Mistress Falcon,

Talin and the mountains. They were so beautiful; they took Ruby's breath away.

"You are only talented, you are," Ruby said and felt a smile warm her face. Grandmother came over to see.

"Deti, did you draw these?"

She nodded, smiling shyly.

"I believe you came from the Valley of Quatar. It's the fifth valley and the place where all the artists go for training."

Deti tipped her head to one side, struck by Grandmother's words.

"I saw your face change when I said the word Qatar. Do you remember that word, Deti?"

"Something about it is familiar," Deti said tilting her head to one side.

"When you are ready, I can have one of the men of Talin take you there."

"Ruby intends to go to Halfhigh," Deti told Ellani. "Could someone take us there first? I want to see Sab-ra and give her these drawings of her babies before I go to this valley of Qatar."

After dinner that evening, Ruby sat at her Grandparent's table to write in her Diary.

Dear Diary:

My last entry was not the last after all. I am here in Talin, the place where Sab-ra was raised. I had to spend near a week in the haymow of a barn, however, before they would bring me up to the house. It was to protect Deti and me from the Mottled Sickness. I have come to a decision. While we were in the barn, they took Sab-ra's Babas to Halfhigh. I need to go there. If the Babas are there, Sab-ra will come.

Deti showed me her drawings of the village of Talin, the Elders and Sab-ra's twins. Deti is bleedin' talented, she is. If I can't get my sister to return to Viridian with me, I'll bring me Ma the drawings so she can see her grandbabies. I keep thinking about my home, me Da, me Ma and of course my beautiful dog. That life seems a million miles away. I have a terrible fear that I am forgetting it.

Some days I have a hard time seeing my Nana's face. I pulled my tickets out of my knapsack last night; to be certain they were there. When I go back to the city of Nam-shay, I will say good-bye to the Garda lads and maybe give Carmac one last kiss. If his stint is up, maybe we'll travel back together. That would get Shane's bowels in tatters, it would.

Signed, Ruby

She grinned to herself thinking of the look on Shane's face when she walked up arm in arm with Carmac.

Chapter 37 – The Lost Lake Valley

As Ruby and Deti prepared to leave Talin for Halfhigh, En Sun told Sab-ra that Ra Khat had not returned.

"This attempt of yours to oppose the will of the Great Dhali Ra is wrong," En Sun told Sab-ra. "I see a frown upon the face of the Goddess."

I felt a wave of fear that the Goddess had cursed this venture. My knees gave way and I collapsed on the ground, breathing hard.

The men emerged from their tents and walked around me. They prepared a simple breakfast and ate silently. I stood up and met their gloomy faces. En Sun stood beside me. I looked up at the thousand thent of rocks guarding the secrets of the great Goddess.

"It will be the darkest day of a hundred year-long winter before all these rocks are moved away," En Sun told the Bearers solemnly. "Those rocks belong where the Goddess placed them. I am going back to Rhan Du. Any of you who wish to ride with me, let us go."

They filed silently from our makeshift camp. As they walked past me, I handed each man his silver parthats. As they were mounting up, I called, "I will pay anyone who will stay here with me double the promised parthats. Six per day."

Two men looked slightly interested.

"We will not enter the snake's hole," one of them said
warningly.

"Agreed."

Ra Khat had still not returned and I feared for his safety.
Only two men dismounted and after talking with each other for a
moment or two began loading rocks into the carts. It was like
emptying the ocean with a child's water pail.

"Cowards," I yelled after the rest of the retreating Bearers
as they rode down the mountain. I went to work carrying rocks to
the wagons. My shoulder ached by afternoon and my hands were
bleeding from granite cuts. The two last Bearers worked steadily,
but the rockfall had defeated us. It stretched from our level almost
to the top of the great mountain and was a hundred thent wide at
the base.

I walked over to Tye and led him to a grassy area where I
found a small spring, bubbling out of the ground, bright and cold. I
knelt and drank with him. I filled my waterskin. The sparkling
water drew my eyes like metal to a magnet. I gazed at the liquid
beauty, envisioning my little ones and their father. How I missed
them all.

Sun on the water, I thought and instantly I saw my
husband's revenant stand before me. Tall and very dark, his eyes
looked down into my soul.

"I have sought you long, my husband," I told him.

His golden eyes flashed. He held out his arms. I stood to
enter his embrace, but the image wavered and was gone. My heart

lifted up. The Vision must have meant that Say'f was still alive. Alive! All I had to do was reach him.

"Goddess of the Winds, what should I do?" I asked. The air was still. The Goddess declined to answer. Leading Tye by his reins, I brought a full waterskin to the two Bearers who stood wiping their foreheads with rags in the hot sun.

"I have been a foolish Lakt. En Sun was right. This rockfall is the work of the Goddess. It belongs here."

Both men nodded.

"I will enter the Lost Lake through the snake's black hole. Will you climb with me in the morning?" I asked. "I don't ask you to go inside, only to wait for me."

"And if you do not return, Mistress?"

"Then you will ride to Rhan Du and take Ra Khat's parthats to his family. Give him twice what I promised him. Tell En Sun to ride to Talin. He must tell my Grandparents the news of my death and give them the remaining parthats for my children."

I had no thought of success. But something deep inside me drove me to try. Like the day of the final battle, I would make one desperate last stand.

The Bearers and I began the climb early the next morning. It was a bright day and the sunshine raised my spirits. I caught the scent of the laelia flower and felt some relief. The Wind Goddess had sent me a blessing. The Bearers climbed behind me, looking apprehensively up toward the black pupil. When we reached the landing outside the opening, all of us breathing hard, the tallest Bearer handed me his knife.

"For the White Snake who took Ra Khat's life," he said.

I thanked him, handed him my small leather sack filled with silver parthats, adjusted my waterskin and feeling for my own small knife in my pocket, I bade them good-bye. The opening was slender, not quite as wide as my shoulders. I had to turn sidewise to make my way forward. What little light penetrated the dimness quickly vanished. I groped my way into the mountain, holding my right arm up so I would know if the ceiling lowered. I found my anxiety rising and fought claustrophobia.

"I will not fear," I told myself. "I am in the arms of the Great Dhali Ra. She will protect me." I began humming a Kosi song. Hours went by in the dense stifling darkness, then my foot bumped into something soft. A horror seized my heart. I bent down to feel a softness. It was a body. I shook all over, but forced myself to kneel and search for a pulse. I found an arm and trailing my fingers toward the hand found the wrist at last. Did I feel warmth? Was there a faint pulse? I worked my fingers back up the arm, across the shoulder and toward the neck. I felt the person's throat for a pulse. It was faint, but it was there—the beautiful sacred throb of life. It had to be Ra Khat; he had been coming out of the dark slit toward the light.

"Ra Khat," I whispered to him and heard a very faint sigh. He lay on his belly, wedged into a crevice. I backed away, careful not to step on him. He was very heavy but the entire time I had been walking up a slanted incline. Pulling him back down toward the opening might be possible because I would be dragging him downhill. I grabbed his hands and began to pull. It took a long time. When I felt my strength fail, I turned and walked toward the light, calling the Bearers.

When I emerged, blinking, they raced forward with their waterskins. I drank and then told them I had found Ra Khat.

"He is injured, but alive. I can drag him no further, I need you to go in and pull him out." They looked at each warily and I felt my rage rise. "Would you let your comrade die? If you will not help him, I tell your wives their gutless husbands refused to help one of their own. He lives, I tell you. Go."

They disappeared into the hole and emerged later, dragging Ra Khat. We carried him down the mountain to the camp and gave him water. He was not fully conscious, but in a few hours began to moan and twitch. I examined him carefully. There was a large blood patch on his right leg. I cut aside his pants and found a bullet hole in his thigh. The bullet had gone straight through his leg. I cleaned and bandaged his wound, packing it tight with feverfew.

"You will live," I whispered to him. "Take heart and tell us what happened inside the mountain?" I gave him more water. He coughed and cleared his throat. I pulled him to a sitting position. He opened his eyes.

"I made it through to the Lost Lake," he croaked.

"Did you see the White Snake? Did you see a Kosi warrior?"

He took a deep breath. "I hid among the yellow trees watching a long time. When the moon rose, I saw the White Snake. The moon hit his hair. He saw me. He raised his long gun and shot me. The pain knocked me down."

"Did you see a Kosi?"

"No, Mistress, I am sorry, it took everything I had to crawl back into the slice."

The next morning one of the Bearers from Rhan Du and I climbed again to the ledge by the black hole. The other Bearer stayed in the camp with Ra Khat and the horses. I brought a burning brand from the campfire as a torch. I was going in. I nodded in farewell to the terrified man, asked him to wait two days for me and walked into the cleft.

This time I had a light and walked rapidly to the area where I found Ra Khat. The torch was still burning when I saw the large blood patch. Suddenly, I felt a draft of wind and heard a huge whopping sound, as if large wings beat the air. The torch went out. Terror seized me again and it took me some time to regain my breathing. The ceiling of the slit was lower, and I had to crouch and then to crawl. I quietly hummed the Kosi song for the Day of the Final Battle remembering our victory at Armageddon. After what seemed like hours, I saw the tunnel grow lighter. I hugged myself in happiness. I was almost to the other end—to the entrance into the Lost Lake.

The egress of the slice was partially blocked with rocks. I was no longer afraid; seeing the light gave me strength. I doused my torch and quietly moved the rocks away, setting them to the side as if they would break. I would not alert Grieg to my presence. At last the whole basin lay before me. More superbly matchless than the lost Skygrass Valley, it lay before me; a gift from the Great Goddess of the Dhali Ra.

Nothing had changed since the last time I looked upon the Lost Lake after Grieg sealed me into the tunnels of the mountain. I had made it to the Lost Lake then by following the sound of Grieg's footsteps. We battled there, almost to the death, yet I survived. I left his body by the lost lake, cut, bleeding and shot. I caused a rockslide to trap him in the valley where I didn't think he could survive the winter. Yet the white snake lived.

Say'f had sought Grieg's death when he learned what the man did to me. Was my husband here also? Who had triumphed in this beautiful place that should have been kept sacrosanct and protected from the terrible acts of blood feuds.

The water in the mountain basin was an unbelievable azure blue color, so clear and bright, I had to shut my eyes. It looked like an enormous blue diamond, large enough to have adorned a ring on the finger of a Goddess. Blue green grasses and trees with white bark surrounded the sapphire water, like the setting for a wedding band.

Carefully surveying the entire basin, I saw a crude shelter made from tree trunks. It was not made by a Kosi. The Kosi make woven shelters of grass on the trail, graceful rounded golden nests. This was Grieg's house. My breath came fast and my heart thundered in my chest. Then I found the fury that lived in me before, when I sought Grieg's death. How dared this demon, this denizen of hell, live when my Say'f was still missing? This time there would be no mistake; this time I would take his life or join my King in the world that lies beside our own, invisible to the living.

I darted silently to some nearby sentinel pines and sat on their red needles, breathing their wonderful scent and drinking water from my waterskin. When the sun went down, I made my way carefully to a spot above Grieg's shelter. When night came and Grieg lay sleeping, I would murder the repulsive worm. My eyes narrowed and my teeth clenched as I saw myself dance in victory around his dead body.

Chapter 38 – Leaving the Valley of Talin for Halfhigh

While Sab-ra waited for Captain Grieg to enter his house and fall asleep, Ruby and Deti assembled their belongings for the trip to Halfhigh.

Deti and Ruby rode out of Talin the following morning. They were going to Halfhigh where Hent and Ambe were camped with Sab-ra's twins. Ruby's grandmother had asked virtually every person in the village if they would guide the girls. All were either too ill, or working hard to provide food and care for those still recovering. Ruby insisted she would go alone if need be, but she was going. Sab-ra was at Halfhigh and she had given her mother a pledge that she would see her. Deti agreed to go along. They left Cloudheart in Talin, afraid of losing him on the trail, but at the last moment decided to take Dusk, the beautiful Kosi gazehound.

Ellani and Silo'am, Ruby and Sab-ra's grandparents, made a detailed drawing of the country. The map was beautifully drawn, but Ruby wondered if the landmarks that were so clear to the People of Talin, would be obvious to her. Such notations as Elder Oak and Gray Sands were not very encouraging.

The first day they rode north toward the final bend in the Wool Road above the Twelve Valleys. Riding on the broad well-travelled trail, Ruby felt her cares evaporate. It was the last stage of her journey; soon she and Sab-ra would be together. Her Grandparents, Ellani and Silo'am, sent food with them and a black dweli. Deti rode a small red pony called Naj and Ruby rode Star, the pony she had ridden out of Namché. It seemed eons ago when she left Maidenstone, a little mouse frightened of everything.

The day was clear and both girls were in good spirits. They had no trouble finding the first campsite, or the spring for drinking water. They set up the black dweli, made a campfire and sitting by the firelight they taught each other songs. Deti found a tree with a white trunk and peeled some sheets of bark. She sketched Ruby's face in the firelight using black char from old campfires.

On the fourth day, they travelled through a northern remnant of the great Kosi grasslands. The whispering grasses moved in the wind, cresting like waves on the sea. In the afternoon, the girls heard the thudding of horse hooves.

"Who do you think it could be?" Ruby asked.

"I think it is a wild horse herd."

Ruby feared it might be the remaining Kosi outlaws from the Green River camp, but when the grasses parted, a glistening wave of color rode through an opening in the high prairie. There were about twenty foals and colts; most were less than a year old. The majority were white, but a few were black or silver gray. A large mare, smoke colored with a black mane and tail drove them.

She raised her head and screamed when she saw the girls' mounts. Despite Deti's efforts to hold him back, Naj trotted forward, his eyes locked in euphoric transcendence on the lead mare. She reared into the air and Naj was transfixed. The mare cantered after the colts, nipping the stragglers, urging them forward. Naj bucked and reared throwing Deti to the ground and disappeared, running after the herd. The stirrups from his saddle flapped in the air; his reins fluttered behind him.

"Deti, are you all right?" Ruby ran to Deti lying on the ground. She sat up, rubbing dirt out of her eyes. They looked around at the endless plains and Star, whose reins were still in Ruby's hand. "Star almost got away too," Ruby said, gripping her reins tightly.

The careful map had blown away in the wind. They looked everywhere on the ground but found only one little scrap of ant'l hide. The rest had been trampled to shreds by the wild horses. The remaining piece showed the way out of Talin and the first day of the trip.

"What are we going to do," Ruby wailed.

"We are only a day or so away from Halfhigh." At Ruby's dismayed expression Deti added, "I remember most of the map." The girls gathered their supplies, Deti mounted Star with Ruby behind her and calling to Dusk, they continued north.

By evening, they reached the edge of a large sand-filled basin. It stretched away to the horizon. The Wind Goddess had scalloped the sand into tiny ridges and miniature gullies. Lines of white crystals tipped the ridges. The sunshine made them sparkle.

"Its salt," Deti cried out happily. The girls ran and picked up the small transparent particles, tasting them on their tongues and laughing. "It must have been a salt lake many eons ago. Perhaps this is where the gray mare was taking the foals."

Early the next morning, they saw the herd again. Naj stood out. He was the only one with a red coat. He trailed the gray mare, still lost in adoration. The girls walked forward silently, with Star behind them, her reins held tightly. When they got within ten thent of the herd, the wild horses moved away, surging like a wave. After an hour of silent approaches, followed by the herd sliding away, Deti tried calling Naj. He didn't even look in her direction. The gray mare pricked up her ears at the sound of Deti's voice and began to direct the herd toward them.

"Naj," Deti called, as the enormous wave came right toward them.

"Deti, run," Ruby cried as she darted to the right of the herd, but Deti stood motionless with her hands outstretched. As the herd parted around her, Naj ran by. She grabbed his saddle horn and threw herself in the air, landing on his back. She strained against the reins, pulling backward and although he bucked, she hung on like a limpet. As the herd dashed away, she rode him back to Ruby. Once he had settled, she dismounted and started to undo his saddle cinch.

"What are you doing?" Ruby shrieked at her. "Don't do that, he will get away for sure."

"I know," Deti said, calmly. "I just need to remove his saddle and bridle. He is mine no longer. He has joined the wild ones."

"Deti, you are crazy as a crow. We are a thousand miles away from Nam-shay, alone in this vast country and you are going to let your pony join a wild herd?" Ruby was incredulous.

"I can't trust him anymore," Deti said. "He will run away again if he ever has a chance."

Deti is one crazy thicko, Ruby thought. Why, oh why did I ever leave Viridian?

They spent the night in the gray sands, rising early the next morning. Dark edged clouds filled the northern sky. They could smell rain on the wind. Adventures, thought Ruby sulkily. Nana said it would be the greatest adventure I could ever have. She failed to mention that adventures are often cold and wet and make you miss your tea. By afternoon, the rain began. The girls were soaked in minutes. Ruby wanted to stop, but Deti persisted. Several hours later, the rain stopped and as the sun went down, huge and blood red. They pulled Star to a stop at the base of a flat-topped mountain.

"I think this must be Halfhigh," Deti was smiling. They could see the tops of white stone houses and a black dweli. They rode Star up the incline.

"Ambe, Hent," Deti called out repeatedly. No one responded. The sky was darkly ablaze, hungry as a forest fire. Deti put Star in the horse boma with Hent and Ambe's ponies. There was no sign of the adults or the twins. The wind rose and a very large black dweli, apparently a permanent fixture at Halfhigh, flapped in the wind. They opened the flap, saw the bedstraw and decided to sleep there. The sound of Ruby's singsong voice woke Deti as the gray light of dawn hit the mountains.

"Black spots run red. The panther roars."

"Ruby, what is it. What do you see," Deti shook her arm. Ruby blinked and returned to the present.

"A panther is here, Deti. I think he attacked Hent and Ambe."

"Goddess, don't let it be the babies," Deti cried softly.

"What do panthers fear, Deti?"

"Fire. They fear fire." Deti opened the flap to the dweli and ran part way across the mesa to a cluster of small trees and silver leafed shrubs. She tore off some branches with dead leaves and brought them back to Ruby.

"I'm going to make torches," Deti said, striking a fire stick against a flint stone. The sparks tumbled against the dead leaves on the branches and the blaze caught. The girls walked hesitantly around the perimeter of the camp holding the blazing branches. A thin scream scorched the air.

"Ambe," Deti yelled. "Hent. Where are you?"

The cries continued. The voice was high pitched; it was one of the babies. The girls ran to the white stone building. The door was ajar, creaking in the wind, leather hinges moaning. They saw a large shadow on the floor. It was a man's body. Ruby thrust the torch into the building. The copper scent of blood filled the room. A massive black panther stood over Hent's body—threw back its head and roared.

Like lightning, the panther came running at the doorway. Both girls screamed and Ruby dropped her torch. The straw on the floor ignited and made a terrifying sound. The flame lit the air making a whoosh sound. The panther darted past the girls. Ruby saw the tip of his curled black tail vanish over the rim. Thin screams rode the wind; the door banged against the doorjamb.

Deti pulled the door fully open and fell to her knees by Hent.

"He's alive, Ruby. His pulse is like a thread, but he is alive. Climb up the ladder into the loft. I think Ambe and the babies are up there."

Ruby stood frozen, as the flames licked the straw in places throughout the stable. Her eyes were huge.

"Now," Deti screamed and Ruby ran, jumping over patches of fire. She climbed up the ladder. Her heart beat so fast she heard thudding in her ears.

Ambe lay curled in one corner, seemingly unconscious. Crimson was sitting beside her body. The baby was screaming. Quinn stood in front of her, a long wisp of straw in his hand like a tiny sword. Ruby got her arm around Ambe's shoulders, lifting her up to a sitting position. She coughed, retched and started to cry.

"Ambe, we have to get the Babas out of here. The panther is gone." Ambe struggled, lurched and got shakily to her feet. Ruby grabbed Quinn, tucked him under her arm like a sack of grain and started to climb down. He struggled to escape.

"Hold still, Quinn," she shrieked. She looked down to see Deti dragging Hent's body outside through the doorway. Ruby's breath came fast and her palms sweated, making it hard to keep hold of the ladder. The fire had heated up the room and smoke rose. Ghostly tendrils of death were already halfway up the ladder to the loft. She forced herself to keep climbing down, reached the bottom rung on the ladder and saw fire all around her.

"Deti," she shrieked. "Come get Quinn." Deti looked up, dropped Hent's feet in the grass and ran back into the house. She coughed and hacked, dodging places where the straw was already on fire. She grabbed the baby hard against her body and raced for the door. Quinn reached his arms back over Deti's shoulder, screaming his sister's name.

Fighting her fears and struggling to breathe in the thick air, Ruby climbed back up the ladder. Ambe was sitting up in the straw, still not fully conscious. The smoke reached half way to the loft by then and Ruby fought her claustrophobia, the heat and the smoke. Sweat ran down between her breasts. Ruby grabbed baby Crimson. The baby put her arms around Ruby's neck and linked her little legs around Ruby's waist.

"Hold on tight," she managed between coughs. Slowly she climbed back down into smoke so thick it looked solid. "Ambe, climb down after me," she shrieked. When she was half way to the bottom, she screamed for Deti. Deti stood in the doorway, fear making her features into a mask.

"I am going to drop the baby. You have to come closer. Catch her." Ruby's voice broke Deti's stillness and she ran to the ladder. Fire jumped toward her feet. Ruby peeled little Crimson away from her body and held her in the air above Deti's head. "Fly down, little one," she murmured and felt the weight of the small warm body fall away. Deti grabbed her and Crimson clasped Deti's neck. Deti dashed screaming from the house, her boots on fire.

Ruby climbed back up for Ambe. She was sitting at the edge of the loft, her legs hanging over into the smoke. She seemed in a trance, watching the smoke climb up to Ruby's waist.

"Ambe, you have to climb behind me." Ambe just looked at her, eyes wide in horror. "Ambe, if you can't climb down the babies will die. You are the only one who has milk."

Ambe coughed and slowly turned around, lowering her feet to the top rungs of the ladder. "I have you now," Ruby told her, linking her arms around Ambe's waist, "I won't let you go." Slowly the women made it to the bottom. Ruby turned on the last rung and reached her foot out into dark air, feeling for the floor. Flame jumped onto her boot. Both of them were coughing.

"Follow me, Ambe," she cried and dropped into the flaming straw. Ambe screamed behind her. The heat was ferocious. Something deep inside Ruby, some basic instinct for life would not let her turn back. She dropped into a crawl and fought her way desperately toward the air. Something hard bumped against her. She winced and pulled away; it was Deti's foot. She was going back in for Ambe.

Chapter 39 – In the Lost Lake Valley

As Deti and Ruby escaped the flaming barn at Halfhigh, Sab-ra crawled cautiously out of her hiding place in the Lost Lake valley.

I cursed the moon as I crept from the sentinel pines, fearing the light would hit my hair and alert Grieg. Stripping off my shirt, I used it as a hat, tying the sleeves under my chin. With all my childhood spy skills re-awakened, I stepped silently from my hiding place. I kept my eyes on the ground beneath the trees, fearful I would step on a fallen branch and it would snap. Moving slowly as a glacier, I reached the area above Grieg's shelter. I tried desperately to keep my breathing silent.

In the bathing moonlight, I saw a white glow on the mountain ridge above the Lost Lake on the other side of the valley. Keeping my eyes fixed on that area, I knew him. It was Sumulus. His white coat glowed in the moonlight, soft as snow. A second Angelion padded behind him. Then I heard a tiny cry from a baby mooncat and the second lion turned back. Sumulus descended the mountain like melting ice, inevitable as the coming of spring.

"Come to me, great mooncat of the high range," I whispered in my mind. "Join me in the hunt." The Lost Lake was alive with the scents of the wind and I sensed the presence of another person. On the western side of the valley, a shadow flowed down the slope, dark as the mountain panther, moving fluidly as water sliding over stones. I recognized that shadow; the man was Kosi, it had to be Say'f. I felt my heart pound loud as the Elders' staves on the stones around the communal flame at Talin. The scent of laelia filled my senses and I swam in its pale aura. My King lived. He and Sumulus sought Grieg's death together.

I forced myself to stay among the trees. I gave the Kosi King my unbounded passion, sending it flying to his heart and mind. He stopped moving for a fraction of a second and looked toward the trees where I hid. His eyes flashed. How I wanted to join him on the death hunt, but kept my feet in flesh-lock. The King sought Grieg's death. It was his right as my Warrior and Protector. I would not take that honor from him. Sumulus kept pace with Say'f on the opposing flank of the mountain. Black and white, they flowed down toward my enemy.

Grieg's door swung open. He stood with his back to his shelter, his long army rifle in his arms. Both the Warrior and Sumulus stopped moving.

"Goddess of the Winds, cover the moon with clouds," I prayed. She did my bidding, but far too slowly. Grieg had spotted the mooncat. He raised his rifle in slow motion, took aim and fired. The bullet raced through the air; Sumulus screamed in cat rage. The shadowed Kosi pulled his knife and the metal caught the moonlight. He roared down the mountain like an avalanche. Sumulus screamed again. The Angelion was injured; I had to go to him.

I would have to circle around the Lake and climb up to the mooncat. Grieg spotted me as soon as I moved and took shot after shot at me, but that night I was invincible. The bullets screamed by my head and chunked into trees. When I reached the edge of the lake, I looked back to see the Kosi charge like a bull toward Grieg. Grieg swung his gun around, pointing it at the Warrior.

"No," I screamed. "Save yourself."

The bullets flew. I heard a cry of wrath. I sank into reeds by the Lake, panting in fear. Looking back I saw the Warrior unhurt, still running toward Grieg. Their bodies collided like stars. It had to be Say'f. I saw my lover's knife slash and slash again. I heard Grieg grunt in pain. They were on the ground, rolling, fighting and bellowing like animals. I heard the Kosi death roar but I did not fear. My lover would prevail.

I reached the other side of the Lake and started to climb up to Angelion. The cloud cover lifted. Every muscle in my body bent to the task of reaching him. Stabs of pain crossed my chest. I dislodged rocks that tumbled down. I grabbed for a tree growing straight out from the rocks and hung for a moment, dangling in the air. I shot a quick glance across the lake. The two men were still locked in mortal combat.

Slowly, hand over hand, I dragged myself to the shelf where the great white lion lay. He was so still. My heart stopped as I fell to my knees beside his great recumbent form. I whispered, "Don't go, great one. Please don't leave me." I felt for a pulse in his soft white throat. It was there, slow and powerful, like the sound of a drumbeat.

The man I was certain was Say'f was injured. I saw blood and bit my lips in fear. He raised his knife again. The scene slowed down. Grieg battled against the Warrior's strength, forcing the knife away. They grappled. The clash went on and on. I heard the Kosi battle cry and I saw my Warrior's dark hands around the throat of the White Snake. I heard my enemy's death rattle. Quietly at first, and then louder, I sang the Kosi song for Victory at Armageddon. The victorious Kosi warrior raised his head and saw me. I raised my arm in a salute. A beautiful white smile lit his dark face. It knew it was Say'f, but when he started to walk, his stride was very different.

I pulled my waterskin from my belt and opened Sumulus' mouth. I poured the liquid over his great tongue. Trying to determine where the bullet entered his body, I felt his ribs. Under my touch, I saw a red spreading stain. Using my small knife, I cut into the wound. I reached inside and pulled the bullet from his flesh. Then I lifted the great white lion's head and gazed into his half-closed silver eyes.

"I must go now," I told him. "Sleep my Champion, I will return with feverfew. You will live to raise your family." I held his great head in my hands and whispered, "My mother sends her unending love to you." I kissed his brow and began to climb down again to the floor of the valley. When I reached the tumbled rocks at the base of the mountain, I ran toward the place where the two dire enemies had battled. I stopped for a moment and looked down. Grieg's body lay dead. I felt his pulse to be certain, but he was a corpse. A shudder, a paroxysm, a *grand mal* of relief flooded my soul.

"Goddess, take this one to the bottom of the earth," I prayed. "The belly of the White Snake stays rooted to the ground. He must never ride the sky worlds."

Chapter 40 – At Halfhigh

*While Sab-ra ran to embrace her King, Deti and Ruby
tended the wounded at Halfhigh fearful no one would survive.*

It was a sober group that greeted a cool windy morning at
Halfhigh. Both Ruby and Deti had burns on their legs and feet.
Hent had been severely mauled by the panther and was
unconscious. Ambe had inhaled much smoke and struggled for
each breath, coming in and out of consciousness. Quinn and
Crimson were in the best shape, but bewildered and frightened by
the injuries of the adults. Ruby propped Ambe up against the
outside of the stone house and put Quinn to her breast. He
latched on lustily, but Ambe was too weak to hold him and he
rolled off her lap. Deti knelt beside them, lifting Quinn up to take
nourishment. Baby Crimson was crawling in the grass, talking to
herself.

Ruby walked over to the baby and sat down beside her.

"The big cat is gone now, little one," she told her. "You
don't need to be afraid."

"Man-ee," Crimee said looking piercingly at her.

Ruby didn't know what she was saying. "Yes. He was a very
bad manee-cat, but we are fine now."

"Man-ee," she said again, louder. She looked intently at Ruby.

Ruby picked her up and held her in her lap, checking her over carefully. She seemed fine, except for some small red burns. Ruby stood up and carried her to see Star in the paddock.

"Man-ee," Crimee called out, holding her arms back toward the edge of the mesa.

"Star, come here," Ruby called and the pony trotted over to the boma fence. Hent and Ambe's ponies followed. Ruby gave them both water from her leather waterskin and the baby petted them. Star's body looked round as a barrel. She certainly hadn't been that round when they left Namché, Ruby thought. Could she be pregnant, she wondered.

"Crimee, can you say, Star," Ruby asked.

"No. Man-ee," Crimee said, looking at her penetratingly.

"Say Star," Ruby said.

Crimee shook her head saying, "No, no, no."

"Ruby," Deti called out. "Come over here will you? We have to get some nourishment into Ambe, or she won't make it. She doesn't seem to have much milk left. Quinn kept squirming away and sitting up instead of nursing."

"I'll check their supplies," Ruby said, putting Crimee down in the grass beside Deti. "See if you can figure out what Crimson is saying, will you?"

Looking through Hent's pannier packs, Ruby found some dried chanry meat and fruit. Walking down to the Aid station in the black dweli, she looked through the medicines. One container had three white pills. She put them in her pocket. She found some bandaging and took that as well. Outside she discovered the spring and filled her waterskin.

"What are these, Deti?" Ruby asked, pulling the white pills from her pocket.

"They are poppy pearls. Give one to Hent. It will ease his pain."

"Man-ee," Crimee said again louder. The girls were confused and ignored her.

Feeling a bit squeamish, Ruby opened Hent's mouth and put a pearl inside. She held his jaw closed until he swallowed. He was semi-conscious and babbled words about the panther attack.

"Should I give him another poppy pearl?" Ruby asked.

"Let's chance it," Deti said.

A few minutes later, Hent opened his eyes.

"What happened," he asked.

"A panther attacked you. Ambe is alive, but ill from smoke inhalation."

"Where is she?" he asked. Helping him to his feet the girls managed to support him until he reached Ambe. He sat down heavily beside her, groaned in pain and sank into unconsciousness again.

Ruby poured some water into Ambe's mouth. She blinked, coughed and tried to speak.

"Manny?" she asked.

"Oh Goddess, no," Deti cried, "That's what Crimee has been saying. Hent and Ambe have a two-year-old; his name is Manny."

Deti and Ruby looked at each other in shock. They hadn't seen any sign of the toddler.

"Ambe," Deti kept yelling until she opened her eyes again. Her eyelids fluttered, wanting to close. "Where did you see Manny last?"

"Dweli," Ambe managed.

Deti and Ruby grabbed the babies and ran to the aid station, praying the little child was still alive. Just as she was entering the First Aid Dweli, Ruby stopped. An enormous warrior on a horse rode the arroyo below them.

"Deti, look," she whispered.

It was a mounted Kosi warrior. He was headed directly toward the Halfhigh trail. The girls stood frozen; terrified it was one of Hozro's allies. As the warrior reached the base of the trail, he looked up. Deti stood as if made of iron, holding Quinn in her arms as the warrior thundered up the trail on his warhorse. Ruby grabbed Crimee and crawled beneath the shelter of a shrub. She curled up in a tiny circle with her arms protecting the baby.

When the warrior reached the top of the butte, he yanked his horse to a stop. The horse screamed. The Kosi warrior controlled him and dismounted. His feet were heavy and the earth quivered as he strode toward the girls. Deti's face was white, but Quinn slowly began to smile. The baby held out his little arms toward the Kosi.

"I am Lord Sta'g, now First Blood Arrow," the man said. Looking over at the brush he said, "Sab-ra, raise yourself. You have nothing to fear from me." Ruby looked up and a frown crossed the man's face. "You aren't Sab-ra. Who are you?" he asked.

Trembling, Ruby stood up. "I am Ruby, sister to Sab-ra," she said, her voice quavering. "This is Deti, and this is Quinn, Sab-ra's son."

The warrior began to smile. "Future King of the Kosi, I salute you," he said and went down on his knees before the small one. Then he stood up and took the baby in his arms. Little Quinn wrapped his arms tightly around the warrior's neck.

"Lord Sta'g, we have survived a panther attack and a fire here," Deti told him. "There are two adults who are badly injured and a toddler missing. We need your help."

"Manny," Crimson said again.

"The two-year-old is named Manny," Ruby told him. "He is missing. We are searching for him."

They found him an hour later, lying unconscious in a crevice in the rocks. Deti pulled his little body out and he made a small sound.

"He lives," the warrior said complacently and carried him to his mother.

Ambe made a soft whisper of gratitude as the warrior placed the little boy in her lap.

"Can you carry Hent and Ambe into the dweli?" Deti asked. Lifting them easily as he had little Quinn, Lord Sta'g placed them both on the soft bedstraw. He came back to get Manny but stopped short when he saw Crimson in Ruby's arms.

"Whose child is this?" he asked, scowling.

"Sab-ra had two Babas," Ruby told him, "But the only milk we have is Ambe's and she is so ill. I fear for their lives."

"Fear kills," Lord Sta'g told her. "Cease to fear. I will go for Wirri-Won." He mounted his stallion, nodded to the girls and thundered off the mesa.

Deti and Ruby spent all afternoon fetching water from the spring and feeding it spoonful by spoonful to Ambe and Hent. Although Manny remained unconscious, Deti forced his mouth open and poured water down his throat. He coughed and opened his eyes. Ruby had found some dried chanry meat in the dweli and cut it in small pieces.

"Eat this, Manny. You must be hungry," Ruby said.

He would not take it and started to cry.

Ruby filled her waterskin and tried to get Quinn and Crimee to drink, but most of it dripped down the front of their little chests. They grew weaker by the hour. Their eyes were enormous. By late afternoon, they couldn't even sit up. Both lay huge eyed and silent on the straw.

As the sun fell slowly behind the mountains, Deti heard one of the horses grunting. She ran over to the boma to see Star lying on the ground.

"Ruby, come and help me. I think Star is having a foal. It seems stuck inside her."

"There's nothing we can do," Ruby said, disgusted by the thought.

"I will hold her while you try to pull the baby out," Deti said.

"No. How repulsive. I am not going to do that."

"Then she will die and the baby will die. We can't let her die, Ruby. Once the baby is born, Star will nurse the foal and we will be able to get milk from her for the babies. Come over here."

"I can't," Ruby kept backing away.

Deti ran over and dragged Ruby back by her hair. "You sit here and help me, or I will tell the Kosi you refused to help the King's son. The babies will die. I don't think you want to face Lord Stag's anger, do you?"

"Oh my God, no. He terrifies me."

"Then grab the baby's hooves and pull. Pull as hard as you can."

Although Ruby's face was a mask of distaste, she grabbed the tiny hooves of the foal and slowly the colt emerged from his mother's body. When his back legs emerged with a popping sound, Ruby fell backwards and the foal landed on her chest.

"I did it, Deti," Ruby cried from under the foal. Her voice was elated. "He's alive."

The little colt struggled to his feet. He was wet all over. The setting sun lit his translucent ears from behind.

"Why he's beautiful," Ruby murmured. The baby's mother lurched to a standing position and as her son nursed, she licked him dry.

Deti cautiously moved close to the mother's side. She opened her waterskin and stripped the mare's teats watching drops fall into the water bladder. Star didn't have much milk yet but the babies were growing weaker. Even a little would help.

"Wirri-won needs to come soon, or the babies, Ambe and Manny—we will all die."

Chapter 41 – The Lost Lake Valley

As Ruby and Deti prayed for Wirri-Won to arrive in time to save Ambe, Manny and the twins, Sab-ra followed a blood trail toward the Kosi she believe to be her husband.

"Kosi Warrior stop!" I called. The moonlight was bright enough that I could see a slick blood trail. Heart pounding, I followed the red road. Was it him? The footprints in blood did not look like his. My palms grew sweaty as I saw the trail grow wider. "Wait" I screamed. He raised his amber eyes, turned and saw me.

"Spirit of Sab-ra, cease to follow me. I cannot come to you."

By the time I caught up with him, he was hunched over at the edge of the Lake. He drank like a lion from the waters. His gaze saw my shirt, still tied on my head and my bare breasts. He reached to touch me and was startled.

"Is it really you, my bare breasted Kosi wife?" he asked and I caught a glimpse of a grin. He held out his hand for mine. "Did I marry a Kosi woman after all?" I helped him stand and examined him as best I could in the moonlight. He was cut and bleeding in a dozen places. He reached for me and we embraced. A huge flower of joy opened in my heart. I had found him.

"My Warrior, I can hardly believe we are together again. I feared the Captain might have injured you fatally, but you will live," I felt triumphant. Nothing could keep us apart now. "I have sought you long, my husband. My heart rises in joy to find you alive."

"The White Snake could not injure me in a hundred fights," he answered, proudly. We sat together on the sand at the edge of the lake while his breathing returned to normal, watching dawn gild the mountain.

"It is a miracle you appeared on the very night I chose to take the White Snake's life." He bent to kiss me and I felt my body respond. "I have seen your spirit a thousand times since I have been in this valley."

"Tell me what happened after the Avalanche drove the rest of us out of Skygrass?" I asked. I was still amazed to be sitting by him, I couldn't move even an inch away and pressed my body tight against his side.

"My shame in allowing Grieg to capture you made me stay behind when the mountain exploded. The fire from the volcano burned much of the skin on my body and I rested for weeks in a cave. When my strength returned, I made my way across the Dhali Ra. Amid the storms of winter, I found Grieg wandering on the other side of the massif."

He looked down at his right leg and I noticed that his foot was injured. He had wrapped it in green reeds from the aquamarine lake.

"I sought his life, and we battled for a long time. Finally, we broke apart, neither of us strong enough to kill the other. I dragged myself into a cave. Late that night, I heard the roar of a mooncat and saw him attack Grieg, but the Captain shot the lion. I saw blood on his leg, but he was strong enough to ascend the cliffs."

Tears of gratitude stung my eyes that Sumulus would fight for me.

"I wanted to be sure the mooncat would survive. It took most of the night for me to pull myself up the mountain, but when I got to the cleft, I heard him growl. I peered inside. He guarded a female and a single nursling. He roared powerfully and I knew he would live. Now, tell me of your journey with the First Blood Arrow after you left the Skygrass valley."

"Lord Rohr and I waited for you for many weeks at Halfhigh after the Avalanche. The rest of the Kosi returned to the Citadel and the miners returned to Talin. When the snows began, Lord Rohr insisted that we leave. I begged to stay longer, but my burns wept liquid and the fever would not leave me. He prevailed. We travelled across the mountain and made it to the Valley of the King by the beginning of the Moon of Snows."

"That was over a year ago, Sab-ra. What did you do in the Valley of the King while the seasons passed?"

I could have told him then about my pregnancy and the babies but decided I would wait until he could see them with his own eyes.

"Lord Rohr and I stayed in the King's service until spring when I received a summons from Wirri-won, Healer of the Kosi people. Although he feared for me, Rohr took me to the Island of the Eaten. Wirri-won had established a leper colony and discovered a vaccine to prevent the disease. She and I were able to save many leper children before the White River tore the Island apart. After that, Lord Rohr and I set out to find you again."

"Why is the First Blood Arrow not with you?" Say'f asked, frowning.

"Lord Rohr never broke faith with you, my Lord," I felt tears fill my eyes. "He protected me as long as he drew breath but a giant leopard took his life," I started to sob. "When he died, I cut myself and stained his arrows with my blood. I placed his quiver and bow on his chest. I promised that I would take his place. I vowed I would become First among your Blood Arrows."

"There is no need for Blood Arrows in the Lost Lake," Say'f said quietly. He looked out across the lake, accustomed to living here, resigned.

"The Kosi nation waits for you, King Say'f. I came into this valley through a pupil in the eye of the Goddess, a hole in the rock wall. If we can get through the opening together, I have my medicines at the Bearer camp. I can treat your foot."

"No," he told me quietly, stubbornly. There was a set to his mouth that boded ill.

I looked at Say'f and felt a trembling come upon me, like shock. The Kosi King looked up toward the range of mountains.

Once again, he did not plan to come with me. Once again, the bars of his pride would not let him escape from the prison of his own making.

"Come with me, my husband," I said. "I beg you."

"Sab-ra, I cannot," he said, pointing to his foot. "I am crippled. No cripple could rule the Kosi."

"Must I get down on my knees again," I asked. My voice was low and I held his eyes with my own. I had said those words to him once before, when I begged for our union on our wedding night.

"I am King of the Kosi no longer," he said. The determination in his face was like rock.

"I think I know a King when I see one," I said keeping my voice calm. "Now I have something to say and you will hear me. I am no longer a terrified bride brought to the bed of a Kosi King. What I have survived has made me a Blood Arrow. Lord Rohr and I survived a trip across the top of the Dhali Ra in winter. After helping Wirri-won with the leper children, I travelled to the Citadel to find you, but nearly everyone was dead. Hozro had been there."

Say'f took in a sudden deep breath, dread clenched his mouth. "Tell me of my warriors."

"When the tide of war turned in favor of the Kosi, Hozro and the other Shunned who fought for the Army retreated to the Citadel. He waited for your warriors to return and convinced them you were dead. He forced them to choose. Either they would honor his sovereignty or they would die. More than thirty chose death.

He killed two women and their infants. He even killed a pregnant woman." I could still see the ranks of the dead in the Citadel and grimaced.

"Were no warriors left alive?"

"Three warriors and one woman were barely alive in a nearby ravine, Ghang, Rohr, Argo and Niffa. They told me what Hozro had done. Say'f," I looked at him with iron in my eyes. "You have no choice. You must resume your kingship. Your people need you."

I knelt before my husband and slowly unwrapped his foot. I was horrified to see that four of the toes were missing. The scars were raised and puckered. Red streaks rose on the sides of the foot. It was still infected.

"How did this happen?" I asked.

"After the Avalanche, when I stayed behind to seek Grieg's death, the Mountain God froze my toes. I cut them off." He sent me an image of removing his left boot and sawing off his toes with a knife in a snowstorm. I saw the blue toes, rock hard, blow away in the fierce winds. I saw his boot, skittering away and his desperate attempt to grab it, before it slid into an icy cleft. I saw his bare foot turn red and then blue as he hobbled away.

"You are a Warrior still," I said. "I applaud your courage."

He shook his head, saying, "I am King no longer, but when I see your face and feel your touch, I would still be your husband. Let us make our home here, in this beautiful valley."

I quieted the rage that was starting to rise inside me.

"As your Queen, I will not permit you to remain here." I felt my body grow hot.

"You are not Queen of the Kosi," he said, shaking his head. "To be Queen of the Kosi, you must be a true warrior; you must have taken the life of an enemy of the tribe."

"When Justyn and I rescued the four Kosi from the ravine, I met Argo, the Kosi assassin. I ordered him to locate Hozro and bring him to trial before the Elders at Talin. I will tell them of his crimes."

"A trial by pacifists will not serve, my wife. Hozro must die," he said softly.

"If no man in Talin will take his life, I will behead him myself," I said.

Say'f looked at me stunned. "You?" he asked. "Your People are peaceful miners and Ghat herders. Your religion bans taking the life of any sentient being or even eating the flesh of an animal that can nurse it's young. What has time wrought to make you like this, Sab-ra?"

"When I saw the Kosi dead at the Citadel something changed deep inside me. Some crimes are so horrendous that they require the perpetrator to pay with his life."

Say'f shook his head and looked at me in admiration, murmuring, "You are more warrior than I, Sab-ra. This night I release you from your marriage vows. Once Hozro lies dead, you can select one of the living Blood Arrows for a husband. Then you will indeed be Queen of the Kosi."

"I am already married to the King. I want no other."

"The Kosi would despise me because of my injury. Injured women and children are cared for, but injured warriors are cast from the Tribe. Most join the Shunned. How I wish I had a son to take my place."

I was sorely tempted to tell him about Quinn then, but held my tongue.

"If you do not return to the Citadel," I said and heard the mooncat growl in my voice, "I will ask the Elders to spare Hozro's life. He will become King of the Kosi in truth. He will claim me as his Queen. He will force me to lie with him and give him sons. If he found my appearance displeasing, he would torture or kill me, even bury me in a pit of garbage as he did to Hodi."

I wanted Say'f to know what his pride would cost. I saw his eyes darken and felt the spark of his anger flare into flame.

"It is your duty to protect me," I hissed, "whether you are King or not. Your injury pales next to your responsibility to your Queen."

The Kosi's golden eyes looked off toward the blue and purple ranges of mountain. He needed time alone to determine his path. I left him to think on my words.

I searched out some willow shrubs, tore off their bark and made a powder from their marrow. The willow powder had a harsh taste, but it eased pain and erased inflammation. I climbed back up to Sumulus who lay where I left him. I forced it down his throat.

After some time had passed, I could tell his pain eased. I sat petting him all afternoon. By the time the sun went down, he was able to stand. He licked my hand.

"Farewell Great Angelion," I told him and bowed. He left me slowly, climbing up toward the cave he shared with his mate. Just before he entered the cave, he turned and we looked long into each other's eyes. "May the Goddess of the Dhali Ra bless you and keep you. With all that I have and all that I am, I honor you," I said. He vanished like white smoke and I wondered if he existed at all—beyond this mythic place.

When I returned to the lakeside, Say'f had made a campfire. He found food in Grieg's small house. We ate in silence. After the meal, I stood and slowly removed all my clothing, piece by piece. I held the glowing eyes of my husband with mine. I lay down beside him. Suddenly shy before his melting gaze, I covered my breasts with my hands, but he pulled my hands away. As he had said on the night we married, he murmured, "I would not have you covered, not for all the gemstones in Skygrass."

Happiness waved across me. I thought him gone to the sky worlds. A warm blood song rose in my body. He gave a shuddering sigh and bent to kiss me.

"I want only you," I murmured. "You are my Lord and King, heart of my heart, blood of my blood. Four toes are nothing to give away—to keep your Kingdom and your Queen."

As we fell asleep, I saw two glowing strands of stars form a great circle. Say'f and Sumulus had ended the life of my enemy. I was at peace.

Chapter 42 – At Halfhigh

While Sab-ra sought to convince Say'f to leave the Lost Lake, Ruby and Deti faced a losing battle for the lives of Crimee and Quinn, Manny and his parents.

The next two days were the longest of Ruby and Deti's life. They tried every medicine in the dweli. They cut up chanry pemmican for Manny but he refused it. He would only drink water. Hent's injuries were badly infected and although he fought bravely, he succumbed to a fever before Lord Sta'g returned. The girls could not bury him. They dragged his body to the edge of the cliff and rolled him over the edge. Deti prayed for his spirit. Ruby asked God to bless him.

Ambe continued to sink lower; the girls feared she walked the dying road. She had no milk left and the babies were silent. They hardly moved any more. Quinn and Crimee's little bodies began wasting away. Their eyes were filled with fear.

Deti tried repeatedly to get Star to let down her milk, but the horse kept moving away. She kicked Deti and nipped at her. By the end of the second day, both girls had given up. They too were sleeping more and more.

In the darkest part of the second night, Ruby woke. She heard singing. The melody was hauntingly beautiful. She shook Deti's shoulder.

"It's Wirri-won. She's here," Ruby told her. They struggled to their feet, only able to stumble to the edge of the mesa. Looking down they saw the white egg shaped head of the medicine woman riding a silver mare. Lord Sta'g rode behind her.

When Wirri-won walked into the dweli and saw Ambe unconscious and the twins in a stupor, she shrieked in rage. She whirled toward Lord Sta'g and sent him racing from the dweli, screaming for him to hunt; to bring meat to the injured ones.

Lord Sta'g returned as dawn lit the mountains with two chanry birds hanging around his neck. He started a fire and cooked them over a spit. He reached to cut a wing away for himself. Wirri-won slapped his head saying, "Kosi Warrior you will eat last," and pushed a small vessel under the dripping meat. She caught the juice as the bird cooked. The scent of the meat floated deliciously over the camp at Halfhigh. The Healer poured the meat juice into a waterskin. She walked back into the dweli and sat across the tent from Quinn.

"Future King of the Kosi," she said. "You must come to me."

Quinn tried desperately to stand, but fell again and again in weakness. Ruby reached for him, but Wirri-won pushed her away. Deti cried, seeing him so weak.

"He must do this himself," she said. "Kings must be strong."

The girls clung to each other trying to keep from rescuing Quinn as he fell repeatedly, but at last dragged himself on his belly to the Healer. She gathered him into her lap and he sucked the juice down. His little body relaxed in the comfort of a full belly.

"Useless Iztar girls, you will chew this chanry meat, but you will not swallow it. When it is a paste, spit it into a bowl and feed it to Ambe and her son. Take none for yourselves. You will not eat until tomorrow."

Both girls quailed before the Healer. She watched their chewing carefully and once hit Deti when she saw her swallow. They took turns spooning the meat paste into Ambe and Manny's mouths and rubbing their throats to make them swallow.

"Blood Arrow," Wirri-won called out for Lord Sta'g, "Get mare's milk for the Kosi Princess."

"I have tried and tried," Deti told her desperately. "The mare only kicks and bites."

"You are no warrior," Wirri-won disparagingly. She turned her gaze on the Kosi. Lord Sta'g leapt to do her bidding.

By morning, Ambe could sit up. Manny had improved miraculously and was walking around the dweli and asking to go outside.

"Where is my husband?" Ambe managed to ask.

"He rides the skies, Ambe," Deti told her with tears in her eyes. "I am sorry, but his injuries took his life."

Ambe started to cry and reached for her toddler. Manny came and sat in her lap. Ruby sat beside Ambe, putting her arm around the woman's shoulders, comforting her.

Over the next few days, the sparkle came back into Quinn's eyes. Baby Crimee was still terribly weak, but she swallowed the mare's milk every time they brought it to her and slowly began to talk again.

"Lord Sta'g, how did you get Star to give you her milk?" Deti asked. "I tried hard. Wirri-won called me Iztar, lazy, but I tried in every way I knew."

"It is good I came here," Lord Sta'g said. "You are small weak girls. The mare required convincing. I crippled her foal to get her attention."

"What? How could you do such a thing?"

Lord Sta'g shrugged. "The children of the King needed milk. The foal will live. He will be lame, but he will live."

Slowly the little band at Halfhigh recovered. Lord Sta'g hunted each day and brought back chanry. The children struggled back to life. Ambe's eyes were lifeless, although she took some comfort from the fact that her son lived. Deti noticed Lord Sta'g sitting beside Ambe often by the evening campfire. Once Ruby surprised them and saw the Kosi's arm around Ambe's shoulders. After a time, whenever Lord Sta'g came to sit beside her, Ambe smiled shyly.

The Kosi warrior made a tiny bow for Manny and short stubby arrows. As Ambe gazed on, still too weak to stand, the Blood Arrow taught Manny how to shoot.

"He will make a good Kosi Warrior one day," Lord Sta'g told Wirri-won.

"And his mother will make a good Kosi mate," Wirri-won said, smirking a little.

Lord Sta'g smiled.

As Lord Sta'g and Ambe grew closer and the babies recovered, Sab-ra prevailed. Say'f left the Lost Lake with her.

We emerged from the White Snake's lair the next afternoon. Say'f told me he had spotted the crevice in the mountain months earlier, but his injured foot kept him from further exploration. I don't know what convinced Say'f in the end, but when I told him I was leaving and stood to walk out of the Lost Lake valley, he limped beside me. He wore only his left boot and cursed his injured foot all the day. I prayed his other boot was in the camp where I left it. Walking into the narrow slice in the rock and then crawling on our knees forever until we saw the light, we made it to the other side. When we reached the camp, all the Bearers had vanished. They had left me only the dweli and some pemmican. Inside the dweli, to my delight, I found my husband's boot. Lord Rohr's horse, Tye, was also at the camp, but little Jemma was gone. Tye pranced in delight when he saw the King.

After a night in the camp, we proceeded slowly down the mountain. I quietly mourned the loss of Yellowmane and scanned the skies for her image dancing in the clouds. I would mourn her for the rest of my life. I knew Say'f still had terrible doubts about his ability to lead the Kosi. I had none. Although it seemed the

Kosi were now an orphan nation, their willingness to defend the sacred Skygrass valley and my marriage to their King had made them my People.

"The Kosi have always been warriors for hire," Say'f told me as we rode. "In the time of my grandfather, the Old King, we were pledged to protect the people of the Twelve Valleys. In those days, one woman a year from your People chose to come to the Kosi. It was considered an honor and the People's women vied with each other for the privilege. When the Old King died and my father became Ruler, he left the Citadel with two guards to negotiate a new agreement with your People for more women, but he never returned. Hozro and my father's guards carried his body back to the Citadel. We gave him a sky burial."

"So you became King then?"

"I was so honored," he nodded. "Months later, one of the Bearer people came to me and confessed that he had witnessed Hozro kill my father. Because Hozro was my nurse brother when we were children, I believed his many lies." Sorrow crossed his face.

"The betrayer must die," I murmured.

"Hozro set up a separate camp near the Green River. He lured warriors away with promises of wives and children. When you arrived, I was making plans to attack his camp and take back my men."

"When Hozro lies dead and your warriors know you live, they will all return. I have seen it," I promised. "I have seen you rule a great and numerous people. We will place his head on a post at the entrance to the Citadel and make the Shunned kneel there. If they would keep their heads, they will swear an oath of fealty to you. We will rule together and the Kosi will once again be the guardians of the People in the Twelve Valleys. Your daughters, Kim-li and Kensing will join us. They are with Conquin and her husband in King Ruisenor's palace."

"I want more children," Say'f said and his gaze made my body warm. I kept the secret of Quinn and Crimson alive in my heart, like two perfect bread rolls warm from the oven of my body.

We rode most of the way in companionable silence for the next several days. The Harvest Moon had begun; my birthday month. I had turned eighteen. On this day two years ago, I left Talin for Maidenstone in disgrace, banned from my People for leaving Hodi in the hands of the Shunned. Today I was returning to the Twelve Valley's country as Queen of the Kosi. My son and daughter, future monarchs of the warrior tribe would be waiting for us at Halfhigh. Together with my husband, we would bring peace to the Blue Mountains. I felt a shiver of intense pleasure cross my shoulders. I had found my destiny.

I watched Say'f carefully for signs of pain and fatigue. When I saw his face turn white, I made him stop, saying I was too tired to continue. The autumn rains had ended and the sky was bright blue. The sun had scorched all color from the dry mountains, but along small streams, the yellow and red trees flamed near blue water.

On the last evening before we reached Halfhigh, we camped by a tributary of the White River. I disrobed and bathed in the water. Say'f joined me and together we washed the dirt from each other's bodies, playing, splashing and laughing. I found a large flat stone lying barely beneath the tumbling water. I laid down on it and let the river wash my hair. I poured water over Say'f and slowly unpicked his coiled braids. I washed his hair with soap grass and left it long to dry. It reached his waist, black and shiny as moonlight.

"I have never been defeated in war, Sab-ra, but this battle you place before me is harder than any I have fought before," he said. "I cannot pretend that I am confident about the outcome."

"You will prevail," I said calmly and he smiled. Then my husband led me by the hand to the sandy riverbank and took me as I lay, half in the water. His hair covered us like a blanket.

"You are my husband and you will be King again," I vowed. The sun went down. We started a campfire and ate our evening meal.

The next morning, I did my hair in the fashion of the Kosi women. I consigned the King's torn dirty shirt to the flames of the campfire and buckled the leather band that held his arrowheads diagonally across his naked chest. I braided his long dark hair. I saw the old healed scars of injury on his body—a warrior's mark of honor. We had washed his leather trousers the night before. He stepped into them, balancing on my shoulder. I had sufficient willow bark powder to fill the toe of his right boot.

When the sun reached its height, I spotted two figures standing ahead of us by the trail. As we approached I saw it was Ghang and Argo. They held a leather bag. When we drew rein beside them, Argo held the bag up to Say'f.

"I greet you, King of the Kosi," Argo said. "In this bag, I have Hozro's head. I fought him to his death. As the fight turned and it was clear that I would prevail, he became a true Kosi again. He refused the help of his followers and died honorably."

I shuddered inwardly, but forced myself not to gag. I made myself look inside the bag. These warriors needed a Queen as brave as their King. The head was there; it was gray and looked almost waxy. I turned away but then quickly back again. This man had a white eye. Argo had failed to kill Hozro; instead he killed the Kosi Wolf who took Hodi's life.

"You have played me false, Argo," I said, in a sudden spasm of fury. "This is not Hozro. This is the Kosi Wolf who murdered my spirit brother, Hodi. While I am grateful he is dead, I ordered you to bring Hozro to Talin. The King demands his trial by the Elders."

"Let me see this head," Say'f said. He bent down and when he raised his face up, I saw him grin.

"Sab-ra, this man is Hozro. Hozro and the man you call the Kosi Wolf, the man who killed Hodi and buried him alive, they are one and the same." Turning to the assassin he nodded, saying, "I am in your debt, Argo."

Argo bent his head and Say'f put his hand on the assassin's shoulder.

Turning back to me he said, "Well done, Queen of the Kosi."

I saw at last my husband's smile of victory, the easy smile of the Kosi King from the days in the Citadel. The death of Hozro had set him free. Just as he had killed my enemy, unknowingly I had ordered the death of his.

Say'f took the leather bag from Rohr and tied it to his saddlebags. I fought the stench and my nausea, but knew it was his talisman. The King's confidence had returned and I had achieved an honorable justice for Hodi. I looked up into the sky and saw my little spirit brother's open-hearted smile.

The King and I, with Ghang and Argo behind us, rode on to Halfhigh as the sun began its sky journey to the west.

We began to see more Kosi warriors. They stood silently on both sides of the trail, astride their horses, bows and arrows strapped to their backs. At first, we saw only two, then three. Soon there were more, twenty, thirty. Some looked afraid, some triumphant. There were women too, bare breasted on their horses, erect and prideful.

"Just as I told you, your warriors have returned, King of the Kosi," I felt jubilant.

As we passed the silent warriors, they fell in behind us, riding two abreast. When we reached the bottom of the trail that leads up to Halfhigh, Say'f stopped. He turned his horse around and faced his Warriors and their women. He raised his bow and gave a huge roar. I did not know the words of the Kosi cry, but the men made a giant dark circle around him. With their horse's heads bowed, they were a ring of satyr's—half man, half horse. It was the vision he showed me the day I asked him to defend Skygrass, the day I knew he would fight for us.

We thundered up the trail and into Halfhigh. I dismounted and walked into the stone house where I saw Ambe with Manny and to my surprise Deti holding Quinn. Then from the shadows at the back of the house, a red haired woman walked forward. She carried baby Crimson. Their hair was identical in color. I knew her as if we were one. She was my twin.

"I see you at last, my sister," she said formally, inclining her head. Leaning forward, she kissed me on one cheek and then the other. It was a gracious welcome.

"Bah-ma," Crimson said and held out her hands for me.

"I am Sab-ra," I told my sister, reaching for the baby, "Welcome to my land."

"I am Ruby, and have come half way around the world to find you, Sister and Twin to my heart. I left our mother, Ashlin, on the Island of Viridian. She sent me to bring you back there with me."

"I greet you, Sister and Twin to my heart," I said, "I honor the arduous journey to have taken to find me." I pressed my forehead against hers, "But I am the Kosi Queen and would have you remain here with me."

"Our mother, Ashlin, is ill and I promised I would return. Your land is beautiful, but it is not my land. My safe harbor is Viridian. Please, I beg you, on behalf of our mother, bring your babies and come with me."

"I hope the day will come when our mother is strong enough to come to visit me here and see her grandchildren, but I must remain with the Kosi."

"Then I must return to Maidenstone. From there I will take the train, what you call the Iron Horse, and then a boat to return to the fair island of Viridian. It is a trip of many weeks, but I long to begin."

"My heart is sad that our lives have touched for such a brief time. Will you stay one day with me?"

"I will," Ruby said and they joined hands.

"When you do leave, I have a dear friend in Namché named Justyn. Would you greet him for me while you are in the city?"

"Do you have a message for Justyn?"

"Yes, tell him please that the King of the Kosi lives, as do my children. They have a father now, but I will never forget the love he gave them," I hesitated, remembering his face, "or to me."

"There was a woman in the Green River Camp who knew you. Nyria was her name."

"She was my spy partner, Hodi's mother. What became of her?"

"I am sad to tell you she died. The Shunned broke her foot because she tried to help me escape."

"I will tell my husband of this. He will find out who did this to Nyria. I would have justice for her."

"Sab-ra, if you will not return to Viridian with me, I was asked to give you a message from our mother. She said to tell you she has lived with regret every day since she left you at Maidenstone. She asks for your forgiveness."

"Tell our mother that she gave me the gift of life and the gift of love for the Angelions. There are no greater gifts. When I left Maidenstone, Mistress Falcon told me to find Sumulus, the baby Angelion she raised with our father. Tell her I found him. I held his great head in my arms and told him of her love."

"Then he is real?" Ruby asked. "I must admit I doubted."

"He lives, but only in the highest ranges. There once were many Angelions but he may be the last. Perhaps he lives only within the mystic Lost Lake valley. Beyond the boundaries of that sacred space, I think he is only white smoke."

"Our mother told me I would understand everything if I could see him, but even without that pleasure, I think I do. Have you any other messages for our mother?"

"Please tell Ashlin, regret must no longer reign in her heart. There is nothing but love between us."

"She will know of your triumph, and you finding Sumulus," Ruby said.

"Don't leave me yet, Sister and Twin to my heart." I found tears running down my face.

"If I stay now, I fear I will never go," Ruby answered, tears falling from her eyes. A long time passed as we held each other's eyes until I broke the contact.

"Tomorrow I will have Ghang to take you to Maidenstone," I said softly.

"Come with me," she pleaded, reaching out to take one of my red curls in her fingers.

"Stay with me," I begged. We embraced knowing neither of us could accede. I turned to my children. "Thank you for bringing my children to Halfhigh. I see that Quinn and Crimmy are very thin, but they are taller than when I left," I said.

"We were all near death from a panther attack that killed Hent and nearly killed Ambe. Her milk dried up and Deti and I tried everything we knew to save them. Ambe's son Manny was lost for a long time. We were lucky to find him alive. When Lord Sta'g came to Halfhigh and saw our desperation, he went for Wirri-won. She came and cured your children."

"You have been brave and loyal, my sister," I said. "I will miss the chance to know you better," my voice quavered. "I am and will be in your debt my whole life long. Come with me, Ruby, I would like for you to meet my husband."

"Did the Kosi abduct you and force you to join with him in marriage." She looked like she was braced for a terrible confession.

"Oh Ruby," I shook my head and smiled. "No. You don't understand. I wanted this marriage in every part of me. He was the reluctant one. I had to go down on my knees to him, but at last he agreed and we married. If you would stay here, I would marry you to one of my husband's Blood Arrows."

Ruby looked at me in amazement. "Dearest sister, I thank you, but there is a man in Nam-shay, a soldier I think I might just love."

"It is good you will marry a warrior," I told her. "When you two are married, bring him to meet me. My husband will make you both honorary Kosi. It is time you met your father," I told Quinn and Crimson, using the Kosi word. I wanted to carry my son out to Say'f, but he was too quick for me. He jumped from my arms to the ground. Ruby followed us holding Crimson in her arms.

Quinn ran out the door, dashed between the feet of the warrior's huge stallions and came to a halt before Say'f. I held my breath, afraid the stallion would stomp on my small brave boy.

"Pad-ma," he said. He lowered his head and went down on one knee. Lord Sta'g must have taught him the proper obeisance to make to a father who is also King. Then he raised his head, his dark green eyes shining and laughed aloud. I looked at Say'f. He was completely baffled. Who was the tiny unknown boy who called him father and knelt to him as King?

"Sab-ra, who is this?" he asked me, frowning.

"This is Quinn," I said. "Your son."

Seeing the still confused expression on my husband's face, I took pity on him. Motioning for him to bend down to me, I whispered, "Conceived on our wedding night in the light of the moon."

I picked Quinn up and handed him up to the King. Holding his son in his arms moved Say'f so deeply that tears sprang to his eyes. "Kosi Warriors, I bring you my son." He held Quinn high over the warriors and the assembled Kosi roared.

Little Quinn, no longer my baby, held his fists in the air and roared right back at them.

Ruby came forward with Crimson.

"Who is this woman? Is she your revenant? Your double?" Say'f asked me, alarm waved across his face.

"This is Ruby, my sister and twin. She and Deti saved our children from starvation."

"Then I am in your debt," my husband told her and she smiled tentatively at him. "Is this your child, sister to Sab-ra?" he asked, looking at Crimson.

"No, this one is also yours, my Lord," I said. "This is your daughter, the Princess Crimson."

Say'f held out his other arm for her and she went to him eagerly, talking in a continuous string of words. Say'f looked at her in wonder.

"What is she saying?" he asked me.

"I believe she is saying she is pleased to meet her father, although she speaks a tongue I do not yet know." I gestured down by my feet. "I also brought your gazehound, my Lord. I named her Dusk. She was still waiting in your sleeping space when we arrived at the Citadel. Starved, dehydrated and nearly dead, she waited for your return. She was prepared to die waiting for you. I am sorry, my King, but your eagle was not at the Citadel. I can only hope someone released him."

When I said the word eagle, Quinn began struggling to get down. Say'f handed him to me and I lifted him down to the grass. He raced between the legs of the warriors' stallions as I held my breath. He dashed to the very edge of the mesa and cried out loudly, "Sky Dog! Down!"

An enormous golden eagle descended, racing down from the sky, talons outstretched. I inhaled sharply, fearing he would rip my son's arm off, but he settled—light as a songbird.

"I believe your eagle has returned, my Lord," I said, unable to keep from laughing. "Apparently, Quinn, future King of the Kosi, can already call him from on high."

Much later that night I rose from the King's furs and tiptoed to the window. The morning fire lit the sky. I turned to look back into the dark room. Say'f lay on his back sleeping, his large hand resting on our son. Quinn lay on his tummy, silent beneath his father's hand. His head was turned away from me. Little Crimson cuddled next to her brother.

"He's back my children," I whispered to them in my mind. "Your father is back."

Quinn turned his head toward me then, his eyes wide open, smiling his baby smile. I already knew he could hear the thoughts of animals; it seemed he could read my thoughts as well. I returned to the bed and joined them.

Just as I closed my eyes, I whispered to Sumulus, saying, "When Quinn and Crimee are old enough to climb the mountain, all of us will come to honor you and tell you of our love. Sumulus, I thank you, for my family."

The destiny I sought for many years was finally mine; the golden cord of wife and the silver cord of motherhood would join the red cord of the Healer and the white of the Far Reader around my waist. I was complete. Sleep came upon us all in the furs of the Warrior King.

Epilogue

Many decades have passed since that dark day when I was very young and travelled with the wool train from the valley of Talin to the terror of what I believed Maidenstone would be. I was young and filled with remorse over the death of my spy partner, Hodi.

Now I have grown old. I sit writing this history in the beautiful white tower of Maidenstone, looking down through the colored web of bridges at the luminous city of Namché.

On one fateful day, a decade after the events I have related here, the Warrior King met the soil in a battle with the Hakan. Against tradition, I ruled the Kosi alone until Quinn was ready to take his father's place. Princess Crimson married into the Hakan tribe and continued my work of bringing the mountain people to peace. As he had known I would, I returned to Maidenstone. Justyn was still waiting. In the evenings, we take tea together and talk of the days when we were young.

Before all is lost in the mists of time, I had to write about the terrible part I played in the fall of Skygrass, the horrors of the war with the Harn Army, the slow disappearance of my People and a near end to the Kosi tribe. Everyone knows of these terrible events. People call it "The Saga of the Fall."

But, I have also told another story. A legend known by very few.

A tale of how a miracle rose from the ashes of war—of how the Lost Lake valley came to the People of Talin—of Sumulus, a being both real and evanescent—of a marriage between a woman of the People and the Kosi King—of our children, the Princess Crimson and Quinn, who in his turn became King of the Kosi.

I have given you a story of how two tribes became one Blended People, and of peace that descended like soft pink twilight on the vast Kingdom of the Twelve Valleys that lie along the Green River high in the Blue Mountains.

Made in the USA
Lexington, KY
28 February 2014